RAVES FOR ELYSA HENDRICKS!

THE SWORD AND THE PEN

"Hook[s] the reader from page one, line one, word one."

—Night Owl Romance

"[F]ans will enjoy this super romantic fantasy."

—*Midwest Book Review*

STAR CRASH

"This space adventure in the *Planet of the Apes* vein has all the required ingredients: crashed spaceships, captive humans in an alien zoo and legends of space travel."

—*RT Book Reviews*

". . . *Star Crash* is an interesting romantic science fiction that is at its best when readers obtain insight into the aliens and how they see humans as being beneath them."

—Harriet Klausner, The Best Reviews

". . . this tale has a lot more going on . . . *Star Crash* is marketed as a romance title but is really a first class science fiction novel."

—Gary Roen, *Midwest Book Review*

HEART'S BOUNTY

"So, ASP has judged me guilty and will hand me over to the Consortium. That's the plan?" Shyanne asked. The open young man with whom she'd fallen in love had never existed; he'd been an illusion created to trap her father. Damn, she didn't want that to matter, but it did, even after all these years. Even after all the pain he'd caused her.

"There are those in ASP who question the evidence and your guilt in these crimes." Greyson snared her gaze. "But you and I both know you're far from innocent."

Staring back at him, Shy fought off the surge of guilt threatening to cool her rage. What did she have to feel guilty about? Surviving? His betrayal had smashed her comfortable, secure world into a million pieces and left her to put her life back together the only way she could. Smuggling was her only option. What else could she have done?

"So they sent you here alone to bring me in." She forced a chuckle. "I think someone miscalculated."

Other *Love Spell* books by Elysa Hendricks:

THE SWORD AND THE PEN
STAR CRASH

Star Raiders

ELYSA HENDRICKS

LOVE SPELL

NEW YORK CITY

LOVE SPELL®

April 2010

Published by

Dorchester Publishing Co., Inc.
200 Madison Avenue
New York, NY 10016

ISBN 10: 0-505-52818-5
ISBN 13: 978-0-505-52818-6
E-ISBN: 978-1-4285-0847-7

Printed in the United States of America.

10 9 8 7 6 5 4 3 2 1

For Mom and Dad,
Thanks for giving me the courage to raid the stars to find my dreams.

Star Raiders

Chapter One

Greyson Dane sank onto the narrow bunk, leaned his aching head against the cold metal bulkhead of his cell and cursed his stupidity. After five years in the field with Earth League Force's Anti-Smuggling/Piracy (ASP) Bureau, he should have known better. His last ten years behind a desk as an administrator had apparently dulled his skills. One minute he was in charge, commanding an elderly man suspected of interplanetary smuggling to take him to his boss; the next he was waking up in a small, locked detention cell with a king-sized headache. How had the old man gotten the drop on him?

As much good as it would do him, at least his hands and feet were free. The steady thrum of an engine told Greyson the ship was moving but gave no suggestion as to where . . . which raised a host of other questions: Even if he managed to break out of his cell, could he escape if things took an ugly turn? Had his captors taken his ship in tow or left it behind?

Left it? Unlikely. These were pirates—no, smugglers, he reminded himself. Not that nowadays there was much distinction. Since the arrest and imprisonment of smuggler Stewart Kedar ten years ago, the line between the two criminal types was often blurred.

Until his final mistake, Kedar had handled his operation like a business, if a criminal one, careful not to break certain laws or tread on the toes of the Consortium of Intelligent Life, recognizing that the leviathan collection of interstellar governments didn't like having its nose tweaked—and that they had the power to secure justice whenever they felt like it. As had ultimately happened.

The new smuggling boss had no such scruples or smarts. Without regard to the danger, from his recent emergence he'd encroached on Consortium space and done as he pleased. But though the culprit had evaded capture so far, eventually his hubris would lead to his destruction. Greyson intended to be the one to bring him down. Just as he'd taken down Kedar.

Not that your run-of-the-mill smuggler would be likely to leave behind a prize like Greyson's ship, he admitted to himself, even back in Kedar's day. His cruiser was small, fast and sleek, and loaded with state-of-the-art technology that a criminal could easily turn into credits on the outer-world black market. And Greyson had been well outside Consortium space when he'd confronted this particular smuggling ship, so he was beyond the nominal protection of the Consortium's legal decrees.

He groaned again, this time more from mental distress than physical pain. What else could go wrong? He'd broken more than a few Consortium rules himself. He ticked them off in his mind: interviewing a restricted prisoner—the smuggler Kedar—without authorization. Using a prototype vehicle without authorization and then losing said vehicle to known criminals. And Greyson wasn't finished. Soon he'd be promising pardons to wanted felons—pardons he didn't have the authority or authorization to offer, working as he did for Earth, who was much too small to have any pull in the Consortium. But there wasn't any choice.

Most of the time Greyson didn't dwell on the negative aspects of Earth being part of C.O.I.L.; in his mind, the good far outweighed the bad. Though some people considered dependence upon the interstellar coalition a drawback, being a member provided benefits that everyone in power recognized—one of those benefits being survival. That's why, with Earth halfway through its one-hundred-year probationary period in C.O.I.L., chances were even if he succeeded in this unauthorized mission, both ELF and ASP would crucify him. His actions were leaving their planet open to expulsion. But the coalition could just as easily revoke Earth's probation if something *wasn't* done to stop the recent attacks.

The door slid open and he was blinded by sudden illumination after hours of darkness. He couldn't make out the features of the person silhouetted in the doorway, but he knew who it was.

Smuggler.

Pirate.

The reason he was on this ill-fated mission. The woman he'd loved and betrayed.

Shyanne Kedar.

Shy Kedar stepped into the holding cell and, studying the man sitting nonchalantly inside, plummeted without warning into the past. Her heart and stomach went into free fall as unwanted memories of laughter, passion and love careened through her mind. Try as she would, she couldn't banish Greyson from her soul.

She couldn't even banish him from her memory—not when she had a constant reminder. From the moment of her son's birth almost ten years ago, Rian was a miniature image of his father, down to the chocolate brown eyes to which she could never say no.

To steady herself in a suddenly unstable universe, she crossed her arms and leaned against the wall. "Greyson Dane," she said, keeping her voice cool and controlled despite the heat growing inside her. "What are you doing here? Last I heard, you were comfortably ensconced in an office as the youngest-ever ASP deputy director." She didn't add that it was a position earned by capturing her father. A position earned through betrayal. A position earned by being a snake.

"Shyanne." He said her name in an all-too-familiar husky tone. "Nice to see you again. It's been a long time. Doing well, I see?"

To keep from lashing out, she tightened her hold on her elbows. "Can the chitchat. Why are you here? And how the hell did you get aboard my ship without being detected?"

"A bit of new stealth technology. I'm sure your engineers will figure it out as they examine my ship. As to why I'm here . . . I have a proposition for you."

"Now, what could you possibly offer me that I don't already have?" she drawled, forcing herself to drop her arms and run her gaze dismissively down his body. But if she was foolish enough to put her hand into that fire again, there was indeed something he could give her that no one else ever could. She just wasn't that foolish.

When she'd first met him, he was a young man of twenty-five, his body tall and lean. He was still lean, but there was more mass to him now. Through the material of his flight suit she could see the outline of his chest, his pectorals, flat stomach and hefty biceps. For a man who spent most of his time behind a desk, there wasn't an ounce of flab to be seen.

Sometime in the last ten years he'd cropped short his thick brown hair. She remembered his shoulder-length locks, how during lovemaking his hair had formed a curtain around their faces and enclosed the two of them in their own small world of passion. For a brief moment she mourned the loss. Then she let it go. Forced her thoughts back to the present.

Her gaze moved to his face. Like most human men, whether under C.O.I.L. influence or not, he opted to use a beard suppressant, so his square jaw remained free of any stubble. Deep lines bracketed his mouth and fine wrinkles sprayed from the corners of his warm brown eyes. Overall, the years had treated him well, turning his youthful good looks into a mature handsomeness.

She shifted away from those eyes that watched her too closely. "I already have your ship. It's a shame to dismantle such a beautiful piece of machinery, but she's worth more as parts. No buyer would dare fly an ELF ship loaded with C.O.I.L. technology out here. Too many pirates would be gunning for them." Something about the ship's design struck her as familiar.

He lifted an eyebrow. "That's what I'm here about."

"Pirates? What do they have to do with me? *You* boarded *my* ship. I'm no pirate."

"Evidence says otherwise."

She bit back a retort. "What evidence?" she asked instead. In the last few months she'd heard rumors that made her uneasy. Learning from her father's mistakes, she was doubly careful to keep her smuggling operation through C.O.I.L. space minimal and undetected, but lately at some ports of call she'd heard her name mentioned in connection with attacks on Consortium ships and outposts. Someone—and she was afraid she knew who—was setting her up.

"ASP detected your ship's locator ID at the site of more than one pirate attack," Greyson said.

Shy snorted. "Locator IDs are easy to fake and totally unreliable as identifers. What do your witnesses say?"

"There are no witnesses. The pirates kill everyone." His tone was icy.

"Do you really think me capable of cold-blooded murder?" The question burst out of her. Though she made her living smuggling, she refused to resort to theft, drug-running, slavery or anything of the like, and she always had. It was one reason she remained strapped for cash. That Greyson knew her so little was yet another slap in the face. Almost as bad as everything else he'd done to her.

He went on without answering. "As long as your activities remained small and caused no real harm, ELF was willing to overlook you. But attacking supply transport ships and small farming colonies, murdering the crews and colonists . . . ? It won't be tolerated. Something has to be done. ASP has to do it."

"And you think I'm responsible," she repeated, searching his face for an answer. His thoughts were closed to her. But then, they always had been. The open young man with whom she'd fallen in love had never existed; he'd been an illusion created to trap her father. Damn, she didn't want his answer to matter, but it did, even after all these years. Even after all the pain he'd caused her.

When he didn't reply, anger burned away her pain. She lifted her chin and said, "So ASP has judged me guilty and will hand me over to the Consortium. That's the plan. *When they catch me,*" she stressed.

"There are those in ASP who question the evidence and your guilt in these crimes." Greyson snared her gaze. "Though you and I both know you're far from innocent."

Staring back at him, Shy fought off the surge of guilt threatening to cool her rage. What did she have to feel guilty about? Surviving? His betrayal had smashed her comfortable, secure world into a million pieces and left her to put her life back together the only way she could. Smuggling had been her only option. What else could she have done?

"So they sent you here alone to bring me in." She forced a chuckle. "I think someone miscalculated."

"My last solo mission went fairly well."

Shy ground her teeth at the nonchalant reference to his betrayal. "Do you think it smart to remind me of that?"

Greyson stood, and despite her height Shy had to tilt her head back to look him in the face. It reminded her of tilting her head back to kiss him, which made things even worse when he said, "What I think doesn't matter. What matters is what ASP is offering for your cooperation. It's your only hope."

She refused to let him intimidate her. "What exactly is ASP offering?" Curiosity made her ask. Not that she'd ever trust ASP or this man. Not after their past. She'd rather let her crewmate Bear pull off her arms and beat her with them. Not that he'd ever do that. The result would be less painful.

"Full pardons from ASP and C.O.I.L. for all crimes past and present."

"You have that kind of authority?" Shy's heart lurched with a hope quickly quashed when he didn't meet her gaze. He did nod, but he had something to hide. Nothing came without price, she supposed. "And what kind of cooperation are they looking for? Who do we have to kill?"

"No one." He chuckled. "Help me track down and arrest the man behind the recent attacks."

Hope crumbled completely, became the dry dust of sarcasm. "Is *that* all? Just find and catch this mystery man? Do you know how many smugglers and pirates there are in the outer worlds? You could search for years and never find the right one. The galaxy is a lot bigger than you pencil-pushing bureaucrats think . . . though the free part's getting smaller every day. Are you even sure it's just one man or crew? Who says this is a coordinated series of attacks? Maybe everyone's getting sick of the Consortium's iron grip." She laughed.

Greyson stared at her. "I've been in the business for fifteen years. Not all of them behind a desk. Believe me, I'm well aware of how difficult it is to catch pirates, slavers, drug runners and smugglers."

Shy's grim humor evaporated. "Don't lump us all together with that human filth. We're not in the same category, smugglers and murderers."

"I don't see the distinction," Greyson replied.

"Then you're blind. Smuggling may be illegal, but aside from lightening the Consortium's well-padded coffers, we don't hurt anyone. In fact, we do just the opposite. Without smuggling, a lot of the smaller outer-world colonies wouldn't even be able to survive. We help keep them supplied. We bring them food—"

"And weapons."

"Yes! Why not? Neither ELF nor C.O.I.L. will protect them, despite their high-handed laws on who can be sold which technologies. Who'll keep them safe from the very pirates you mention—or from the less honorable members of the Consortium?"

She'd seen firsthand what happened to colonists without any means of self-defense, and pirates were the least of their worries. That type might raid a colony, but they usually moved in and out quickly, taking what they wanted and leaving the rest intact for later visits. But more than one colony had been wiped out by a greedy C.O.I.L. member, its infrastructure destroyed, its people killed or sold into slavery. Part of C.O.I.L.'s charter said no member planet could claim a world if it held sentient beings unless after first contact that world refused membership. Then the charter allowed anything, including outright conquest and murder.

By the time Earth chose to join C.O.I.L., humans had spread far and wide throughout the galaxy. Many had become independent worlds and despite the risk of remaining separate entities were unwilling to forgo their independence and turn their government back over to Earth. Nor did all wish to join the Consortium.

"If they'd agree to unite with Earth rather than insist on maintaining their independent planet status, ELF would provide protection."

"Not everyone wants to be part of the great

Consortium or submit to Earth rule." Shy sneered. "Some people prefer true freedom."

"Then they have to be willing to accept the accompanying risks. Freedom is never free—as some of us have always believed."

The corners of Shy's lips twisted at the memory of her youthful idealism. Nothing was as clear-cut as she'd believed at the tender age of eighteen. "Yes, I think we've had this argument before."

"And we agreed to disagree." Greyson smiled, too, perhaps unconsciously, and the expression transformed his face from merely appealing to dazzling. Unbidden and unwanted, warmth curled inside Shy as she remembered what had usually ended each and every one of their arguments.

After a pause Greyson went on. "I have some information that will help narrow the search."

"And what might that be?"

"A name. Simon Dempster."

Shy flinched. Her breath hissed through her teeth and she bit her bottom lip; her fingernails cut into her palms. Simon Dempster—her father's former right-hand man and her personal nemesis. As a child, she'd disliked him. Though he smiled and treated her like a princess whenever her father was watching, other times she had seen his hatred. It had lurked always beneath the surface of his genial charm, waiting for release.

Because of her father's regard for the man, she had never mentioned the look in Dempster's eyes, or her uneasy feelings for him, but after her father's arrest she'd learned the true extent of his evil. When she managed to escape Greyson, Simon was waiting. At first she'd thought he was there to help rescue her father, but she quickly learned that he had a different agenda. He'd tried to use her father's arrest to gain control of her. She'd managed to elude him.

Over the years she'd continued to evade the man, watching helplessly as he built his own smuggling organization, one that erased the line between smuggler and pirate. Last year she'd had a run-in with him from which she barely escaped. His interest had grown from mere hate to obsession. He no longer wanted her dead; he wanted to possess her. And for a few endless days, he did. Screams—her own—still echoed in her mind. She preferred death to a return to that.

"You know him?" Greyson asked.

To ward off the headache growing behind her eyes, Shy pinched the bridge of her nose between her thumb and forefinger. "Yes, but why come to me for help in finding him? Why not appeal to C.O.I.L. for assistance? Isn't that what they're for?"

"Until Earth gains full membership, C.O.I.L. only provides limited assistance in what they consider internal planetary matters. To prove ourselves worthy of membership, the Consortium charter requires Earth to police its own borders, to maintain control of its rogue planets and criminals. If we won't or can't do so, they'll step in and the result won't be good for humanity. Failure to stop this renegade could cost Earth everything."

"What good is being a C.O.I.L. member if you can't count on their protection?" Shy sneered.

He ignored her and continued. "We've destroyed some of Dempster's ships, but he's smart enough to never enter our space himself."

Shy shook her head. "ASP isn't restricted to Earth or Consortium space. Why don't they send ships in pursuit of him?" She'd be happy to see Dempster destroyed.

"In the last few years there's been a dramatic increase in smuggling and piracy inside Consortium space. ASP is overwhelmed. We don't have enough agents or ships to protect Earth ships and legitimate colonies."

"And so they sent you out alone to track down and capture him."

Just as it always had, his rich laugh warmed her like hot chocolate after a long, cold, space walk. "No, they don't expect me to do it alone. That's why I'm here. You have contacts throughout the outer worlds, access to places and information no ASP agent could ever hope to have. Once I know Dempster's location, I can call in backup. We're going to take him down."

"Contacts . . ." His words turned to acid in her stomach. "You want me to be a Judas goat. Again."

She'd worked hard to bury the pain of betrayal by both Greyson and her father. Her father's duplicity cut deep. His lies about who and what he was had left her vulnerable. If she'd known the truth, maybe she wouldn't have let slip the information that led to his arrest and imprisonment. She'd forgiven him, incarcerated as he was on a Consortium prison world, but with a standing warrant out for her arrest it was impossible to ever see him again. To initiate or accept any contact would be foolish, as the Consortium had spies everywhere. The fact that Greyson had found her proved as much.

Greyson. His betrayal was beyond forgiveness. Whereas her father had lied to protect her, Greyson had lied to entrap her. She was no longer a naive, trusting little girl enamored of a handsome face. Experience had taught her a hard lesson: Never trust anyone. It had taught her well.

And yet the past was the past. What Greyson offered had to be considered, if it was genuine. Ten years of living a smuggler's life had taken their toll. Long months spent away from her son. Dangerous encounters with desperate men. Never being able to relax, knowing there was always someone out there trying to take away everything you'd worked for. There was also her small crew: the loyal few who hadn't scattered into the outer worlds to make their own way when her father's organization shattered. They deserved more than she could offer. Their smuggling operation earned enough for them to survive, but with little put aside for the future. Still, not one of them objected when she used their hard-earned credits to rescue slaves or help resupply a devastated colony. They were good men. For them, she had to consider Greyson's offer.

But he'd lied to her before. Was he lying to her now?

To another man, Shyanne's face might appear expressionless, but Greyson could see the emotion flickering in her pale blue eyes. He remembered how those eyes darkened from their normal color to a deep azure when they'd made love and she came apart in his arms. For ten years he'd pushed those memories away. Now, in her presence, they came rushing back.

From the first time he saw her he'd fought an instinctive urge to possess and protect her. A willowy young girl with summer-sky blue eyes and golden blonde hair floating around a smiling face, she'd seemed so fresh and innocent. He'd found it hard to believe the Consortium's most-wanted smuggler could be her father, but his superiors claimed she was not only the man's daughter but deeply involved in his operations.

That charge had been false. He knew it now. But at the time he'd been young and idealistic, and he'd believed in ASP and ELF without reservation. He still believed in their purpose, though experience taught him that the men who ran the organizations made mistakes, mistakes that cost him and others dearly. And honesty forced him to admit that at times they were not just inept but also corrupt. But what alternative did one have if one believed in the law? Every planet and every people needed the rule of law.

For months he'd played the part of a student. Ignoring what his heart and conscience told him, he'd courted and wooed Shyanne until she fell into his arms. At the same time he'd fought against what was growing in his heart. He'd convinced himself that by bringing her father to justice he'd be saving her as well. He really was an accomplished liar. And now he needed every bit of his considerable skill to convince Shyanne to help him.

The years had treated her well. Her fresh-faced prettiness had blossomed into womanly beauty. She now wore her blonde hair in a short cap, a style that emphasized her high cheekbones, wide-set eyes and full lips. Though her frame was still willowy, giving her a feline grace, her breasts and hips appeared fuller as they strained against the snug confines of her metallic silver flight suit. The toe of her soft-soled ship boot tapped impatiently as he continued to stare. He pulled his gaze up to meet hers.

While years ago Shyanne had been blameless in her father's crimes, today that wasn't the case. She freely admitted to being a smuggler. Nor was she the trusting innocent he'd lied to before.

"Why did they send *you*?"

Her question snapped him out of his thoughts. "Because of our history, I volunteered."

"You betrayed me before. Why should I trust you?"

He shrugged and answered, "You shouldn't . . . but what choice do you have?"

"I could space you." Her hand rested on the hilt of the pistol at her waist. "No one would ever know what happened."

"They'd have a good idea," Greyson replied. "And what purpose would killing me serve? ASP isn't going to give up. They can't allow murder and piracy to go on like this, unpunished. Even if they wanted to, the Consortium wouldn't let them. On the other hand, if you agree to help capture Dempster, you gain pardons for you and your crew." The old Earth custom of clasping hands to seal a bargain was long out of fashion, but he wanted an excuse to touch her. "Do we have a deal?" He held out his right hand. When she stared as if it might hiss and strike, he let it drop to his side.

"I'll consider your offer. But don't think this means I trust you. I don't. Make one wrong move and you're out the air lock."

Chapter Two

Greyson didn't miss the way Shyanne rubbed her palm against her thigh, surely stifling the urge to touch him, and he suppressed a smile. She wasn't as immune to him as she'd like to be, even if she hadn't given in and shaken his hand. He'd made it past the first hurdle.

"Come on," she said. "It's time you met my crew."

He gingerly rubbed the back of his head and grimaced as his fingers touched a small knot. "I've already met one of them. What did he hit me with?"

"You've met two. Eldin and Bear. Eldin, face-to-face. Bear, fist-to-the-back-of-your-head."

Greyson could hear the amusement in her voice. He followed Shyanne out of the cell into the ship's main corridor. "He hit me with his fist? Felt like an iron pipe."

"Good analogy. You'll understand when you meet him."

She led him through a maze of corridors. The fact she trusted him enough, despite her words, to let him walk behind her gave him hope this relationship might work. But then, as if she heard his thought, she looked over her shoulder and said, "Don't get cocky." Her eyes flicked behind him.

The hairs on the nape of his neck rose. Prepared

to defend himself, Greyson whirled. A body thumped into his, clearly surprised by his sudden stop, and both of them lost their balance and went down in a tangle of arms and legs. Greyson ended up on the bottom, flattened beneath an enormous weight.

Shyanne's laughter echoed in the corridor. "Greyson, meet Bear. You can let him up, Bear."

The large man heaved himself up and off Greyson, who gasped air into his crushed lungs and stared mutely at the hirsute giant towering above. At nearly seven feet tall, Bear had to hunch his massive shoulders to keep his head from brushing the ceiling. Few men who went into space were as large as this; most ships couldn't accommodate even Greyson's six feet two inches. The brute's black hair hung in feltlike ropes around a face that had never used a beard suppressant. Dressed all in black, the figure radiated strength . . . and menace. Then he grinned, his white teeth a shocking contrast against his ebony skin and hair, and held out a huge paw.

Greyson clasped the man's hand with a bit of apprehension. Inside the giant fingers, his own felt like a child's, but Bear's grip, while firm, was gentle. He pulled Greyson to his feet.

"Thanks," Greyson murmured, absently rubbing his hand.

"You can go, Bear," Shyanne said.

Bear's smile disappeared. He fixed his stare on Greyson, the warning in his eyes clear: Harm her and you die. Then he turned and left. For all his bulk, he moved without sound.

Until Bear disappeared around a corner, Greyson hadn't realized he'd been holding his breath. He considered himself fit and capable of defending himself, but in a fistfight against Bear he wouldn't stand a chance. Maybe not even if he had a weapon.

"He's from Cardew," Shyanne remarked.

Greyson searched his mind for the history he'd learned early in his career. All ASP agents had to be familiar with the known outer worlds and their occupants, as well as the thousands accepted into the Consortium. "Cardew. A planet colonized over two hundred years ago by descendants of an African tribe looking to preserve their native culture. When Earth joined the Consortium, they refused to unite with Earth or apply to C.O.I.L. as an independent world." He paused as he remembered Cardew's fate. "They were wiped out when Alphus Prime claimed the planet forty years ago. I didn't know any Cardewians survived."

"Bear's the only one left. During the attack, his parents escaped in a small ship. Brave Alphus Prime warriors—with the full blessing of the Consortium, I'll remind you—tracked them down, boarded the ship, killed his father and tortured and raped his mother while he lay in hiding a few feet away. Before she died and they blew up the ship, she managed to get Bear onto a space raft. They missed his escape in the explosion. A few days later my father found and took him in. He was only five. He's never spoken a word."

Shyanne's monotone recital of the facts didn't hide her rage and disgust for the Consortium. Quite a few citizens of Earth felt the same way, Greyson knew, but until Earth was a full member they had no representation in C.O.I.L.'s main council. Earth League Force feared any move on Earth's part to object might result in expulsion, and there were too many planets who coveted Earth's rich resources to lose C.O.I.L. protection. Again, toeing the line was compulsory at this junction.

Regardless, Greyson decided not to argue the finer points of interstellar politics. Unlike their spirited discussions of ten years ago, when they'd both been young and idealistic but without practical experience, they'd each now seen and done things that put them firmly on opposite sides of this fight—a fight he couldn't afford to lose.

And they couldn't make up the way they used to.

When Greyson didn't rise to her bait, Shy let the subject drop, turned and proceeded down the corridor. Was allowing him to stay aboard her ship foolish? She didn't fear that he'd attack her physically. He'd be an idiot to do so. After meeting Bear, he had to know if he hurt her he'd never make it off the ship alive. Besides, the Greyson she'd known would never sink to using violence against anyone he considered weaker than himself. That personality flaw was what had allowed her to escape ten years ago.

Of course, he could have changed in that time. She herself certainly had. But even now he seemed more diplomat than warrior. No, the danger he posed to her wasn't physical. Words had always been his most powerful weapon. She remembered their arguments when they'd sat up half the night debating the pros and cons of Earth's membership in the Consortium. Even then she'd taken the side against C.O.I.L., but her childhood had been free of the trauma and tragedy she'd seen since. She'd had no idea what she was talking about while parroting her father's words. Now she did.

Yes, during those youthful discussions Greyson's knowledge and logic had easily defeated her idealistic rhetoric, but she'd managed to circumvent his complete victory by other means. Her body heated as she recalled just how she'd always silenced him.

That wasn't an option anymore. It was no more an option than was letting him go.

His offer of pardon tempted her. Not that she trusted him, exactly, but the thought of living with her son—of living without fear, without constantly having to watch her back, finally able to trust someone outside her crew—held an inescapable lure. As well, she had to find out how he'd tracked her. If he could find her, so could Dempster.

"Nice ship." Greyson came abreast of her in the narrow corridor, and his shoulder brushed hers. She sucked in a breath, attempting futilely to break contact, but he didn't seem to notice and ran his hand along the wall. "She's old but well designed and maintained. I don't recognize the make or model."

"Kedar designed and built her himself. She may be older, but she's as good as anything being built today." Since his arrest ten years ago, she'd never again spoken of Kedar as her father. In her mind his lies had stripped him of that title. Unfortunately, the message hadn't quite reached her heart. She referred to him as Kedar, as did his former crew, not only to remind herself of his betrayal and distance herself from him, but to remind herself of who she was—his daughter.

Greyson gave a whistle. "With this kind of talent, I'm surprised he turned to smuggling. Earth League Force would have paid him well to be a designer."

"They never gave him the chance. He was four when Earth joined the Consortium. He and his parents lived on Delta. When the planet officials objected to having their independent-planet status revoked after seventy-five years and becoming a second-class Earth colony, ELF sent in troops to forcibly remove them. During the fighting, Kedar's family was killed." She hadn't known any of this until after his arrest. For all the good it did, he'd tried to protect her by keeping her in the dark. Only as she tried to rebuild her life had she learned of her father's past.

"History is full of tragedy and injustice," Greyson agreed. "Earth League Force had just come into being. Any human colonized planet less than a hundred years old had to come in under Earth's umbrella. Perhaps in their zeal to bring everyone in line with the new law, ELF overreacted."

His weak attempt to explain away the horror of the event enraged her, and Shy whirled to face him. "*Overreacted?* Every person from Delta was judged a criminal and sent to a penal work colony, including Kedar. He spent the next fourteen years doing hard labor for ELF. To court favor with C.O.I.L., they stole his planet, his home, his family and his future. When they finally released him as an ex-convict, he couldn't find work on Earth or any Earth colony. And other C.O.I.L. worlds don't accept ex-cons as immigrants. Is it any surprise he turned to smuggling to survive and had little love for Earth or the Consortium?"

"I'm sorry," Greyson said. "I don't doubt they made a mistake."

Unable to accept his offered sympathy and understanding, Shy turned and strode off down the corridor. At that moment she didn't care if he followed or not; she had to get away from him and the memories.

But which memories was she running from? When she'd learned of her father's past, some of her anger with him died. She'd forgiven him for his crimes, if she couldn't forgive him for abandoning her and betraying her trust in him, for not being the man she'd believed. But those memories, while still tender, weren't the ones that haunted her days and tormented her nights.

She counted her life as rich. Not in credits but in personal relationships. As odd a collection as they might be, she viewed her crew as family. So, why did scarcely a moment in her life pass when she didn't grieve for what might have been if Kedar and Greyson were honest? If they'd been the men she'd thought them to be? It was a question she wasn't ready to forget.

She reached the lift at the end of the corridor and stopped. Despite his heavy gravity boots, Greyson made no sound as he moved over the metal grate flooring, and she sensed rather than heard him come up behind her. The subtle smell of him, reminiscent of rich, dark chocolate, teased her nostrils. Heat from where his hand hovered over her shoulder sent a bolt of longing through her for him to touch her, but when she turned to face him, he stood at least three feet away, his arms hanging loosely at his sides.

Miserable and aching, Shy swallowed a groan.

The sadness in Shyanne's eyes stirred Greyson's emotions. Guilt and pity threatened to drown hope.

During their interviews, Kedar had never spoken of his past to Greyson, or of his reasons for becoming a smuggler. Nor had he discussed his daughter, so Greyson didn't know what to say to erase the pain in Shyanne's expression. Pain he'd helped put there.

He knew her youthful arguments against the Consortium were based on a childhood of being raised by a parent who was anti-C.O.I.L., and now experience had hardened her once idealistic views into antiestablishment dogma. The Consortium was far from perfect, and Earth League Force had its share of sins to answer for, but he believed in the greater good both organizations were set upon accomplishing. C.O.I.L. worlds provided better and safer lives for their inhabitants than the outer worlds. As long as they complied with C.O.I.L.'s simple laws, each member planet was allowed to govern itself without interference.

Of course, break those laws and the imposed penalties were swift and harsh. Earth was particularly vulnerable, as it was still in its probationary period. Greyson didn't claim to understand all the power dynamics, but he knew there were forces that wanted Earth to fail: The manner and localization of the recent upsurge in piracy and other criminal activity was a clear indication of that. It was also why ELF, desperate to avoid drawing negative attention from the Consortium, was coming down hard on ASP. They had to put an end to it.

Greyson spared a moment to wonder what would happen if the ELF officials who drooled over the ships Dane Enterprises built for them learned who designed those ships. Despite his words to Shyanne, he'd recognized the design of her craft immediately. She was right; despite her age, the *Independence* was as good as or better than the battle cruisers being built today. Kedar was a sly dog holding back on his current designs to give his daughter the edge she needed to survive. Though Kedar was a convicted felon, Greyson quickly learned things were not always what they seemed with the man.

For years, Greyson had been bringing Kedar's designs out of prison and helping him bank the proceeds—another black mark against him if it ever came to light.

The door opened, and he followed Shyanne inside the lift. Crammed together in the tiny cubicle, they rode upward in silence. She stood at the front with her back to him. A blast of air from the circulation system ruffled her short hair and he inhaled sharply. Her familiar scent filled his lungs.

Soap. Clean female. A sudden urge to wrap his arms around her and pull her against his chest left Greyson shaken. Years had passed since he'd felt the nearly overwhelming need to touch, smell or taste a woman. No—his hands curled into fists to keep from reaching for her—who was he fooling? The only woman he'd ever felt this way about stood right in front of him. Since she'd blindsided him and run away that day, he'd never again wanted a woman the same way he wanted her. He just hadn't admitted it until this moment. Which meant he was in serious trouble. If he was wrong and she was responsible for the attacks, he'd have to bring her in. If he was right and she was innocent, even if he obtained the pardons he promised, she'd never forgive him for this second betrayal, for his lies.

The lift stopped and the doors slid open. The corridor revealed was better lit than the one below, the metal of the walls buffed and clean.

"*Independence*'s bridge, galley and crew lounge are on this level. Medical bay and crew quarters are on the next deck down." Shyanne pointed out the rooms as they walked. Greyson peered into the open doorways they passed.

Kedar had designed a unique, comfortable and functional craft. Even some of Earth's premier luxury space liners weren't as well laid out or appointed, and the design of *Independence* rivaled the best ELF had to offer in either cargo or military ships. It was a shame he hadn't turned to his talent for ship design sooner rather than becoming a smuggler.

"How many in your crew?"

"There are seven of us."

"That's all?" There was no possible way seven people could be responsible for all the attacks currently being blamed on them. If she was telling the truth, the small size of her crew went a long way to establishing her innocence.

"Despite what you might have heard, we're a small operation."

"This is a pretty big ship for such a small crew," Greyson pointed out. Though his gut told him she was being truthful, he couldn't help wondering why she was being so forthcoming with information. Working his job had given him a healthy dose of skepticism about people and their motives.

Shyanne shrugged. "Kedar built her for his operation, which was much larger than mine. She'll house a crew of up to thirty comfortably. But he also designed her so only two people can fly her if necessary. We prefer to run our business undetected. The less ELF and C.O.I.L. know about us, the better."

"You're not as invisible as you think. Even before this rash of attacks, ASP was aware of your activities."

"Then why haven't they tried to shut us down?"

"As long as you bribed the right officials and hurt no one, I guess they didn't care about the things you smuggled." He didn't mention he'd buried many of the reports he'd seen. "But during one of the recent attacks, slavers abducted a shipload of schoolchildren."

Shyanne stopped walking and stood with her fists clenched at her sides. "I don't kidnap children or run slaves." Her physical reaction told him more than her words.

"One of those children is the six-year-old daughter of a Regalus senator." An older member of C.O.I.L., Regalus held a seat in the Senate and wielded considerable power. With their home planet situated in a barren region of space surrounded by other longtime C.O.I.L. worlds, Regalus had few colonies and little opportunity to expand. They coveted Earth's rich mineral resources. If Earth were expelled from C.O.I.L., Regalus was reputedly prepared and eager to stake a claim. "His screaming was what attracted the Consortium's attention."

Shyanne started to say something but paused, shrugged, then suggested, "And like the good little puppet it is, when the Consortium talks, ASP listens and acts."

Greyson didn't respond.

She sighed and moved forward. "Two levels of *Independence* are cargo holds. The lower level—where you were—houses the engines, weapons systems and a transport bay. We have four smaller ships for moving cargo on and off planets. *Independence* never goes planet-side." She stopped in front of an armored door. "This is the bridge."

He watched as she placed her palm against the ID screen and peered into an eye scanner. The door gave a sharp click but didn't open. As he stepped forward to give it a push, she stopped him before he could. "There are three levels of security. Hand." She held up her palm. "Retinal scan . . . and voice." She spoke a phrase in a language he didn't recognize and his translator chip couldn't interpret. "Miss the third and try to open the door and you're incinerated by lasers from six different angles." She pointed to the front and back, above and below and to either side of the door. "There won't even be enough left of you to sweep up."

Greyson shivered. "Thanks for the warning. I forgot Kedar wasn't the trusting sort."

"He had his reasons," Shyanne replied, eyeing Greyson coldly. "But this goes far beyond what you think. Even if enemies boarded this craft, once he was on the bridge he could escape. The bridge is a self-contained ship of its own."

"Did he ever use it?" Greyson asked.

"I don't know. He never shared that part of his life with me, and Eldin and the others don't know."

"Have you used it?"

"No."

Curiosity made him ask: "How do you know it works?"

"I don't."

"Shouldn't you test it?"

Shyanne smiled and shook her head. "It's not an easy in-and-out. To launch the bridge as an escape shuttle would tear a hole in *Independence* that would disable her and set off a self-destruct sequence."

"Oh," Greyson said. "Well, that's one way of defeating would-be boarders."

"If we need to run, we have four other ships available, remember. Not that we plan on ever doing so. *Independence* is ours, and we'd never give her up without a fight. Now . . . ready to meet my crew?"

Shy watched with interest as she introduced Greyson to the members of her bridge crew: Eldin, Bear and Terle. Each of the three responded according to his personality.

For the last ten years Eldin had been her mentor, friend and substitute father figure. He'd guided her through those first rough years when she struggled to find a way to survive. Though he'd advised against her smuggling, when she'd insisted he'd taught her everything he knew, which was considerable.

Eldin rarely met a man he didn't like. Dempster was one exception, and so he smiled and nodded a greeting to Greyson while monitoring for any other ships in the area. After Greyson's craft slipped up on them without their knowledge, he'd become a bit paranoid. She'd have to let him know about C.O.I.L.'s new stealth technology.

Though Bear's name fit his hulking form, it didn't reflect his nature, which was gentle and quiet. He was an island, rarely interacting with anyone. He was born Theodore Berski, and her father had nicknamed him Teddy Bear. As he'd grown in size, only Bear stuck. He grunted now but didn't look up, lying as he was on the floor beneath a console, busy repairing some ancient wiring. Unless Greyson posed a threat to Shy, the crew or the ship, the man likely wouldn't even acknowledge him. If Greyson became dangerous . . . well, the result would be ugly.

Terle glared at Greyson and then snarled at Shy for bringing him on the bridge. His wild red hair and green eyes only hinted at the temper she knew the man held in check—most of the time. On occasion rumors of his planet-side drinking, whoring and fighting drifted back to her, but never once in all the years she'd known him had he acted out aboard ship or made a pass at her. He was trustworthy.

Swearing one more time, he swung back to his console.

"Ignore him," Shy told Greyson. "Terle's our pilot, but he doesn't work or play well with others."

Eldin let out a bark of laughter.

"Where's the rest of your crew?" Greyson asked, moving about the bridge.

"Checking us out, jerking viper?" Terle snapped.

ASP personal were both proud and sensitive about snake references. Shy caught her breath at the insult and awaited Greyson's reaction. Even Eldin went still and Bear peered out from under the console.

Greyson's lips thinned but he ignored the slur.

To defuse the tension, Shy said, "The rest of the crew—Damon, Able and Silky—are out on deliveries."

Greyson continued. "ASP has a proposal to put forth, but it's for the whole crew, so they should hear it before you all agree."

"You can wipe your ASP with your fujerk proposal." Terle gathered his saliva and prepared to spit until Shy caught his eye. He swallowed, shot a crude hand sign at Greyson and hunched once more over his console.

Eldin leaned back, crossed his arms over his thin chest and gave Greyson an appraising look. "Now, just what kind of proposal would ASP have for the likes of us?"

Greyson met the older man's eyes. "A full pardon

for all crimes past and present against ASP, ELF and C.O.I.L."

Eldin straightened in surprise, his arms dropping to his sides. "And who do we have to kill for this boon?"

Greyson shook his head and grinned at Eldin's response. "No one."

"What makes those jack-offs think we want their slimy pardon?" Terle snarled. "They can take it and—"

"Speak for yourself, ass-wipe," Eldin snapped. "Some of us are getting on in years, are tired of running and always having to watch our backsides. Let the man talk."

Bear crawled out from under the console and crouched near Shy's feet to listen as Greyson explained the proposition. Eldin stroked his chin and regarded Greyson thoughtfully.

"Sounds fair for as far as it goes," the old man admitted. "But if we stop our smuggling operation, what does ASP suggest we live on? Despite what they believe, our profits are small. The thought of giving up the criminal life is attractive, but I for one don't relish the idea of living in poverty. Even without ASP's gracious offer, if we had the means we long ago would have found a place to retire and live out our lives."

Eldin was right. Though they had a place to go, that place relied on them for supplies to survive and none of them had enough put aside to provide those supplies; they needed to continue smuggling. It cost a lot of credits to maintain *Independence*, its shuttles and the home she kept for Rian, not to mention the more charitable activities she and her crew undertook. While she and Damon were still young enough to start new lives, what would happen to Eldin, Bear,

Terle, Able and Silky? Their ages and criminal pasts, as well as some of their physical peculiarities, would make it difficult for them to fit into any normal law-abiding, human community or lifestyle.

Perhaps she could sell *Independence*. No. Selling the ship was out of the question. It was her home and her last tie to Kedar. She knew every inch of the old girl. Losing her just wasn't an option.

Greyson turned as Terle faced him. A shrewd gleam had replaced the anger in his eyes, and the man said, "Even if we agree to help ASP bring Dempster down—which I'm not saying isn't a good idea; the man's scum—we'll be risking everything we have. A pardon isn't enough to make it worth our while. We'd be agreeing to give up our livelihood."

Greyson nodded. "There's a substantial reward for the capture of the pirate responsible for the attacks in Consortium space. I imagine that will help you all resettle in more . . . legitimate careers." The reward was real; he just didn't add it was posted for Shyanne rather than Dempster. They probably already knew about the price on her head.

Eldin asked, "What do you think, Shy?"

Greyson saw the respect in the old man's eyes, and the other two men also as they looked to Shyanne for guidance. Even Terle, despite his macho attitude, waited before saying anything else.

"It's something to consider, but as Greyson suggested, we need to discuss it with the others before we come to a decision. That's only fair. When are they due back?"

"Able and Silky should be coming in anytime. Damon's scheduled to rendezvous with us tomorrow," Eldin answered.

"Good. We'll convene then and decide. In the meantime, I'll get our guest settled." She faced Greyson. "Come on. I'll show you to your quarters."

"The brig is nice and comfy," Terle muttered.

Greyson followed Shyanne off the bridge. The door slid shut behind them with a solid thunk, cutting off Eldin's chuckle, and the pair walked silently down the corridor and into the lift. The door closed and they were sealed inside.

What happened next came as a surprise. With a muffled thump, the lift jolted, dropped, then jerked to a halt. Thrown off balance, Greyson staggered. His right shoulder rammed painfully into the wall and Shyanne fell against him. Instinctively he wrapped his arms around her, to keep her from falling, as a series of what sounded and felt like explosions rocked the ship. The lights flickered and went out, leaving them in complete darkness.

For a few seconds Shyanne didn't react. Her back pressed against Greyson from shoulder to hip. He could feel the rapid thud of her heart beneath his palm.

When the emergency lights kicked in, washing the small lift in a ghostly reddish hue, she straightened away from him and touched her fingertip to her left temple, where a communication chip was embedded. A moment later she said, "Damn. Com system is down."

Greyson's arms felt empty without her. "What happened?"

Busy with the lift control panel, she didn't look at him. "I don't know. *Independence* is old. Sometimes bits of her electrical system short out, but . . . I don't think that's what happened this time. Those felt like explosions. We're under attack." She turned to him, calm as could be, and pointed toward an access panel at the top of the lift. "The controls are fried. Give me a boost up."

"Let me go first. I don't think you'll be able to lift me out."

"Maybe that was the plan." In the glow of the red light, her grin was wicked. Then she put her hands together, and he put his foot into her cupped palms.

"Not much of a plan," he muttered. "Even without your help I could get out of this box."

The access panel slid aside in a shower of rust. Coughing, Greyson pulled himself through the narrow opening and up into the dark shaft beyond; the dim emergency lights from the lift barely penetrated. Fortunately the ship was only four decks high, and the lift seemed to be stuck halfway down, so they didn't have far to climb.

"Not if I blocked the access panel from the outside," she called up, continuing the joke.

"Good thing I went first, then." He lay across the roof of the lift, leaned his head through the opening and reached down. "Give me your hand."

Her fingers felt cool and slim, her grip firm. His injured shoulder protested as he hauled her up.

"Where to?" he asked.

"Follow me." Without hesitation she scrambled up a flimsy-looking ladder almost invisible against the wall of the shaft. Greyson eyed the thin space between the lift and the shaft wall and hoped the power didn't decide to kick in. If it did, they'd end up a lot thinner.

Decades of dust and grease coated the walls of the shaft and the rungs of the ladder. Where in the vacuum of space had it all come from? His heavy gravity boots gripped the metal, but he could see Shyanne struggling to maintain her hold and balance with her soft-soled ship boots.

Twenty feet above the lift they reached the end of the ladder. Standing on the top rung, she reached up to pry open the outer lift doors. Her feet slipped. One foot slammed into Greyson's cheek. The other hit his injured shoulder. The impact knocked his hand loose and jarred his feet off the ladder. He dangled by his left arm.

At the same time, Shyanne scrambled to regain her balance. Trying to grab the ladder, she couldn't get a solid hold on the slick rungs. With a strangled scream, she fell. Greyson's heart lurched as she went past. In a moment of terror, his arm flashed out and grabbed the back of her shirt. She jolted to a stop. Pain shot up his arm. He gritted his teeth and swung her toward the wall.

"You can let go. I've got the ladder again," she said. "Thanks."

Her head pressed against the side of his hip, she guided his feet back to the ladder. He unclenched his fingers from the back of her shirt, but when he tried to raise his arm to grip the ladder again, his vision started to go black. He leaned his head against the top rung and fought to remain conscious.

"Are you all right?" Shyanne asked.

"I think I dislocated my shoulder. You need to climb back up around me and try again to open the doors."

She didn't argue. Slipping up past him, she brushed against his injured arm. He bit his lip to keep from groaning.

Though he could only grip the ladder with his left hand, he moved up behind her so his chest pressed against her hips; maybe that would keep her more secure as she pried at the doors. Her tremors echoed his own. His heart raced at the thought of what had almost happened. The fall might not have killed her, but landing across the lift support beams would have broken her body.

The doors slid open with a creak. Light flooded the shaft, and Greyson blinked against the glare. Hands reached down and pulled Shyanne up and through the opening. Greyson could hear voices but couldn't make out words. He struggled to remain alert.

"Careful. His shoulder's probably dislocated," Shyanne was telling Eldin and Bear. They gripped Greyson and yanked him out of the shaft. Barely conscious, he groaned and slumped against the wall of the corridor.

As much as Shy wanted to see to Greyson—he'd saved her life!—the safety of her ship and crew took priority. "What happened?" she asked Eldin.

"Damn slave ship fired on us! They came out of subspace sending Spitfire's locater ID. By the time we had visual and realized it wasn't Damon's ship, they'd already attacked. Caught us off guard."

"How much damage?" Her gaze strayed to where Greyson now sat listening. His cheeks were colorless and his gaze, though pain-filled, was clear again.

"Minor. Knocked out a couple of thrusters, put a few dents in the hull and shorted some electrical systems—that elevator's unfortunately among them. Probably used the Spitfire's locator ID in an attempt to slip by us. They obviously weren't looking for a fight they couldn't possibly win, just trying to put us out of commission long enough to get away. Must have heard our reputation of confiscating human cargo. They missed the weapons system."

"Did you get a shot at them?"

"No, we didn't fire. Even a small blast would have blown the poor buggers apart."

She knew he referred to the slaves, not the slavers. Having been one himself, with the scars both inside and out to prove it, Eldin had little sympathy for those who traded in human flesh—and maybe too much for the slaves themselves. "Might have been more merciful," she suggested.

"Probably." Eldin sighed. "Just couldn't do it. Where there's life there's hope."

"How long for repairs?"

"Four or five hours."

"Do we know who they were?"

Eldin shook his head. "I didn't recognize the ship: a small, older ranger-class model, held together with spit and a prayer. No markings. Can't hold more than a crew of three, along with ten or twenty slaves in the hold."

Shy sighed. Unfortunately, running slaves was still far too easy, especially out here. Few outer-world governments cared, and even fewer did anything to stop it. The slave trade was huge both in the outer worlds and in Consortium space. Though Earth and its colonies had banned it, many other worlds still used slave labor. And so long as the slavers didn't break any other C.O.I.L. laws, the Consortium didn't see fit to interfere.

"Any idea where they were coming from?"

"No, but Terle tagged them with a locator beacon. Looks like they're headed toward that shit-hole, Verus."

Only someone desperate to unload their human cargo would land on Verus. Selling a slave there was barely worth the trip. Inhabitants of the resource-destitute desert planet were scum: criminals, mental cases, those unwelcome anywhere else in the outer worlds. Few women lived there, and those who did rarely lasted very long.

"Damn." Shy rubbed a hand around the back of her neck. Her head ached where she'd hit it against the ladder. "We're behind schedule, and we've already got enough complications." She looked down at Greyson, who eyed her with interest.

"What do you want to do?" Eldin asked, as if he didn't already know.

She couldn't ignore this problem, but she didn't need another drain on her already waning resources. "Get going on the repairs. Send a message to Able and Damon to rendezvous with us behind Verus's fifth moon."

"What about him?" Eldin glanced at Greyson. "Want me to take a look at him?"

Shy shook her head. "No. I'll take care of him. Bear, help me get him to the med bay."

Chapter Three

Greyson winced as Bear gripped his uninjured arm. He flexed it and groaned. He was pretty sure his shoulder was dislocated. When he tried to look, the pain made him nauseated and light-headed. Still, he said, "I don't need to go to med bay. I'm fine."

Shyanne glanced over her shoulder at him and muttered something that sounded like "Men . . ."

Bear's hand tightened in warning. It didn't look as though he had a choice. Greyson sighed and let the giant help him to his feet. Dark spots blurred his vision. Maybe a sling and a few painkillers wouldn't be such a bad idea. He followed meekly.

When they got there, Shyanne pointed at the room's examination bed. "Sit. You can go, Bear."

The man glared at Greyson, then nodded and left the room. The door slid shut with a soft *snick*.

Greyson sat on the edge of the bed and watched while Shyanne moved around the well-stocked and organized medical bay. Though the rest of the ship might be showing age, the equipment here was state-of-the-art and more than adequate for even the most delicate surgery.

Shyanne came to his side to help him pull down the top half of his flight suit. When she probed the tender flesh around the swollen joint, he flinched and swore. "So much for my macho image."

She grinned. "Partially dislocated. Lie down and I'll move it back into place."

He did as she instructed.

She bent his arm at the elbow and rotated it externally. Every inch sent pain streaking down his arm. He gasped. Sweat beaded on his forehead.

She paused and asked, "Do you want something for the pain?"

"No," he ground out. "Just get it done."

She nodded and continued. When his arm reached a thirty-five-degree angle, he heard and felt a pop. He closed his eyes and went limp in relief. Though his arm still ached, the excruciating pain stopped.

Something cool moved down his arm from shoulder to elbow. With each pass, the ache lessened. He opened his eyes to see Shyanne running a small silver-colored rod over his arm. The rod gave off a milky blue glow.

"What's that? What are you doing?" he asked.

She didn't answer, instead saying, "I don't think there's any muscle or ligament damage." She leaned away from him. The rod's glow faded. "How does your arm feel?"

He sat up and tentatively flexed, surprised to find he had full motion with little residual pain, no more than he'd have from a heavy workout. He rotated his arm. "What did you do? What is that thing?"

"Something I picked up a few years ago. Handy. Repairs most muscle and ligament injuries without surgery."

"How does it work?"

She shrugged. "I haven't a clue. Got it from an alien

whose spacecraft was disabled by a meteor. We rendered a bit of assistance and he gave it as payment, though we didn't speak the same language. I thought it was a bar of metal, maybe platinum. Was going to sell it. It's not. Can't quite determine what type of metal it is, though, and discovered its use by accident."

"Can I see it?

"Sure." She tossed the rod to him. "Won't do you any good, though. When it's working, you can't examine it. When it's not, there's nothing to see; it's just a solid piece of some unknown metal."

She was right. He rolled the wand around in his palms. Aside from being warm to the touch, it appeared to be nothing more than a solid rod, without any indication of seams or internal parts.

"We've scanned it but there's nothing inside."

"What species of alien did you get it from?"

"Don't know. Like I said, we couldn't communicate well. Not even my translator chip could decipher their language. Trying just gave me a raging headache. Silky had a long interaction with them, but she never let on if she learned much."

"Then they're not from a C.O.I.L. world. And if your translator didn't work . . ." He tossed the rod back. Realization washed over him. "You've been in the Beyond."

"Yes. Why shouldn't I?"

"Consortium law strictly regulates first contact with nonaffiliated worlds and species."

She threw back her head and laughed. "And I should care about C.O.I.L.'s stupid laws why? I'm already a criminal, and their stupid laws—"

"Laws are what allow mankind to live civilized lives."

"Granted, but some lawmakers are corrupt and unjust."

The sparkle in her eyes warned him this would be no easy battle. Greyson struggled to keep from continuing the dispute. Cooperation, not conflict, was his goal. Reengaging her disdain of all things C.O.I.L. wasn't the best way to achieve success. And he couldn't help but fear a debate with her would no longer be a sure win.

"I think we'll have to agree to disagree about Consortium law," he said. Trying to get things back on track, he asked, "When will you and your crew decide on my offer?"

Disappointment washed through Shy. She'd hoped to engage him in a war of words. When they were younger, his greater knowledge had allowed him to demolish her arguments against the Consortium, but now she could hold her own. So of course Greyson had ended the discussion. It figured.

She crossed her arms over her chest, leaned back against the med cabinet and muttered, "Still the single-minded ASP agent."

He avoided her gaze. Not that she was looking at his face. The sight of his chest, where his flightsuit gaped open, revealing an expanse of smooth golden skin, distracted her. How did he manage to maintain his coloring? And did he do it all over? She glanced at her own arm and remembered how pale it had looked against his. Memories made her tremble. Warmth surged through her. Her breasts grew heavy and moisture gathered in her mouth and groin.

She stiffened. *No.* Her current attraction to Greyson was only the aftermath of the adrenaline rush from almost falling to her death: Sex was the ultimate reaffirmation of life. She wouldn't succumb to the need pounding in her veins. For ten years she'd buried her craving for human contact, for *him*. She could do it again. Why did it get harder each time their eyes met?

Straightening, she asked, "Why are you so determined to capture Dempster? What's in it for you?" That was the relevant question.

Greyson snared Shyanne's gaze and began. "The current director, Williams, is convinced you're behind these attacks. He's gone on the record saying as much. He didn't object when I decided to pursue another direction, though." Of course the man hadn't objected; Greyson hadn't asked permission. "If I'm wrong, only I'll be discredited and he doesn't lose anything. If I'm right and we bring Dempster in, he'll say I was working under his guidance. He'll use the credit to further his political ambitions and I'll become the new director."

"What if you're right but you can't capture Dempster?" Shyanne asked.

"I doubt it will matter; I'll probably be dead. I'm sure the director will find a way to blame everything on me, though."

"What about your deal with my crew? What happens to them if we prove our innocence but can't capture Dempster?"

Greyson hesitated. He knew she deserved the truth, but he couldn't take the risk of losing her cooperation. Too many lives depended on him succeeding. He looked away and lied. "ASP will honor my agreement with you. But . . . it won't matter."

"What do you mean?"

"Well, if at the end of the month the attacks continue, the Consortium will get involved. They have a plan. That's what ELF is trying to avoid."

"What is it?"

Greyson reached out and grabbed her hand. About this he wouldn't lie. She deserved—needed to know the truth, what was at risk. "Their intended cleanup won't be limited to Earth space and a track-down of these killers. The outer worlds will be purged of all sentient life and opened to colonization by C.O.I.L. members. It's a proposition they've been considering for some time, and this is just the excuse they need. This is why Earth's government didn't want to agree to their plan. At least not right away."

Shyanne's fingers tightened on his. "Th-they c-can't do that. They wouldn't. There are millions of people in the outer worlds!"

Greyson shrugged. "C.O.I.L. can and will. It isn't common knowledge, but they've done similar things in the past. I've read the records. And if they decide on this plan of action and Earth objects . . . well, as a probationary member it's subject to the same treatment. At the very least, Earth will be expelled from C.O.I.L. Even if they do nothing more, which isn't a sure thing, Earth will get no protection from them when other planets attack. Over the millennia the Consortium has deemed more than one species unfit to be a member and wiped them out of existence. That's why ELF is determined to stop the problem before C.O.I.L. gets involved."

"Isn't there anything ELF can do to stop this atrocity?"

"Most Consortium technology is far beyond ours.

They've only shared small bits with us, things like the MAT units and the stealth technology. There's little chance our troops could win such a battle—if anyone even decided to stand up to them. And without Consortium backing, Earth stands no chance against all-out war with other more advanced planets, so in the end it's unlikely Earth's government will interfere with C.O.I.L.'s plans."

She sagged. "It all means nothing. Freedom. Independence. Those things are nothing more than a mirage. Earth. Its colonies. The outer worlds. We're all in thrall to the Consortium, whether we know it or not."

Greyson slid off the table and walked to her side. When he cupped her cheek in his palm, she looked into his eyes.

"Yes and no," he said. "Certainly the Consortium has the power to make and enforce its laws. And, right or wrong, Earth voted to join. In doing so, we took on the obligation to obey those laws. As long as we do so, we're free to live our lives without interference. Every law-abiding member is free to live his or her life."

Shy glared at Greyson, but she couldn't bring herself to move away. Oddly, the warmth of his hand eased the icy fissure his words had torn in her heart. She also knew he meant what he said, though she believed his government was turning a blind eye to evil. "*I* didn't join C.O.I.L.," she whispered.

"No, but our species made the choice. Like it or not, we now have to live with the consequences. Though I agree there's a lot wrong with their methods, I still believe the benefits to mankind outweigh the negatives. And Dempster needs to be destroyed. This is an excellent incentive." He gave a wry smile.

Shy shook her head. "Tell me that after the Consortium kills everyone in the outer worlds."

She tried to pull away, but Greyson wrapped his arms around her and tugged her into his embrace. "With your help it won't come to that, Shy."

For a moment she let herself relax in his arms, absorbing his strength. It had been a long time since she'd leaned on anyone, let anyone else be strong and carry her. Being in his arms felt good. *Too* good. Leaning on anyone made her weak. She jerked out of his hold and stalked away. When he didn't try and restrain her, part of her felt forsaken.

She sensed him watching her as she paced the small chamber. If he was telling the truth, what choice did she have? Despite her outrage and sometimes bravado, she knew neither Earth nor the outer worlds were a match for the Consortium. In existence for thousands of years, with a membership of species numbering in the thousands, C.O.I.L. ruled vast reaches of space and could call upon endless resources. Earth and the outer worlds were mere specks, insects to be swatted as soon as they became an annoyance.

Also, even if Greyson was lying and there was no planned attack by C.O.I.L., she knew her choice still had to be the same. Even if Dempster weren't casting the blame in her direction, she couldn't allow him to continue preying upon the weak and helpless, murdering and slaving and increasing his power. For years she had run away from the man. It was time to make a stand.

* * *

Greyson watched and waited while Shyanne paced. He could almost hear the argument raging in her mind. Had he misjudged her? Had the years changed her from the idealistic young woman she'd been? Was her loyalty to her species and the innocents of the outer worlds strong enough to overcome her distrust of ASP and ELF? What options did he have if she refused to help?

None. It was a rueful admission, but alone he didn't stand a chance of locating Dempster in time, forget capturing him.

Her expression determined, she turned to him. "I have work to do. You can stay here for now. Don't leave without an escort," she warned.

The words were unnecessary. Greyson had already noted sick bay locked from the outside.

"I can't be responsible for Terle if he catches you wandering around by yourself," she added.

"Worried about what I might do to him?" Greyson asked.

Shyanne gave an unladylike snort, and her determined look faded, replaced by amusement. "Hardly. He'd chew you up and spit out the hair—what little of it you have left."

He smiled and ran his hand over his close-shorn pate. After she'd disappeared, every time he'd combed or brushed the shoulder-length strands out of his eyes, memories of her surged up. Finally, in a fit of disgust he'd shaved it off and kept it short ever since.

"Easier to maintain," he lied. "Yours is shorter, too." Unable to stop himself, he reached out and threaded his fingers through her hair. The short, silky strands wrapped enticingly around his fingers. Her scalp felt soft and warm beneath the pads of his fingers. He felt the catch in her breath as she tilted her head into his palm, and her eyelids drooped. "It used to reach the middle of your back."

Memories of how her hair had brushed against his bare chest as she moved above him made his body swell, and compelled by a need stronger than common sense, he let his hand slip to the back of her head to tug her toward him. At the same time he stepped closer.

With a desperate little moan, she tried to retreat. Fresh and sweet, her scent rose on her body heat to surround him in a sensual haze. His chest barely touched hers as they stood together, their harsh, rapid breaths mingling.

Her hands came to rest on his chest. For a torturous second he feared and prayed she was going to push him away; then she wrapped her arms around his neck and pressed her hips to his in an age-old gesture of need.

"Damn," he whispered as he brought his lips down over hers.

Shy swallowed Greyson's muffled curse and took control of the kiss. She stroked the seam of his lips with her tongue until he groaned in surrender and granted her entrance. Rich and warm, the taste of him exploded in her mouth, just as she remembered. Liquid heat rushed to her groin. Hot and insistent, desire boiled through her. Reason dissolved under need.

For ten long years she'd denied herself the comfort of a man's embrace. Aside from her son, she allowed no one to touch or hold her, physically or emotionally. She gave her crew her loyalty but refused to acknowledge they owned more of her heart than that. Loving people made you vulnerable.

She wanted this man, though. *Now.* For the moment the past didn't matter. Her body needed—demanded—what only he could offer. Consequences be damned. She'd deal with the future when it arrived.

"Shyanne, stop." Greyson put his hands on her shoulders, but rather than pushing her away, his fingers tightened as if to hold her in place. "Mixing business with pleasure isn't a good idea."

"It's the best idea I've had in ten years. Fuck business. Better yet, fuck me," she murmured against his lips. At that moment she didn't care what her words revealed.

"You'll regret this."

Somewhere in the back of her mind she knew he was right, but physical need trumped rational self-preservation. A whole decade of need. "The only thing I'll regret is if you don't fuck me right now." She used crude words to keep from revealing what she really wanted, and she silenced his weak objection with her mouth over his.

Sliding her hands inside the open front of his flight suit, she stroked them down his chest. Her hand moved lower and surrounded his sleek, hot sex. At the same time she nibbled kisses down his throat and chest until she reached his nipple. With one hand cupping his testicles and the other dancing over his cock, she nipped the hard nub. He groaned a protest when she moved back and let go of him, then went motionless as she peeled away his flight suit and tugged off his boots.

When he stood naked before her, she sucked in her breath. Avoiding his eyes, she let her gaze travel down his body. Smooth skin stretched over his muscled chest, which heaved with every breath he took. His fists clenched at his sides. She smiled in feminine satisfaction.

Despite his words, he was far from unmoved. A narrow line of hair arrowed down from below his navel to his groin. There, thick and bold, his cock, pale against its nest of dark chocolate curls, stood at attention. A bead of moisture glistened at its tip. She licked her lips and raised her eyes to meet his. His heated look scorched her.

"Are you sure this is what you want?" he asked in a strangled voice. Despite his obvious arousal, he was leaving the decision to her. It would have been easier if he'd taken command. This way left her no excuse.

His question increased her apprehension. Want? No, she screamed silently. She didn't want to want him. After all the pain and grief he'd caused her, how could she want him? No, she didn't want this . . . she *needed* it, the release his body could give hers.

"Yes," she said.

A small smile touched his lips, and the tension radiating off his body vanished. He took a step toward her.

When she tensed, he placed his palm against her cheek and looked into her eyes. "Trust me. I won't hurt you."

Looking into his eyes, she wanted to believe him. Wanted to feel what she'd felt all those years ago: pure, innocent love, untarnished by lies or deceit. But that time was long gone. Those feelings were long dead, the people who'd felt them long discarded. Whatever they shared now could be only physical. Lust: Yes. Sex: Hell, yes. Trust? Hell, no.

She stood in silent anticipation as he peeled away her clothing. She shivered. Not from the cool air swirling over her bare skin, but from the heated look in his dark eyes. Her breasts swelled. He leaned forward and captured one hard nipple between his lips and sucked. Wet heat sizzled through her. Her knees buckled. To keep from falling, she grabbed his shoulders, then gasped as he swung her into his arms and deposited her on the exam table.

He crawled up and over her. His cock brushed against the inside of her thigh where, slick and hot, moisture gathered. Desire churned in her belly.

She reached up and pulled his mouth to hers. Their tongues tangled in a silent battle, and she realized her control was an illusion. Under the assault of his hands, lips and tongue, rational thought deserted her. His lips left hers to trail down her throat. She arched her neck to grant him access. Breath shuddered out of her as he rolled one aching nipple between his fingers and sucked the other into his mouth. The suction sent frissons of long forgotten sensation coursing through her, like the tiny bubbles in effervescent wine they tingled in her veins.

Need built the pressure inside her, need dammed up without release. Her skin felt supersensitized. Greyson stroked his fingertips down her chest and belly and explored the indent of her navel. Lower, he combed through her damp curls. One finger moved past the hair and delved into the slick folds.

When he circled her clit, the surge of energy from the brief touch jolted her and she gasped. He tried to pull his hand away, but she grasped his wrist and held him there. She felt him grin against her breast.

Twisting her body, she flipped him onto his back,

then rose on her knees and straddled his hips. Air cooled the heat on her breast, but the feel of his hard cock pressing against her pubic mound sent a surge of heat into her belly. Though his cock throbbed, bouncing gently against her, and his breathing was rapid, he smiled.

Every nerve coiled in anticipation, but his command of his passion angered her. She wanted him as frantic for satisfaction as she. Desperate to take back control, to get what she needed from him, she lifted her hips over him and plunged downward.

She gasped at the small spear of pain from his intrusion into her body. Years of going without had left her tight. Still, unwilling to wait for her body to adjust to his size, she rode him fast and hard.

Clasping her thighs with his hands, he met her stroke for stroke, pushing her ever upward. The bubbles in her blood turned to sparks of fire. Inside her an inferno raged, burning away the last of her reason, her doubts and her fears. Nothing mattered but reaching this summit and plunging into the abyss beyond.

With a burst of inner light, she climaxed. She cried out and fell forward over him. He thrust upward one last time and she felt his liquid heat flow into her. She pressed her face against his sweat-slick body and murmured, “This doesn’t change anything. I may still space you.”

He chuckled. “I’ll worry about that tomorrow.”

She didn’t object further when he enfolded her in his arms and held her close. Her breathing returned to a semblance of normal. Both drained and filled, they lay tangled together until sleep claimed them.

Chapter Four

Shy stared at the man dozing on the narrow med-bay bed beside her. She'd wanted him. Oh, how she'd wanted him, and she'd taken what he could give her with little hesitation. In her moment of need she'd ignored his past and possibly present betrayal. Had it been wise?

What was it about Greyson Dane that spoiled her for any other man? He wasn't the most physically attractive man she'd ever met. His body was above average, lean and firm, strong enough to make a woman feel secure in his arms, certainly, but not muscle bound. His features were even and pleasant. With his eyes closed, though, he looked almost ordinary, the kind of man you'd see anywhere and barely notice. Her crewmate Damon was far better looking than Greyson. But for all his golden good looks, perfect body and charm, Damon—even if she hadn't considered him a brother—didn't stir her blood that way. No other man ever had.

Her mind told her this had been a bad idea, but her body still tingled from their lovemaking. No, not *love*making. Love had no part of her relationship with Greyson. She'd gone that route once and lost everything. They'd had sex just now. Great, mind-blowing sex, but just sex. Sex her body was already beginning to want again.

Shy groaned.

But, her body argued, as long as she didn't trust Greyson, why shouldn't she enjoy a physical relationship with him? Why shouldn't she use him to satisfy needs long denied? And as long as she didn't love him, he couldn't hurt her again.

Satisfied she'd resolved the conflict, she curled up next to him and closed her eyes. She had a few hours to rest before she needed to act.

Greyson woke with his body sated and content but his mind in turmoil. Shyanne sprawled on her stomach asleep beside him. The smell of their passion lingered in the air.

He stroked his hand over her back. Her skin felt like satin. He knew he shouldn't have taken her to bed—scratch that; let *her* take *him* to bed—but in spite of the complications a renewed relationship between them would cause, he didn't regret a moment of what they'd just shared. Nothing in his life compared to the feeling of completion she gave him. In comparison, the last ten years felt like a cold, barren wasteland. How had he survived so long without her? How could he keep her in his life?

Their first affair had been the fault of his youth and inexperience: Taken with her innocence and joy in living, he'd fallen hard for her. He smiled as he remembered their courtship. She'd been a virgin when they first came together, but apart from her name there'd been nothing shy or retiring about Shyanne

Kedar. As with everything else in her life, she'd approached sex with curiosity and abandon. Once she decided to be with him, he hadn't stood a chance.

But what had drawn her to him? What had she seen in him all those years ago? He didn't consider himself outstanding in the looks department. Though he kept in shape, his body wasn't bulging with muscle. With brown hair, brown eyes and pleasant, even features, he'd made the perfect undercover ASP agent. Like a chameleon he faded into whatever environment was necessary, careful not to stand out in a crowd or in people's minds.

His original job had been to watch her and report back, not to get involved with her. He'd never expected her to approach or even notice him. She was a bright golden flame, the most popular girl in school. Nonetheless, she had fallen for him, and once she did, he was lost—to both her and his superiors in ASP. Having to eventually betray her trust had gone against everything he thought he stood for, but at the time his allegiance to authority had been unquestioning and his rage against Stewart Kedar unwavering. Now he realized what blind loyalty and the thrist for vengeance had cost him.

She'd changed. The woman she was today was much more reserved and cautious—until he kissed her, at least. For those few minutes while they were physically connected, he'd collapsed the walls she'd built around her heart and mind. But what excuse did he have for courting her trust?

She *was* why he was here, of course, putting his career and his life on the line. It wasn't just fear of the Consortium's plan that moved him. With both ASP and ELF out gunning for Shyanne, it was only a matter of time before something terrible happened. Even if she was truly guilty of the crimes she was accused of committing—which he found impossible to believe—he wouldn't allow her to be killed or captured. He owed her a life. Too bad that life could never be with him. No matter what happened, ELF was going to be extremely angry he'd disobeyed his director. He'd end up in prison, but it would be worth it.

Though her life was a crucial consideration, his motive went deeper than Shyanne. As he'd told her, if C.O.I.L. got involved in the cleanup, human life on the outer worlds would be totally eliminated. His adopted father had told him of it, and of the enforcers C.O.I.L. would use. No one knew for sure what these creatures were. They operated out of their ships, never making physical contact. Very few planets survived their arrival. And if Earth objected they could be destroyed as well or expelled from the Consortium, left fair game to any greedy C.O.I.L. member. Maybe it was foolhardy of him to attempt to capture Dempster on his own, but Greyson saw no other choice.

Shyanne murmured something in her sleep and curled closer to him. Thoughts of Dempster, the director and C.O.I.L. faded from Greyson's mind as her body brushed against his. Soon enough he'd have to deal with his lies and deception, but selfish or not, for now he'd grab what he could.

His intent was interrupted as the door slid suddenly open. Greyson tensed, sensing another presence enter the room. Turning to look, he nearly bolted upright in surprise.

Beautiful and deadly, its sleek body covered in silvery fur, a hundred-pound cat crouched on the floor just inside the door. Its tufted ears lay flat against its head. The tip of its tail twitching, its body was bunched and tense, ready to attack. Almost unnoticed at the creature's feet crouched six normal-sized cats. They also watched Greyson, their shoulders hunched, eyes piercing and tails swishing.

Greyson blinked, meeting the creature's gaze. This was no ordinary cat; intelligence gleamed out of those sea green eyes. He searched for a weapon. Pound for pound, cats were the most dangerous predator. He and Shyanne wouldn't stand a chance against this one's teeth and claws, especially naked.

He shifted until his body blocked Shyanne's. The movement woke her. "Don't budge," he whispered.

Shyanne rose on her arms and peered over his shoulder. Her soft chuckling made her breasts rub against his back, and the cat snarled, showing its long, gleaming canines. Greyson tensed.

"Go away, Silky," Shyanne told the cat. "Take your friends and find another bunk for the night."

The cat hissed and rose on its hind legs. Greyson watched the outline of its body blur and begin to change shape. His stomach roiled at the impossible sight. Dizzy and unable to watch, he closed his eyes. When he opened them again, the cat was gone. In its place, instead of a four-legged animal, there was a bipedal humanoid. Only the silvery fur that covered its body and the emerald eyes were the same.

Be vigilant, human.

Like icy daggers, words stabbed into his mind. He groaned and pressed his palm against his temple and translator chip.

The cat glanced at Shyanne, then whirled and left the room. Tails high, the other cats followed.

Reeling from pain, Greyson looked at Shyanne. "Who or what was that? I'm familiar with every C.O.I.L. planet and their native inhabitants." Or at least he'd thought he was. Maybe he'd missed a few; there *were* thousands. "I've never seen or heard of anything like that creature."

Seemingly unconcerned about the cat-thing, her nakedness or the fact that they'd made love, Shyanne sat up. The sight of her body drove the pounding blood from his head lower into his body. He tugged the sheet over his hips to hide the reaction.

"We're not sure what Silky is," Shyanne admitted. "I found her in a bar on Tartala a couple of years ago. The owner had bought her off a passing trader to help keep down the local rat population."

"She's a bit big to be chasing rats."

Shyanne grinned. "You haven't seen the rats on Tartala. Besides, back then Silky wasn't quite as large as she is now. Apparently, the idea didn't work out the way the bar owner hoped. When he made the deal, Silky was drugged. After the drugs wore off, Silky became less willing to do his bidding. He chained her and stuck her in a cage, charged his patrons to watch her fight. By the time we came along, she was near dead from starvation and fighting. The bar owner was happy to let me take her off his hands."

"How did you tame her?"

"*Tame* her?" Shyanne chuckled again. "I don't think so. Silky isn't an animal. She's a member of my crew. Also, just so you know, we refer to Silky as a she for convenience. We're not sure of her sex."

"Did you ask her?"

"Sure, but either she doesn't know or doesn't care to answer. Eldin took care of her injuries, but he hasn't been able to figure out her gender—or if she even has one."

Greyson rubbed his aching head. "What did she do to me?"

Shyanne touched his temple with her fingertips. Warmth coursed through him.

"She's telepathic. Translator chips amplify her thoughts. If she likes you, she whispers so it doesn't hurt so bad. If she's angry or doesn't like you, she shouts."

"Makes sense." He didn't understand the micro-technology involved, but he knew TCs translated the electrical impulses of thoughts, so telepathic messages would definitely be picked up.

Residual pain flared behind his eyes, and he groaned and asked, "How do I get her to like me?" Shyanne's trill of laughter caused his head to pound. He closed his eyes and waited to die.

If Shyanne felt anything about what had transpired between them, he couldn't tell. Calm and collected, she rose from the bed, dressed and requested him to accompany her. Still reeling from Silky's mental assault, and from the bizarre queasiness brought on by watching the cat-thing's body morph, he complied without protest. At some point he'd have to ask about the creature's shifting ability and his reaction to it. He dressed and followed Shyanne out of the room.

Greyson's ability to separate his personal and business lives had made him an excellent field agent and an even better administrator. Now, with Shyanne, he found he didn't have that balance. She didn't seem to be having the same problem. Her manner had been one of distant courtesy, as if they hadn't just made love. It gave him an odd twinge: If she and her crew decided to reject his deal, would they really space him?

He couldn't say he didn't deserve it.

Verus's fifth moon came into view on the main screen, and Shy nodded. Though little more than an oversized rock caught in Verus's gravity well, the satellite had a dense metal composition that would block *Independence* from detection.

Terle and Able manned the controls. Greyson stood to one side, observing without comment. Bear was down in the shuttle bay getting the ship *Liberty* prepped, while Eldin prepared the med bay—even though the ship that had fired on them was small, capable of holding only a few slaves, they were headed for a slave auction on Verus. No telling how many slaves they'd end up bringing back.

After a quick look at her account, she hoped there were only a few up for sale. The rest of the crew had offered to contribute, but she'd rather not take their money if she could help it. Despite their constant comments, this was her cause, not theirs. They shouldn't have to pay.

There were other ways to gain custody of slaves besides paying, but Shy and Bear usually posed as an acquiring madam and her enforcer and took the easiest and least dangerous method of outright purchase. Sometimes a grateful family paid a reward for the return of a loved one, but those situations were few and far between; if a family had money, slavers usually took a ransom. Most of the slaves Shy rescued came from devastated colonies, and slaves auctioned on Verus were usually the poorest of the poor.

"Damon just checked in, babe," Able said.

"He's early." She bit her tongue to stop herself from grousing about his endearment. Nothing she did stopped him from using the nickname he'd given her as a child.

At her expression, Terle snickered. What she tolerated from Able didn't extend to him. "You have something to say, Terle?" she asked.

"No, Captain." He gave her a mock salute and fell silent.

Managing this crew was like herding cats. Shy sighed and turned back to Able. "I hope his delivery came off without a hitch. I think I'm going to need the credits."

Light glinted off Able's smooth bald head as he swiveled in his chair to face her. His broad smile revealed a gold-capped tooth. "Damon never comes home empty-handed."

"Yes, but it's what's in his hands when he gets here that worries me," she said.

Terle grunted and hunched farther over his console.

Aside from herself, Damon, at thirty, was the youngest in her crew. His devastating good looks, charm and easy smile hid an inner darkness Shy had never been able to penetrate. She'd been eight when her father first brought him home, a handsome but quiet boy of ten. At the time she knew nothing of the evil that pervaded the universe; she'd just been thrilled to have a playmate. For the next few years they'd been almost constant companions, until at last he joined her father's business. She loved him like a brother. She knew little more about his background now than she had as a child. Whatever his scars, he hid them deep inside.

"Hope he hasn't picked up any more strays." Terle rubbed his thumb over the scar on his lower lip. "Last one he brought home bit me."

Able threw back his head and laughed. The hearty sound boomed around the bridge. "If you hadn't tried to kiss her, there wouldn't have been a problem. Poor little gal was terrified."

"She didn't have no problem cozying up to Damon," Terle grumbled.

"Yeah, he does have a way with the ladies. Must be his face."

"I'm good looking," Terle protested.

"Who can tell under all those pretty pictures you've got all over you?" Able teased.

"Look who's talking," Terle shot back.

The older man's tanklike body sported as many tattoos as Terle's, if not more. Only Able's face and hairless head seemed to be off-limits. The bickering between the two men was good-natured and harmless, a way to blow off steam and bond. But at times Shy found the testosterone-charged air annoying.

She glanced over to where Greyson sat quietly, a small smile on his lips. He hadn't said a word since she'd informed the crew—aside from Damon, who'd yet to arrive—her recommendation was to help Greyson track down Dempster. No one had argued. As much as they disliked ASP and ELF, none of them wanted to see the outer worlds obliterated. Even Silky had agreed to help.

Though he didn't let it show, the detour to Verus disturbed Greyson. They didn't have the time to spare. Though Earth and its colonies had banned it, slavery was a sad fact of life in the outer worlds and on many

C.O.I.L. planets. As long as the practice didn't violate any other laws, the Consortium preached toleration. Too bad their policy of noninterference didn't extend to allowing planets to practice freedom of choice in their affiliations.

In his mind, the fate of a few slaves couldn't take precedence over the destiny of all mankind, but he was wise enough to hold his tongue and hide his impatience. Shyanne's crew didn't trust him. Her words had swayed them to help. If he lost her support, which objecting to this rescue mission would cause, they would turn on him in a heartbeat. He couldn't risk it. His best option was to help them get in and out as quickly as possible.

The bridge doors slid open and a man strode in. A thick mane of tawny blond hair tumbled in disarray around his face and rested on a pair of broad shoulders. Blue-gray eyes set in a handsome face sparkled with humor. A half smile played around full lips. Half wildcat, half angel, the man sizzled with energy and at the same time radiated a sense of peace. The dueling effects were unsettling.

"Where's my favorite kitty cat?" he asked. "I brought her some kitty treats."

Able laughed. "Probably hiding from you."

"When are you going to give up?" Terle taunted. "All the treats in the universe aren't going to get Silky to like you."

"Never." Damon grinned. "Defeat is not in my vocabulary. Someday that cat will eat out of my hand."

"More likely she'll take off a few fingers," Terle said.

"Can't figure why you bother." Able shook his head. "Isn't it enough every woman you meet falls at your feet? Why worry about whether or not one little alien likes you?"

"I like a challenge. Women are too easy. They see only what they want." Damon lifted a shoulder. "Silky is . . . different. She sees the truth."

"Yeah, and that's why she don't like you," Terle laughed.

Damon didn't respond to Terle's goading, but his smile faded. For a moment the mask slipped and Greyson caught a peek of a lost man beneath.

When the newcomer turned and caught sight of Greyson, he discarded his carefree demeanor. The man's narrowed gaze revealed nothing, but his body language spoke volumes. His hand went to the pistol strapped to his hip. "Who are you?"

Prepared to defend himself, Greyson tensed and straightened. Before a confrontation could occur, Shyanne stepped between them.

"Damn it, Damon. When will you learn not to shoot first and ask questions later?"

"It keeps me alive." Humor and affection flashed in his slate blue eyes.

"Until it gets you killed," she muttered. "Greyson Dane, this is Damon Wilde." She quickly laid out the situation.

As she spoke, Greyson watched but could detect no further flickers of emotion in Damon's eyes or facial features. When she finished, his happy-go-lucky mask snapped back into place and he let his hand drop from his pistol. Greyson let out a breath of relief.

"Welcome to our merry little band of thieves," Damon said.

"We're not thieves. We're smugglers." Shyanne's tone held a note of exasperation.

"Minor distinction." Damon waved his hand in dismissal and turned his back on Greyson. "So, if we're going after Dempster, why are we hanging around this shit-hole of a planet? There's nothing on this rock to interest him." He leaned over Terle's shoulder as if to study the console, but Greyson sensed it was more to annoy the other man. Terle growled a warning a split second before he jammed his shoulder into Damon's midsection. With a strangled cough that did little to hide his laugh, the blond man straightened.

"Slave auction," Able answered.

Greyson saw reaction ripple across Damon's shoulders. "I'll go down with you," he said.

Shyanne shook her head. "No. Able, Bear and I are going. You'll stay aboard *Independence*." When Damon started to object, she held up her hand. "I won't have a repeat of what happened last time."

He fell silent. Terle snickered. Able shushed him.

Greyson wanted to ask what had happened but held his tongue. There was no sense stirring the pot before it began to boil. Shyanne didn't know it yet, but he was going along as well.

Chapter Five

"You're not coming along. That's final!" Shy strode down the corridor toward the shuttle bay. It annoyed her greatly how easily Greyson kept pace.

Just before they reached the lift, he grabbed her arm and swung her around to face him. "I'm going."

"Why? Your presence isn't necessary. Able, Bear and I can handle it. We've done this alone dozens of times." All along she'd sensed his restlessness about the delay this side trip would cause, but he hadn't voiced any objections or made a single demand until now.

"Not this time." He cupped her face in his palm.

The concern in his eyes weakened her resolve. Having him with them was a complication she didn't want or need. She and Bear had a well-rehearsed routine. She played the role of brothel madam, while he became her enforcer. The sight of him usually discouraged anyone from objecting to their presence. Even she wasn't foolish enough to land on Verus by herself.

Counting on her crew was one thing; letting herself rely on Greyson was a blueprint for disaster. She'd trusted him once and look where that had gotten her.

"I can't afford to lose you," Greyson continued.

"Without you I don't stand a chance of catching Dempster."

Pain killed the tender feelings the first part of his sentence had engendered. As always, she was nothing more to him than a means to an end. To hide the hurt she knew flared in her eyes, she jerked around and punched the lift button.

"Fine. Come along. But keep quiet and stay out of my way."

They met Bear in the shuttle bay where her ship waited. Though old, *Liberty* was fast and maneuverable, able to move in and out of a planet's atmosphere. One person could fly her, but she could hold a crew of two for long distances comfortably. Four would be a squeeze.

Years ago, when Shy had taken over and expanded her father's habit of rescuing slaves, she'd converted a good portion of the cargo bay to a dormitory capable of holding twenty or so people. Though the accommodations were primitive, a cot, group lavatories and MAT unit, they were still luxurious compared to the squalor in which most slaves lived.

She landed *Liberty* in a secluded valley about a mile outside Discoll, Verus's largest town. From what she'd heard, calling Discoll a town was an exaggeration. Once every few months when a ship came by with goods to sell or trade, Verus's population converged there. The rest of the time it consisted of a mercantile store with empty shelves and a tavern with home-brewed liquor that would kill you quicker than the planet's inhospitable climate. By listening to the radio chatter, she'd learned the auction was to take place there.

While Able stayed aboard to keep *Liberty* safe and

ready to fly, she, Bear and Greyson set out on the walk into town. They traveled in silence. Opening her mouth to speak let hot, gritty air invade her mouth and scrape her throat raw. Her eyes watered from the stinging sand that swirled around her in the endless wind whose whining drone made her head pound and her heart race with some unknown dread.

Above, the planet's two suns beat down without mercy. What little vegetation the planet claimed grew low to the ground, its foliage as dry and dusty as the turf around it. Stinging nettles and barbs guarded the plant's precious moisture from the planet's meager animal population.

"Why would anyone choose to live here?" Greyson asked.

"Because they ran out of choices," Shy said. "Without water or any marketable resources, once someone lands on Verus, they have no way of making enough credits to get off again."

"Then why would a slaver try and sell his product here? There can't be much profit in it."

"They must be desperate to unload their cargo."

"I wonder why," he mused.

The reason made her nervous, too. This smelled like a trap. One she had no choice but to step into. Though she knew she couldn't save them all, once slaves crossed her path she couldn't walk away. She knew the pain and suffering of being *owned* by another.

The pathetic little town came into view. In the middle of the dilapidated buildings people gathered around a raised platform upon which a group of ten female children, all about six years old, huddled together. All were humanoid, though several weren't

Earthlings. Shy couldn't determine their planets of origin. An older girl, probably no more than seventeen, attempted without success to guard them from the hungry eyes of the milling crowd.

Though she was female, the men's gazes didn't linger on Shy. Dressed in rough clothing, weapons openly displayed, her hair hacked short—the men moved aside for her to pass. Having Bear behind her didn't hurt.

While the younger girls appeared unharmed, though obviously frightened and dirty, the older girl's clothing was torn; her lower lip was split and her thin arms sported nasty bruises. The haunted look in her eyes told its own tale. Despite that, she stood straight and glared at the men ogling her.

Shy hated that she'd been forced to let the slavers who'd abused the girl get away. They'd dropped their cargo and left immediately. The whole situation made her uneasy, but rescuing the girls took precedence over retribution. Someday there'd be justice done. The tag on the slaver's ship would allow her to track them down eventually.

At Shy's side, Greyson radiated anger. She put a warning hand on his arm and whispered, "Let me handle this." Lips tight and eyes hard, he gave a nod.

They reached the edge of the platform just as the auctioneer began. "Well, gents," the skinny, weasel-faced man began. "We have quite a treat today. It's not often we get such a selection of merchandise here on Verus." He grinned and motioned to the cowering children. "Open up your wallets and let's get the bidding started . . . on *this* lovely little one."

The man's assistant yanked a girl out of the group. When the oldest objected, he smacked her across the face. Cradling her cheek, she fell to her knees but didn't cry out. The children all started to sob. Greyson sucked in his breath but stood rigid. Shy appreciated him letting her handle this.

She could feel Bear's reassuring bulk behind her. Without him she was sure the milling men of Verus would have long since made a move. Many of them had guns, but his own impressive array of weaponry and intimidating size would make even the bravest man hesitate.

"Young and healthy, this one will give you years of service." The auctioneer picked up the crying child and held her aloft for the crowd to see. She dangled in his grip like a broken rag doll. "Let's start the bidding at a thousand credits."

The crowd muttered in anger and shifted forward. The auctioneer had miscalculated, or was perhaps playing a dangerous game. Not one of the men here looked to have a hundred credits; Shy doubted they could come up with a thousand credits between them all. Besides, the older girl was what interested them. She had curves and was old enough to provide labor outside of bed. The young girls would drain limited resources for several years before the men could recoup their investment—if the girls even lived that long. What was the auctioneer playing at?

As the silence grew, sweat beaded the man's oily skin. "Five hundred credits? Two-fifty?"

Several men to Shy's right argued quietly, and then one shouted, "Fifty!"

"I have a bid of fifty credits."

Shy could hear relief in the auctioneer's voice.

"Do I have one hundred?"

"Fifty-five," another man called out.

The price rose bit by bit as the men pooled their resources. Finally, the bid reached one hundred credits. The time was nearing to act.

Greyson shifted in place. Though he'd always known the slave trade existed, when he'd been a field agent his jobs had focused on the smuggling of goods, so he'd never seen the results firsthand. The last ten years had been spent behind a desk. Slavery statistics on paper didn't convey the miserable reality.

With each bid, his tension grew. He couldn't allow these innocent little girls to fall into the hands of Verus's men. Though every minute of every day he regretted the death of his mother at the hands of pirates, he preferred knowing she was in a better place than this.

Shyanne had to do something or he would. What was she waiting for? Her calm demeanor in the face of this horror made him question who and what she'd become since he'd last met her. The fate of these children was in her hands. Why didn't she bid? Could she be so coldhearted as to let one become a disposable sex toy? Maybe all of them? Could she have changed so much from the young, idealistic girl he'd known? Did she have some plan he didn't yet know?

"Trust me," she whispered.

Trust her? How could he? She didn't seem to be reacting to this at all.

Yet what choice did he have? Outnumbered, the three of them didn't have a chance of stealing the children away. If Shyanne didn't bid, he could only stand and watch in disgust. Why hadn't he thought to bring money on this mission? Could he risk accessing his credit line and revealing his location to his superiors to purchase the girls? Would this backwater planet even accept anything other than hard credits?

He looked up in surprise as Shyanne stepped up onto the platform and plucked the girl from the auctioneer's hands. She buried her face in Shyanne's neck and clung to her.

"A thousand credits"—she paused for a moment as the number sank in—"for the entire lot."

"Th-this is most unusual. I d-don't know," the auctioneer sputtered, but greed glinted in his beady eyes. A thousand credits was a bargain for eleven female slaves even this far off the beaten path, but the auctioneer knew a good deal when he heard one. Grumbling started in the crowd.

Shyanne smiled. "A thousand credits to you. And . . . a month's worth of free passes to every man here at the pleasure house I plan to open!" As her words sank in, the grumbles turned to cheers.

Greyson let some of the tension ease out of his body. He had to admit Shyanne's plan was inspired. In one stroke she'd stolen the girls away from the men but proposed to give them back without any hassle or expense of maintenance. The auctioneer would get his money and the men would get their sex. Who could object?

Even better, it was all a lie.

"No!" the older girl screamed, and launched herself at Shyanne. Greyson jumped up and caught her before her nails raked Shyanne's face.

"Let me go!"

The girl twisted like a wildcat. She clawed his arm and sank her teeth into Greyson's wrist. The crowd laughed and cheered him on as he subdued the frantic girl and handed her to Bear. Once in Bear's grip she slumped in defeat.

Greyson turned his attention to helping Shyanne with the younger girls. As he approached, they crouched and huddled together on the platform, whimpering in fear. The girl Shyanne held, with her white blonde hair and sky blue eyes, reminded him painfully of the little girl who'd died along with his mother in the pirate attack so many years ago. Afterward, the girl's parents had generously taken him into their home and named him their son, but he knew he'd never replaced their daughter in their hearts. Where Anna's eyes had been full of laughter and courage, this little girl's eyes held nothing but terror.

He wanted to gather them all in his arms and chase away the demons he knew would haunt them for the rest of their lives. But he realized if he showed them any scrap of kindness or compassion, they'd crumble into hysteria. Instead, using a firm voice and hand, he herded them off the platform and through the crowd. Cowed by their experience with the slavers, they obeyed without question. Their submissive attitude broke his heart.

After paying the auctioneer, Shyanne, with the blonde girl still in her arms, led the way back to the ship. Greyson herded the other children behind, while Bear brought up the rear with the oldest. Though in general the crowd seemed pleased with the arrangement, Greyson noticed a few men watching them leave with calculating looks. Trouble brewed. The sooner they were off this planet, the better.

The girls' small legs struggled to keep pace with

Shyanne's long stride. Finally, Greyson picked up two of the smaller children. Bear put down the oldest and scooped up three others, and the oldest lifted another. Between them they were carrying seven of the ten children. The remaining three moved faster to keep up.

Their pace increased, but the trip back to the ship took twice as long as the trip into town. At last *Liberty* came into view and Greyson breathed a sigh of relief. Carrying the children had left them unable to access their weapons. He didn't like being vulnerable.

He stood at the bottom of the boarding ramp with the older girl while Shyanne handed the children through the narrow door to Bear and Able. Suddenly, Shyanne dove down the ramp and crashed into him and the girl. They went down in a tangled heap. Laser-fire bounced harmlessly off the ship's hull instead of bursting his head. Together, Greyson and Shyanne grabbed the girl and rolled beneath the ramp.

Above, they heard Bear and Able returning fire. Able urged them to get aboard ship, but Greyson knew better than to try; they were pinned down.

"What are you doing?" Shyanne asked as he pushed the girl against her and crawled toward the edge of the ramp.

"I'm going to take a look."

"No," the girl cried, and grabbed at him. Apparently, sometime during the trip from town, the girl had decided he and Shyanne were the lesser evil. "You'll get shot."

"She's right," Shyanne said.

"Probably, but we need to know their positions. If they move, this ramp isn't going to be much protection."

Shyanne nodded. "Be careful."

Greyson wriggled around and peered out to pinpoint their assailants' locations. The flat land surrounding the ship gave them little cover, so the men crouched low to the ground. A shot buzzed over his head and he pulled back.

"There are two of them about thirty yards at three o'clock," he said. "Take the girl out the other side and up the ramp. I'll cover you."

"You take the girl and lift her up. You're stronger, and I'm a better shot." She grinned at him and, before he could argue further, rolled out from under the ramp and came up firing.

"Damn stubborn woman!" he swore but didn't hesitate; grabbing the girl's arm, he lifted her up to the top of the ramp. Able reached out, snagged her and dragged her inside, keeping her out of the line of fire the whole time. Greyson then turned his attention back to Shyanne.

The acrid smell of laser-fire burned his nose. Their attackers were firing blind, and it was striking the ground all around them. It was only a matter of time until one of them was hit.

"Come on!"

He leapt onto the ramp and reached for her. Firing off one last volley, Shyanne whirled, grabbed hold of his hand and swung herself onto the ramp beside him. Five feet separated them from safety.

Laser-fire pinged against the ramp and the side of the ship. Greyson pushed her ahead of him through the opening. From inside the ship he could hear Able yelling and the girls' sobbing. He turned and shot. A man screamed.

Another blast and Shyanne's gasp wiped away Greyson's smile of satisfaction. He caught her as she fell and carried her inside. Able smacked his hand against the ramp controls. The ramp slid upright and the door closed.

"Get us the hell off this rock," Greyson commanded.

Shyanne's crewman hesitated long enough to ask, "How bad is she hurt?"

"I don't know." Greyson stared at Shyanne, saw a long burn mark on the side of her head near the temple. "Alert Eldin I'm bringing her to sick bay."

"It's just a flesh wound," she muttered, opening her eyes and shaking her head. "Put me down. It just grazed me." Then her eyes closed and she went limp.

The sound of his captain's irritation motivated Able. He nodded at Greyson and ran for the bridge.

The smell of laser-seared flesh burned Greyson's nostrils. Shyanne's ashen complexion and shallow breathing were worrisome. He smoothed a strand of hair away from the wound. Off to the side, Bear waited with the children. Still awed by his size, they huddled together, but their sobs along with the continued ping of laser-fire hitting the ship's hull pierced Greyson's brain like icy daggers.

"Can the crying," he snapped.

The older girl stopped sobbing to ask, "Is she dead?"

"Why the hell do you care?" The rage and pain churning inside him revealed just how much he himself cared. His concern made his tone harsher than he intended.

The girl straightened her shoulders and growled,

"I don't." But the tremor in her voice put paid to her words. Tears spiked her lashes and streaked the dirt on her face. Her lower lip trembled, though she met Greyson's gaze without flinching.

Greyson put his fingers against Shyanne's neck. The strong, steady beat eased the ache in his heart and he said, "No, she's not dying, but when she wakes up she'll have a hell of a headache." He couldn't stop his grin of relief.

The girl smiled back, then jumped as another volley blasted the ship.

"What now?" the oldest girl spoke up.

Greyson examined her. She was older than he'd first thought, closer to twenty than seventeen. "What's your name?" he asked.

"Brina."

"Well, Brina, would you please help Bear get the children settled?"

Brina turned uncertain eyes toward Bear. To her credit, she hesitated only a second before nodding and moving to the others. They went eagerly into her arms.

Greyson watched in admiration. The girl had been through a horrible trauma, probably seeing her family and friends killed, had been beaten and probably raped and still she sought to care for and shield the younger girls. Who was she? Who were these children? Where had they come from, and why did this whole situation feel as if it had been a trap from the get-go?

Liberty lifted off. Shyanne groaned, and Greyson stroked her cheeks and forehead. Answers would have to wait.

"Go on with Bear," he urged Brina. "He won't

hurt you or the children. I know you have a lot of questions. We'll talk more later, but you're safe now. I promise."

He couldn't help flinching. If this was a trap, had he made another promise he wasn't sure he could keep?

Chapter Six

Simon Dempster watched with satisfaction as the blip appeared on his scanner. How easily she'd taken the bait. And as directed, the slavers had tagged her ship. He had her now. For over twenty years he'd been waiting to obtain his goal: possession of Shyanne Kedar. Success was only a few steps away.

When she was a child, she'd stolen the one thing he desired above all else—Stewart Kedar's love. He'd worked hard to position himself at Kedar's side, to eliminate all others who'd command the man's attention or affection. Then she'd come into his life, and Simon had ceased to matter. Then she'd caused Kedar's downfall.

Years it had taken for Simon to recover and rebuild her father's empire—the empire that should have been his. He'd earned it with hard work, and her womanly mistakes had destroyed it. That womanishness now meant something different to him.

Oh, on more than one occasion he'd come close to getting his revenge. Last year he'd had her in his grasp, but she'd managed to slip through his fingers. Again.

He rubbed the jagged scar on his cheek. Others wondered, though none dared ask, why he didn't have it removed. He kept it to remind him of whom it was he chased and how dangerous she could be. Only after she paid for his pain and humiliation with her own would he visit the surgeon and have the scar eradicated.

This time, he'd set his trap with a sweet bait he'd known she couldn't resist. The bait was taken, the trap sprung. Now he just had to reel in his catch.

Greyson paced the corridor outside the *Independence* med bay. Memories of what had gone on in that room only hours earlier fought with the image of Shyanne lying pale and still on the examination bed.

The door opened and Eldin came out.

Greyson started to go in. "How is she?"

Eldin blocked him from entering. "She'll be fine. I've given her something to make sure she rests. She'll be asleep for some time."

"I won't disturb her." Greyson tried to move around the older man, who laughed.

"Oh, you'll disturb her all right." The old man's humor faded and he pinned Greyson with a hard stare. "Leave her be."

Greyson's shoulders sagged. Eldin was right. He had no rights where Shyanne was concerned. Eldin and her crew were her family, not him. He'd given up that chance long ago.

"How often does she pull this kind of stunt?" he asked. His own inability to rescue the children frustrated him, while Shyanne's clever plan had saved them all, but it also had almost gotten her killed.

Eldin shrugged. "As often as necessary. It's made her unpopular in a lot of places." He patted Greyson on the back. "Fortunately, they didn't recognize her on Verus. You never know when someone will. Word gets around. Things would have gone down differently if they had. Usually she just raids slave ships and auctions, but when that's not possible she'll do this sort of operation."

"The crew backs her up on this? Don't they object to her spending their cash?"

"Most of us know firsthand what it means to be a slave. Shy's father rescued us, so now we're returning the favor."

"What will happen to the girls?"

"We'll see if we can locate any family for them, but with the way things have been going lately, that's not likely." Eldin shot Greyson a sly look. "I have it on good authority the pirates who likely collected this group haven't been leaving anyone alive."

Greyson's first instinct was to end his mission and take the girls back to Earth, but if he did, Shyanne and her crew would end up in prison and things would only get worse. "Kedar rarely operated in C.O.I.L. space. He kept to the outer worlds. That's why it took so long for ASP to track him down and arrest him. Why has Shyanne been smuggling so close in?"

The angry look on Eldin's normally genial face told Greyson he'd touched a nerve. The man looked ready to punch him. Had he pushed too far?

"The only reason Kedar surrendered," the old man hissed, "was to keep ASP from shooting up innocent students in an attempt to capture him. Deceit and betrayal brought him down."

"Granted," Greyson admitted. He liked to think the ASP operatives would have shown restraint, but the risk to the student population had been real. Ten years ago, Williams, the current director, had been the agent in charge of the operation. His ambition, then as now, made him blind to all but the obvious. "But that doesn't answer my question."

Some of the fire went out of Eldin's eyes and the old man sighed. "Because of Simon Dempster. Ever since Shy was a child, he's hated her. Last year, during one of her runs, he caught her. We barely got her back in one piece."

Greyson shuddered. He'd read the reports of what had been done to the men, women and children of the ships and colonies attacked by Dempster and his men. He'd known immediately upon reading those reports that Shyanne couldn't be responsible. What had the bastard done to her?

"Since then, we've moved closer in," Eldin continued. "It's easier to avoid him in C.O.I.L. space. Our operation is small, so we can move in and out quickly. If it wasn't for Dempster's trickery, we'd have gone unnoticed by you folks."

"Oh, ASP noticed," Greyson countered.

He'd been following Shyanne's criminal career since its start. Bringing down her father had resulted in promotions for both him and the current director, despite her escape. In his position as Williams's deputy, as long as her operation remained small and didn't go beyond the smuggling of food, equipment and medicine, Greyson had been able to avert any direct action being taken against her. Even after he'd learned of her trading in weapons, he'd managed to shield her from exposure. Only after these current rash of murderous attacks had he become unable to help.

Nothing he'd said to the director convinced the man that Shyanne wasn't responsible. If Williams ever learned of the buried evidence regarding Shyanne's previous crimes, he'd be facing treason charges. Of course, going behind the director's back to see Kedar and now running with known criminals had Greyson facing the same fate anyway.

"Dempster's actions have made it impossible for ASP to ignore her," he told Eldin. "If we don't track him down, Shyanne will end up paying for his crimes."

The old man gave him a considering look. "Why do you care?"

"Why? Easy. Bringing in Dempster puts me in line to be director of ASP."

"I don't buy it. If all you wanted was to make director, you'd just try and bring her in. She's the one they think's doing it. What's your real goal?"

Greyson weighed his options. Eldin and the rest of the crew deserved to know the truth, or at least part of it, but he wasn't ready to reveal his deception. If they succeeded in stopping Dempster, Greyson hoped his superiors would honor the agreements he'd made, giving everyone pardons. If they failed . . . well, at the very least he hoped to help Shyanne and her crew escape the resulting holocaust that would result from C.O.I.L.'s actions.

Leaving out his deception about the pardons, he quickly explained the situation with ASP and C.O.I.L. Eldin whistled and nodded. "The rest of the crew needs to hear this," the old man said. "Come on." He headed toward the lift.

Greyson hesitated. "When can I see Shyanne?"

The old man shook his head. "She should sleep for at least a couple of hours."

On the bridge, Greyson fielded questions about

the situation. Eldin and Bear were neutral; their inquiries revolved around planning and logistics, if they were still going to go forward with the assault on Dempster's operation. Able and Damon's questions were guarded, and more about C.O.I.L.'s possible plan, but they were receptive. As Greyson expected, Terle's questions bespoke hostility.

"Where's Silky?" Greyson asked when the questions stopped.

"She and her crew are keeping watch over the children," Able said.

"Her crew?" Greyson asked.

They ignored him.

"We need a moment to discuss this," Eldin said. "Alone." Terle muttered an anatomically impossible suggestion and glared until Greyson stepped off the bridge to await their decision.

A few long minutes later, Eldin called him back. The crew apparently all agreed tracking down and capturing Dempster was still their best option. Shyanne being wounded hadn't changed anything.

"What about the children?" Greyson asked. "We can't take them with us. It's too dangerous."

"Shy usually shuttles them to a planet on the fringe of the outer worlds," Damon said.

"How long will it take to get there?" Greyson asked.

Able punched some numbers into his console. "From here, about three standard weeks."

"That's too long. We have less than a month to capture Dempster and stop C.O.I.L. intervention! Isn't there someplace closer?"

Damon shook his head. "Most of the outer worlds near Earth or C.O.I.L. space already have more refugees than they can handle. Those planets that might take the children are little better than Verus."

Greyson thought for a second. "I know where we can take them."

"Where?" Eldin asked.

Greyson pulled up a star chart and pointed. "It's only a few hours away."

Terle swore.

Able shook his head. "That's an Earth outpost. We can't take *Independence* that far into Earth space."

"Yes, we can. I know the commander. Carter Kincaid has little love for ELF, ASP or C.O.I.L." *Or me*, he added silently. "The risk is minimal. The station is small and *Independence* is more than a match for it. But even better, you don't have to take *Independence* in. We can use one of the smaller ships to shuttle the children to the station."

"And if the commander decides to further his career by taking our craft and its crew prisoner?" Eldin asked.

"I'll shuttle the children down myself. If I don't come back, you're well rid of me."

"And we've lost a ship," Terle snapped.

"But you have mine in exchange. I'm assuming you've got it in your docking bay."

It was an odd negotiation, Greyson admitted. No one mentioned that all the commander had to do was call for reinforcements and *Independence* would be trapped.

"How do we know the children will be safe with this commander?" Damon spoke up. "We don't know where they're from. If they're from the outer worlds, will he see to their needs or turn them over to ASP? They might end up treated no better than criminals."

The questions startled Greyson. He wouldn't have thought the pretty boy would put the children's welfare ahead of his own. Still, he had an answer ready: "Carter Kincaid would never let a child come to harm." Not the Carter Kincaid he'd once known.

Of course, he hadn't spoken to the man in over five years, and the last words Carter had spoken were a threat to get even. Still, Greyson didn't believe Carter would use innocent children to even the score between them. At least, he hoped not.

Eldin nodded. "We'll do it your way. But stars help you if you're wrong."

Able grinned as he plugged coordinates into the ship's nav computer. " 'Cause we sure won't."

"Shy's going to ream us all new ones when she wakes up," Damon pointed out.

Terle just hunched over his console and swore.

Shy rolled over and groaned. Her head throbbed in unison with the steady thrum of *Independence*'s engines. What had happened?

She touched the bandage on her temple. Memory came back in a rush of pain. Her eyes flew open. "The children! My ship! The crew!" She bolted upright, then fell back and closed her eyes on another groan.

"Easy there. The children are fine. The ship and crew are fine."

Greyson's voice soothed her anxiety as the feel of his fingertips brushing the hair from her forehead eased the ache in her head. She cracked an eyelid and peered up at him. "What happened?" she croaked.

She wasn't sure why she trusted his words, but she did. Perhaps because no alarms sounded. *Independence*'s engines still hummed in their reassuringly familiar way.

"You got shot." His voice wobbled almost imperceptibly. "Grazed your temple. Slight concussion, related shock issues."

She didn't object when he wrapped an arm around her shoulders to help her sit up and held a glass of water to her lips. The cool liquid slid down her throat like a magic elixir, relieving the dryness, but it was the heat of his body against hers that banished the chill of having come so close to death. This was the nearest she'd ever experienced.

"Was anyone else hurt? Were we followed?" she asked.

"No."

Without her volition, she turned her head and pressed her lips to his chest where his flight suit gaped open. He sucked in his breath and started to pull away, but, the need to reaffirm life pounding in her veins, she gripped his arms. If she didn't know better, she'd almost believe he'd arranged these accidents to stir her libido.

What crazy musings! She almost laughed. As if she needed a reason to crave this man. She'd again take up the reins of command when she was better, but obviously the ship was manned and Eldin had everything under control. For now she'd abandon duty and responsibility. Now was time for her to heal. It was just for her, for what she wanted. And what she wanted was Greyson.

Ignoring his stillness, she trailed kisses up his

throat and over his chin until her lips were a whisper from his. "Make love with me," she begged.

He stroked his hand over her hair, trailing his fingertips like feathers along the edge of her bandage. "We shouldn't. You took a nasty blow to the head. A fraction of an inch and you'd have more than a nasty headache."

A ripple of longing went through her. She wound her arms around his neck and tugged him onto the bed beside her. "It's not my head that aches." The blanket pulled away as she leaned over him, and she realized someone, probably Eldin, had removed her flight suit.

Maneuvering, she stripped off her camisole. She cupped her aching breasts, fuller and heavier than before Rian, and lifted them—an offering to a hungry god. Her nipples peaked in anticipation. The fevered look in Greyson's eyes as he watched her play with herself promised her victory, in this at least. Later, she'd consider what it meant to their relationship, making love more than once.

Much later.

Greyson knew he should pull away, should refuse what Shyanne offered.

"I want more than your body," he said instead. Had he spoken his desire aloud?

"Take what you can get, ssssnake," she said with a distinct hiss. "I will."

But he wanted more than her body. He wanted more than a momentary release from the tension riding both of them. He wanted what she'd given him so freely ten years ago, something that—once she knew the truth, once his lies were exposed—she'd never offer him again. Her trust. Her love.

She leaned forward, the heat of her lithe body hovering over him. It weakened his resolve, stirred the banked fire burning in his groin. Through the thin material of his flight suit the hard points of her nipples brushed his chest. Moisture seeped through her thin panties and dampened his thigh when she moved to straddle him.

Her unique scent teased his nostrils, the acrid tang of engine oil and laser burn, along with the clean, fresh smell of soap and the heated aroma of aroused woman. With the tip of her moist pink tongue she stroked the edge of his ear and blew. He shivered and groaned in surrender. For this moment he'd selfishly take what she offered. Soon enough she'd hate him again.

He rolled her beneath him and the battle for control began. He failed, and her thin panties tore. He looked in disbelief at the flimsy cloth dangling from his fingertips.

Laughing, she helped him struggle out of his flight suit. He barely noticed as the fastener scraped the skin of his belly, leaving an angry red scratch on the tender skin from his navel to his groin, for she squirmed lower, her body undulating along the length of his. His breath caught as her warm tongue laved the length of the mark and eased the sting. Then her mouth closed over him and rational thought burned away.

Her tongue danced and stroked over his engorged shaft until he had to grit his teeth against the explosive need building inside him. When he could take no more, he pulled away and pinned her to the bed.

"My turn," he growled against her thigh.

With a laugh she spread her legs to allow him access. "I've always believed in taking turns."

He nuzzled her. Her warm, damp curls tickled his nose and he breathed in the heady aroma of her desire. He parted the fiery curls with his fingers. Moisture glistened on her swollen nether lips. With slow deliberation, he tasted her. Her hips bucked upward. He pressed her thighs farther apart. His tongue stroked, probed and swirled over her sensitive flesh until she writhed against the bed.

"Come to me! Now!" Her fingers fisted in his hair.

He slid into her heated depths and began to move. Her body surged in time with his. The slick slide of his flesh in and out of hers drove him relentlessly toward his release. The cords in his neck stood out. Every muscle in his body clenched as he held back.

"Ah-h-h!" Her cry of satisfaction filled the room as her inner muscles constricted in spasms around him, milked him.

"Shyanne!" In a flurry of sharp thrusts he let go and collapsed over her.

They lay together, bodies damp and limp, limbs tangled. Greyson's face rested against Shyanne's throat. Her pulse now beat an irregular tattoo against his lips. He kissed the throbbing vein and tasted the salt on her skin.

Though he knew they couldn't last, emotions filled him. Fulfillment. Satisfaction. Completion. Tenderness. Affection. He could stay this way forever. He snuggled against her warmth, enjoying the feel of her body under his, the smell of sex lingering in the room.

"Ugh. Get off me. You're heavy, sweaty and you stink." Shyanne pushed him away and curled into a ball. In seconds he heard her breathing even out as she fell asleep.

He chuckled and stretched. Apparently he was alone in his more tender feelings.

The rarely used communications link in the room squawked for attention, waking Shy. Greyson was shaking his head and coming awake beside her.

She touched her temple, then flinched as her fingers encountered the bandage. She tapped again. Nothing happened. Her com chip wasn't working. The shot to her head must have damaged it. She'd have to have Eldin implant a new one.

"Shy," Terle's voice snarled over the room's com speaker at the same moment *Independence*'s proximity alert started to wail. "You'd better get to the bridge. Now! And bring that two-timing ASP snake with you. We've got company. And they don't look friendly."

"I'm on my way," Shy answered as she tugged on her flight suit and boots. "Who are they?"

"Ask your friend," Terle said.

She shot Greyson a questioning look. He wouldn't meet her gaze, but he dressed and followed her to the bridge.

Once there, Shy quickly took stock of the situation. An ELF fighter stood nose to nose with *Independence*. But that's not what made her gut burn; the fighter, though heavily armed, was an antiquated model and no match for *Independence*'s firepower. Trouble would come later, when ELF learned of the fight—and Shy didn't doubt that they would. They were in Earth space.

Just beyond the fighter was an ELF space station.

Little more than a far-flung outpost, it had a small communications array, which was probably already broadcasting *Independence*'s location to ELF, ASP and C.O.I.L.

She whirled on Able. "What are you waiting for? Take out their communications. Now!"

Able looked at Greyson.

"No need to blast them. We used my ASP override code to block their transmissions," Greyson said.

Shy sensed a *but*, which Terle soon supplied. "Before we blocked them, they sent off an emergency beacon."

"Then what are you waiting for? Disable their fighter!" she directed Able. "And get us the hell out of here before reinforcements arrive."

"It'll take a few hours for the call to be received, and several more for a response team to arrive. By that time we'll be long gone. Terle, would you open a channel?" Greyson said.

Terle muttered something, but to Shy's surprise he complied. "When did you all decide to mutiny?" she asked.

None of the crew answered.

"No mutiny," Greyson said. "Just common sense. We need a place to unload the children. This outpost is the closest, safest place, and I know the commander. He'll see to their well-being."

"And why should he just let us unload the children and leave? Capturing the *Independence* would be a coup for an outpost commander. Might even get him a better posting."

Greyson gave a humorless laugh. "Believe me, ELF isn't going to promote Carter Kincaid. Even if they did, he wouldn't accept. He won't fire on us first, either. He knows he can't capture us; we outgun him."

"Channel open," Terle said.

"This is Commander Kincaid. State your business, pirate," a man's voice demanded over the com. Shy could hear the anger and frustration beneath his controlled tone.

When Greyson didn't respond, she raised her eyebrows in question.

"It would probably be better if you dealt with him," Greyson said so only she could hear. "Kincaid and I have . . . history."

"What kind of history?"

"Pirate!" Kincaid interrupted whatever Greyson might have answered. "Why are you here?"

Shy keyed the com. "This is the captain of the . . . cruise ship *Alliance*." She supplied the false locator ID they were broadcasting. "We have a group of children that need assistance."

"Cruise ship, my ass. I don't care what locator ID you give. I've got eyes. What game are you playing? This outpost has nothing of value for you to steal. And what little we have will cost you dearly."

Shy ran her hand around the back of her neck to relieve the tension. "No games, Commander. We have ten children and one young woman rescued from slavers that we need to unload. Then we'll leave peacefully."

Kincaid fell silent for a few minutes, then said, "Close your gun ports and dock on port three."

"I think not." Shy laughed. "We'll send the children over via a shuttle. And our gun ports stay open."

"I look forward to meeting you, Captain . . ." His voice trailed off.

She didn't supply her identity. "I'll have to forgo the pleasure this time. I'm no fool. A friend of yours will deliver the goods."

"What friend?"

She ignored Kincaid's question, cut the connection and turned to Able. "Strip the *Spitfire* of her weaponry and valuables and get the children aboard."

"Why my ship?" Damon protested.

"Because it's the smallest and oldest one we have." She grinned. "If it doesn't come back, you can have Greyson's."

Chapter Seven

Greyson stood outside *Spitfire* as Eldin strapped the children into some makeshift seating. This trip was bound to be interesting.

Going to the outpost and seeing Kincaid again was a gamble. Though he knew Kincaid would see to the children's welfare, the man had little reason to grant him any favors. Five years ago he'd testified at Kincaid's hearing about the incident at the Largon colony. His testimony kept Kincaid from spending time in a penal colony and helped him maintain his rank, even if he was then posted as far from civilization as possible, but that didn't mitigate the fact that Kincaid felt Greyson had betrayed their friendship.

At the time, Greyson had felt compelled to reveal the truth, but time had a way of blurring the sharp lines of right and wrong. If he'd kept his mouth shut, kept the truth hidden, Kincaid might have walked away from the hearing without penalty, his career with ELF intact. Instead, because of Greyson's actions, a good man and a brilliant soldier was reduced to running an unimportant outpost.

"I'm not going." Brina's voice jarred Greyson from his memories. "I want to join your crew," the girl continued.

"You don't know what you're asking," Shyanne said. The two women stood just out of sight, down the corridor and around a corner, but their voices were clear. "We're smugglers. Outlaws. Go back to a more safe, comfortable life. You'll prefer it in the end."

Brina snorted. "I'm not a child. I know what I want. What life would you have me go back to? The one where I was a slave? Is that safe or comfortable?"

Greyson heard Shyanne gasp in surprise. As he started to move toward the pair, Brina continued.

"That's right. I was the senator from Regalus's slave. One of my duties was to care for his daughter. She d-died in the attack." The young woman's voice broke for a moment, then hardened. "How warm do you think my welcome will be when I'm returned?"

"Don't you have any family?" Shyanne asked.

"I don't know. My colony was raided when I was eight. It wasn't a sanctioned Earth colony, and I don't even remember its name. Please, let me stay with you. I'm a good cook and have some limited medical skills."

Greyson heard Shyanne heave a sigh and then say, "All right. You can stay with us until we can find your family or a place for you."

"Thank you."

Greyson couldn't see what happened, but he heard Shyanne cough and the rustle of clothing being straightened.

"Go help Eldin get the children settled for the trip. Afterward he'll set you up with a cabin and some clothing." A few seconds later, Brina rushed past Greyson into the ship.

Shyanne followed and stopped beside him. "You heard?" she asked.

He nodded. "You should have sent her with the children. Kincaid would have seen to getting her settled somewhere safe. Earth banned slavery ages ago. No one would send her back to Regalus."

"Maybe, maybe not. Who knows what the Earth government might do to prevent that senator from making a fuss? I couldn't take the chance."

As much as Greyson hated to admit it, she had a point. With the threat of C.O.I.L. intervention hanging over their heads, the fate of one girl wouldn't amount to much.

Eldin and Brina came out of the *Spitfire*. Eldin eyed Greyson. "The children are ready. I gave them all a mild sleeping draught, so they shouldn't give you any trouble on the trip. You're sure your friend will see to them properly?"

Greyson nodded.

Eldin said to Brina, "Let's get you settled in. I know just the quarters that'll work for you."

As they left, Greyson turned to board the *Spitfire*. Shyanne's hand on his arm made him pause.

"Come back," she said.

"I didn't know you cared." Before he could control his tongue, the wisecrack slipped out, masking his real feelings. As much as he'd like to deny it, he wanted her to care.

She snatched back her hand. "I don't. But without your assistance it'll be harder to take down Dempster. And if you're not around to back them up, will ASP honor the pardons they promised? I'd hate to test that."

Knowing what he did, Greyson felt the same way.

A short time later Greyson docked at the ELF outpost. He took a deep breath and punched the control panel to open *Spitfire*'s hatch. Behind him, the children slept peacefully.

The hatch swung open. After the dim illumination of the transport craft, Greyson squinted in the bright light of the docking bay. Five armed men stood waiting, their weapons leveled at his chest. He raised his hands and took a step down the ramp. The chilly air didn't stop the sweat from trickling down his spine.

"Hold," a familiar voice ordered.

Greyson blinked and the man came into focus. "Carter Kincaid."

Five years hadn't changed his old friend. With long dark hair, swarthy complexion, scarred face and the dagger always strapped to his waist, he looked more like a pirate than an ELF officer. His disreputable appearance hadn't won him any points with the judges during the hearing, but it was his disrespect for authority that really sealed his fate. Few people who saw him would guess at his strong sense of justice. That same inner code was what had led him to disobey direct orders on Largon. And though his action saved lives, it had ruined his promising career and landed him here.

"Dane?" The barrel of the man's laser rifle dropped a notch. "What in the blazing galaxy are you doing running with pirates?"

"Long story. Will I have time to tell it?" Greyson gave the weapons a pointed stare.

"At ease," Kincaid told his men.

Greyson let his arms drop, too.

Kincaid's gaze narrowed as he glanced back toward the *Spitfire*. "Are there children aboard, or was that a ruse to gain access to this station?"

"No ruse. There are ten. All have translator chips, so your medic should be able to track down their families. They're asleep in the cargo hold. They're Regalian nationals."

"Nice of you to drop miniature bombs in my lap."

Earth relations with Regalus were strained. Regalus slavers regularly raided human colonies that refused to unite with Earth and acknowledge Consortium authority. Despite Earth's protests, the Consortium hadn't seen fit to intervene. As a C.O.I.L. member for more than six hundred years, Regalus had more clout in the council.

Kincaid heaved a sigh and ordered, "Dyson, go aboard and check."

One of his soldiers nodded. Weapon ready, he moved past Greyson into the ship. A few minutes later he reappeared. "Confirmed, and all clear, Commander."

Greyson waited as Kincaid touched his temple and spoke. A few minutes later, an older woman and two men dressed in medical whites entered the docking bay. Without addressing Kincaid, the two men directed several automated antigrav stretchers up the ramp into Spitfire. The woman paused next to Greyson and asked, "What were the children given?"

"Meloton," Greyson said, naming the mild sedative Eldin had administered. The woman's stern look softened. She nodded, then followed the men inside the ship.

It took less than ten minutes for the medics to offload the children and whisk them away. After Kincaid dismissed his soldiers, he turned his attention to Greyson, who stood near the top of *Spitfire*'s ramp. Seeing the look in the man's eye, Greyson wondered if he should make a break for it. He glanced from Kincaid to the open hatch. No. Even if he managed to get inside the ship, he couldn't launch with the bay doors closed.

Kincaid cocked his head and grinned. "Not thinking of trying something stupid, are you? Come with me." Raising his rifle, he motioned Greyson ahead of him.

Inside his office, Kincaid racked his rifle and plopped into the worn chair behind his desk. Greyson took a moment to look around. From his less than military appearance and general disregard for military protocol, no one would guess Kincaid was a neat freak, but like the rest of the small station, Kincaid's office was clean and well organized if old and outdated. Behind the desk a large view screen showed an expanse of empty space, making the tiny office appear larger than it was.

"Sit," Kincaid said.

Greyson complied. He'd known getting on and off this station wasn't going to be easy. The confrontation between himself and this man was five years overdue.

But instead of bringing up the past, Kincaid leaned on his forearms. "What the hell are you up to?"

"The less you know the better. If it blows up on me, you don't want to be involved."

Kincaid looked surprised. "So, by-the-book Dane has decided to skip a page?" Some of the tension left his body, and he leaned back in his chair and studied Greyson.

"More like a chapter. Or two."

It was an old joke, him being a stickler for the rules, and it made Greyson smile. When they were students together at the military academy, they'd spent hours debating the finer points of Earth and C.O.I.L. laws. They'd met at the age of ten, at primary school, and become inseparable, brothers in all but blood. Greyson was the privileged foster son of a wealthy businessman, Kincaid the son of an abusive drunk. With Greyson's foster father's assistance, Kincaid and Greyson both attended Earth's finest military academy. After graduation, Greyson had opted for service in ASP, while Kincaid enlisted in ELF.

In hindsight, based on their personalities, their choices struck Greyson as odd. With his looks and disregard for military protocol, Kincaid would have been a better fit for ASP's undercover operations. And with Greyson's need for order and discipline, serving in Earth League Force would have made more sense. Odd, how things didn't always work out logically.

Kincaid interrupted Greyson's musing about their past. "Just give me the high points and let me decide whether or not I want to be involved."

Though Kincaid made no mention of their history, Greyson wasn't fooled into believing he'd forgotten. The man knew how to hold a grudge. Apparently, however, he wasn't looking to immediately exact revenge. He took a chance and briefly explained the situation.

Kincaid let out a low whistle. "You're up to your neck in it, aren't you, old friend? I've heard of Shyanne Kedar and Simon Dempster. Of the two, I'd put my money on Dempster as the culprit, but all the recent evidence points the other way."

"Evidence isn't always reliable. And the truth is . . . often less obvious than it seems." Greyson wished he could go back and handle the Largon case differently.

Kincaid's mouth tightened but he nodded. "I've had years to think about the difference between evidence and truth. And, as much as I hate to admit it, because of you I haven't had to think about it in an eight-by-ten cell."

Greyson shook his head. "If I'd kept the truth to myself, you might have walked away without censure. You'd probably be a general by now."

Kincaid laughed. "Unlikely. The next time I decided to twist the rules to suit my purpose, would you have been there to bail me out?"

"Your actions saved innocent lives."

"And put others at risk." Kincaid stood and turned to face the black void of space. "Only pure dumb luck kept that whole fiasco from backfiring on me."

"You did what you had to do in a difficult situation. We both did."

Kincaid turned to face Greyson. "What do you need from me?"

"Need?" Greyson was taken aback. "Nothing. You don't need to get involved."

"If what you say is true about the Consortium sending in their troops, it'll affect every human in Earth space, and all those people in the outer worlds. I'm already involved, whether I want to be or not. And I want to be. So what do you need?"

Greyson knew once Kincaid made up his mind, there was no swaying him. He supposed he should count his blessings.

"I could use remote access to ELF and ASP files." When he'd left headquarters, taking what the director thought was a leave of absence, Greyson had been forced to sign off the system; otherwise his UTD—the undetectable tracking device installed in every

ASP agent—would have showed his every move. While on leave, a UTD still recorded an operative's movements, but no one monitored them. Only if the operative failed to report back at the specified time, or if the operative activated his emergency beacon, would those records be viewed.

"I'll set you up with a long-distance link. Anything else?"

"Cancel the emergency call you made."

"Already done."

Greyson started. "When? How?"

Kincaid grinned. "Right after you docked. After I took over this station, I made a few modifications to the communications system. ASP and ELF overrides don't work here anymore."

"Still playing fast and loose with regulations, eh?"

Kincaid shrugged. "When it suits my purpose."

"There's one more thing—favor—I need."

"What?"

"If this all falls apart, do you have connections to get Shyanne and her crew out of Earth space and someplace where they can start a new life? Someplace safe."

"Fujerking hell, if Consortium troops come knocking, I'll take them there myself."

Chapter Eight

Pistol in hand, Shy awaited the *Spitfire*'s return in the docking bay. When Greyson exited the ship, she let out the breath she hadn't realized she'd been holding. Too much could have gone wrong. The thought that he might not have come back bothered her more than she liked.

"Let me know when you make up your mind if you're going to shoot me or not," he said with a grin.

Anger at his carefree mockery burned away her softer feelings. "Don't worry, you'll know when I decide. It'll be the last thing you ever know." Holstering her pistol, she strode out of the bay.

He followed. In the lift, he started to speak, then fell silent.

She got them past the security measures and onto the bridge by rote. Able and Terle manned the helm; Eldin was still helping settle Brina into her quarters. Though the engine could be controlled from the bridge, Bear liked to be down with it whenever they were under way, in case anything went haywire. His presence in the engine room had saved their asses more than once. The man was a genius with anything mechanical.

She had no idea where Damon and Silky were. She

wasn't worried, though. Neither was critical to in-flight operations and the two were more than capable of looking out for themselves.

Damon had no interest in flying *Independence*. Though he was a competent pilot, his true talents lay in other directions. A slick negotiator, he always got them the best prices for their goods and made sure the right palms were greased so they could move smoothly through any interstellar bureaucracy they encountered.

Silky really served no real purpose on board. She came and went as she pleased and kept her own counsel. But since her arrival, the rodent population on the ship had taken a nosedive. Shy wasn't sure if the kills were Silky's or those of the feline crew she'd assembled. To date, Shy had counted a dozen feral cats slinking through the ship's corridors.

"Status?" she asked Able.

"The ELF fighter has powered down its weapons and moved off. Communications are quiet," came the answer. "We're clear to leave."

Shy shivered. "Then get us the blazes out of here. Being this close to an ELF outpost makes my skin crawl."

"Aye-aye, Captain. Where to?"

Shy cocked an eyebrow at Greyson. He was the one with the plan.

Greyson nodded. "According to Commander Kincaid, Dempster's last attack was three days ago, on the mining asteroid Nexis. He slaughtered the miners and seized their transport, which was filled with unrefined ore."

Able spoke up. "The right place to dump stolen ore would be Ramin Five. They have a refinery and all the right contacts to dispose of any finished product."

"Like Verus, another fujerking garden spot," Terle remarked.

On the far edge of the outer worlds, because of its inhospitable conditions and lack of usable resources, few worlds had any interest in adding the planet to their territory. Where Verus was dry, on Ramin Five it rained twenty out of every twenty-four hours. The temperature hovered around a hundred degrees. While Verus was devoid of life, Ramin Five teemed with flora and fauna: two-legged, four-legged or otherwise, feathered, furred and scaled, most everything hostile to humans.

The planet's claim to fame was its large ore refinery and reputation for not cheating customers. There were credits to be made there, but humans didn't fare well in the mineral-laden air. In order to breathe on Ramin Five, humans needed to wear an oxygen filtration unit: an OFU. Otherwise, they'd drown. Those with the credits to do so lived in bio domes. Even with these precautions, though, after a few years the native bacteria caused skin to rot, and lungs got saturated and developed chronic pneumonia.

Able made some calculations. "It would take him at least four days to get from the Nexis system to Ramin Five."

"Dempster's unlikely to still be there, but it's a place to begin the hunt," Greyson agreed. "Someone will know where he headed next."

"Yeah, that fujerking Ramin-fish Fiske will know."

Fiske. Terle referred to the human in charge of the planet. He'd used illegal genetic research to have his DNA modified so he could exist there, but now he could never leave. Shy thought it seemed a poor choice, but then she didn't have to live on Ramin Five.

Terle glanced at her. "He could tell us, but are you willing to pay his price?"

She ignored him. "Set a course for Ramin Five. How long?"

"At FTL . . . three days," Able said.

Greyson leaned over the man's shoulder to study the console. "If you boost our power and take this route, we can cut it to thirty-six hours. Then we might catch Dempster still on planet. He wouldn't trust a transaction this large to an underling."

"I don't know," Able said. "That'll put a strain on the old girl and take us right through the center of an area lousy with pirates, slavers and the flotsam and jetsam of a dozen different worlds. Using FTL, we can't shield or use our weapons, either. Anyone can take potshots at us. We've tweaked a few noses there, so we're not the most popular kids."

Greyson shook his head. "Even if they see us—which is unlikely, since they won't be looking for us—it'd take pinpoint accuracy to hit something in the FTL stream. I'm pretty sure we'll be fine."

Though she wanted to disagree, his reasoning was sound. And any time they could make up was valuable. "Do it," Shy said. "The sooner we catch up with Dempster, the sooner we can retire *Independence* and ourselves."

"If we don't get her blown up first," Terle muttered.

Shy left Greyson, Able and Terle on the bridge, arguing the best way to program the FTL, Faster Than Light, drive, and she headed to the crew quarters deck to check on Brina. Letting the girl remain on board was a mistake, but faced with her pleas, she hadn't been able to refuse. Shy knew what it was like to be hurting and alone with nowhere and no one to run to.

It bothered her how easily Greyson fit in with her crew. In a matter of days he'd become one of them, the one they looked to for direction. Even Terle acknowledged his innate authority. But what truly disturbed her was how quickly he'd disarmed her, eased her doubts, calmed her fears and worked his way back into her life. For the last ten years, suspicion and maintaining a distance between herself and others had kept her alive and free. She wasn't the innocent young girl who'd trusted him with her heart. So why did she want to believe him now?

Was helping him track down Dempster worth the risk? To her crew? Her ship? Herself? Her son's future? How could she be sure Greyson wasn't lying to her about the Consortium's plans? Just because her body responded to his as it did with no other man didn't mean she should trust him. Had she learned nothing from his first betrayal?

Yet, even if he was lying about the Consortium, she knew he wasn't lying about what Dempster was up to. She'd seen the evidence. The man was a monster. He wanted to own her, body and soul. The few days she'd spent as his guest still gave her nightmares. After her crew rescued her from Dempster's prison, it had taken her weeks to shake off the effects of the drugs he'd forced her to take, drugs that had twisted her mind and body into knots. And drugs weren't the only weapons in his vast arsenal.

No, she had no choice. No matter if Greyson lied,

no matter the risk, she had to bring Dempster down. Greyson could only break her heart. Dempster intended to destroy her and everyone she loved.

Thirty-four hours later, Greyson stood by as Able slipped *Independence* unnoticed out of the FTL slipstream and hid her behind a small moon. Traffic to and from Ramin Five was light, so they should be safe from detection for a few hours.

"Good girl." Able patted the console and leaned back. "Told you she could do it."

Terle snorted. "For all the good it did. I scanned the area. We're too late. Dempster's ship isn't in orbit. Not much other traffic, either. Must be a slow time."

"It was a long shot that he'd still be here," Greyson admitted. "I'll go planet-side and find out where he was headed."

"You?" Terle laughed. "They'd peg you as a snake in two seconds and skin you even quicker. Let us do a few scans first, see if he's hiding like we are."

Greyson nodded his agreement, but his thoughts were elsewhere.

Skinning. He couldn't repress his instinctive shudder. After having had their cover blown, more than one ASP operative had met the gruesome fate of being skinned alive. It had been a constant fear during his early undercover work, and he winced, remembering the past.

He'd shown considerable skill at blending in with the dregs of the universe, of course. Back then, after he'd graduated from the academy, being undercover had provided him a sense of freedom: freedom to be someone—some*thing*—different than was expected of the foster son of a prominent businessman and former high-level politician. Freedom to release the beast he feared lived inside him. Freedom to exact revenge on the scum who'd torn his life apart.

Chalmer Dane had never blamed Greyson for his daughter's death, but Greyson blamed himself. He'd spent years beating himself up over it. If he'd reacted quicker when the pirate snatched little Anna from his side, he might have saved her. Instead, he'd frozen in horror as his mother charged the man and was shot and killed. The bright-eyed four-year-old died in a subsequent explosion, her small body vaporized. The little girl had idolized him; in return, he'd failed her.

Ten years ago, both Chalmer and Greyson had believed Kedar was behind that attack. That was why, years later, Greyson was practically drooling over the assignment of infiltrating Shyanne's school: He'd bring Kedar to justice. After the operation, however, Kedar was never charged with the murders of Greyson's mother and little Anna. It was for that reason Greyson made it his mission to discover the truth about the attack. Though his superiors weren't happy about it, Greyson had taken Kedar's further testimony in prison. He'd come to the conclusion that, though Kedar was guilty of many crimes, he hadn't orchestrated that attack. But he'd never indicated who had, despite all of Greyson's questioning.

An even more surprising occurrence had come about, too: A strange friendship developed between the men. Without the promotion resulting from Kedar's capture, Greyson probably would have continued to work as an undercover operative until he made a mistake and was killed, skinned just as Terle joked;

ASP field agents generally didn't live long. For that reason, the arrest of Kedar had in some ways saved Greyson's life—just as his time with Shyanne had stolen it. He couldn't help feeling grateful.

As well, during those visits, despite his dislike of Kedar's activities, Greyson found he legitimately liked the older man. Intelligent and thoughtful, always soft-spoken, Stewart Kedar seemed an unlikely sort to have controlled a massive smuggling empire. But he never spoke or acted in haste. At his trial, the government was unable to substantiate more than a few of the charges leveled against him because his colleagues were loyal to a man. Yet Kedar hadn't fought all of the charges brought against him. He'd used the stand to make a statement, and after pleading guilty was sentenced to fifteen years.

Though Greyson rose in ASP rank, his visits to Kedar continued. It was then he'd learned of the man's skill in ship design and made the deal to see his spacecraft put into production. Their meetings had become rare these days, but when the recent raids resulted in ELF's attention being focused on Shyanne, Kedar had requested Greyson come see him. At the same time, Greyson had learned from his stepfather of what was to come with C.O.I.L. He'd learned almost more than his brain could assimilate.

During their last meeting Kedar seemed older, his calm demeanor shattered. He'd insisted his daughter wasn't behind the current attacks and finally named the true culprit: Simon Dempster. At the same time, he'd revealed that Dempster was behind the attack that killed Greyson's mother.

Kedar had asked him to find and protect Shyanne from both ASP and Dempster, but now Greyson wondered if he was pursuing the man to save Shyanne and Earth, or to exact revenge. The latter was a distinct possibility.

Shy looked over as the door to Brina's new quarters opened. Damon stood outside.

"Hello, ladies. Miss Kitty," he greeted them all, leaning against the doorjamb.

Silky was curled on the bunk, and she lifted her head and hissed. Her tail twitched in agitation. The cat had adopted the girl and hadn't acted pleased at either Shy's or Damon's intrusion.

When he crossed his arms, the satiny material of Damon's flight suit stretched taut over his broad chest. Brina glanced up, and he graced her with a heart-melting smile.

Considering him a brother didn't stop Shy from appreciating Damon's male beauty. But she knew his angelic features hid a darkness only those who crossed him truly saw. She made a mental note to warn Brina not to take Damon's flirtations seriously. He loved the hunt and enjoyed the capture, but he never kept his catch. Still, from what she'd seen, he always managed to leave his prey happy.

Brina's expression didn't change, however. She showed no surprise or interest. If anything, her already cool gaze turned icy, and Shy suddenly realized Earth's sun would go dark before the girl would let another man near her. Without a word, the blonde went back to making up her bunk and organizing the clothing and supplies Eldin had collected for her use.

Damon straightened, his smile faltering, and Shy chuckled. The look on his face as Brina totally ignored him was almost worth the aggravation of letting the girl remain on board. "We'll leave you to get settled." She tugged Damon into the corridor with her. "If you need anything else, let Eldin know."

Brina turned. "What I need is to keep busy. Put me to work."

Her words were brisk, but they revealed to Shy the lost, hurt little girl hiding behind the hard exterior. She understood the need for action, the need to bury the pain, fear and anger by working until you were too exhausted to think or feel. She wanted to tell Brina it wouldn't work but knew the young woman had to find out for herself.

"Give yourself a few days to figure out what you want to do. Staying aboard *Independence* isn't your only option," she reminded the girl.

As if oblivious of what the girl had been through, Damon suggested, "I could keep you busy. I'd be all too happy to help."

Silky growled. Shy jammed her elbow into his side, and he grunted. Liquid oxygen was warmer than Brina's glare. She slammed the door in both of their faces.

"You're a real ass, you know that, don't you? That girl has been through hell. The last thing she needs is some sleazy Lothario coming on to her." Shy followed Damon down the corridor.

"I'm exactly what she needs!"

"You really think she's going to fall into your bed?" Shy snorted in disgust.

"Doesn't matter." Damon's shoulders lifted, then dropped. "If everyone treats her like fragile, damaged goods, she'll explode. She needs a focus for all the rage brewing inside her."

"So you decided to volunteer for the job?" This

was a side of Damon Shy rarely saw: the sensitivity buried beneath his carefully crafted wild demeanor, the lost boy he'd been when her father first brought him home. He'd never spoken of his past, but she guessed he'd suffered as much as Brina, if not more. So perhaps he knew what he was talking about.

She pressed her palm against his cheek and felt his almost imperceptible flinch. With his aversion to being touched, she wondered how he managed to seduce and bed so many women.

"What can I say? I'm a glutton for punishment. Besides . . ." He gave her a cocky grin, the moment gone, the bad boy back in place. "Maybe I'll get lucky and she'll succumb to my charms."

"In your dreams." Shy let her hand drop along with the subject.

A short time later, she entered the docking bay to prepare *Liberty* for the jaunt down to Ramin Five. They needed to discover where Dempster was headed, and to do so, a trip planet-side was definitely necessary. Able and Terle had completed a few other scans and been unable to track Dempster's ship.

The sight of a man she didn't recognize standing just inside *Liberty*'s hatch made her pause. She pulled her pistol and crept forward along the wall. Who was he? No one could board *Independence* without raising an alarm.

Wait a minute. . . . She stopped and looked closer. Anger drowned out relief. She holstered her pistol and stormed up the ramp. Grabbing the man's arm, she swung him around to face her.

"You jerking idiot! I could have shot you!"

The man gazed calmly back and smiled. Covered as he was from head to toe in Ramin Five rain gear, an OFU hanging around his neck, she didn't recognize him. Stubble darkened his face, giving him a rakish air. But despite the changes he'd made to his appearance, she knew it was Greyson.

"Where's Terle?" she asked. "He's supposed to go down with me."

"Terle had a small accident. He cut his hand while replacing a damaged circuit board. It's just a scratch, but it's too dangerous for him to be exposed to the bacteria on Ramin Five," Greyson explained.

"What about Able? Or Bear? Why you?" she asked, though she already knew the answer.

"Able told me he can't handle an OFU, because of some residual lung damage, and Bear's size would raise too many questions. Eldin's too old, and Damon, well . . . he's just too pretty. That leaves me." He cocked an eyebrow. "Any other objections?"

"No," she growled. "Let's go." She shoved him aside and stomped up the ramp.

Even though *Liberty* was more valuable and a more attractive target for anyone looking to steal a ship, because of her greater firepower and faster speed Shy had opted to take her rather than *Spitfire*. Greyson's ship would have been an even better option, but it would have raised too many red flags. Better to drop in without drawing any attention at all.

She fired up the engine while Greyson secured the hatch. Once he was seated next to her, she launched.

After they'd been traveling for a while, Greyson asked, "How do you suggest we find out where Dempster's headed next? Did you have any ideas?"

The silent treatment didn't seem to work with this man. Not that she could ignore him. No matter how hard she tried, every fiber of her being was aware of his presence. The soft rhythm of his breathing tingled in her ears. She inhaled his warm male scent with each and every breath. To dispel the memories that scent engendered, she blew out a sigh of frustration.

"How much do you know about Ramin Five?" she asked.

"Not much. Just that it has the largest ore-processing plant in the sector, and that, even though they deal with pirates as well as legitimate businessmen, there's been no trouble with people getting what they pay for. With everything else going on, it's never been a priority for ASP or ELF."

Shy nodded. That all sounded correct. Now it was time to fill him in on her plan. "Dempster's powerful, but he doesn't control every pirate or smuggler. Out here he's just one among many. He has a lot of power, so he gets few direct challenges, but the truth is most of us distrust him.

"Because they focus attention on *all* pirates and smugglers, his forays into C.O.I.L. space make him unpopular. More and more, other groups have had to curtail their activities or join Dempster's group for the protection he can provide. Of course, once they join they can never leave, except in a body bag. ELF and ASP think it's me behind all the attacks, but the people out here know the truth." She glanced at Greyson. "You guys need better informants."

When Greyson didn't respond, she continued. "In this sector, Fiske is the . . . big fish. He's bigger than Dempster, even, so if Dempster wants to do business here, he has to play by Fiske's rules. Dempster wouldn't get payment for the ore until it's inspected, assuming he's just selling it, so unless he wanted to wait around he'd have to file his next port of call. Fiske will have that information. He's finicky about record-keeping."

"So we just go see this Fiske and ask?"

Shy laughed. "Hardly. Fiske now dislikes 'air-breathers,' giving up humanity as he has. Unless the deal is *extremely* lucrative, he conducts his business through middlemen."

"So we'll ask *them*?"

She shook her head. "No matter the bribe, they won't tell us anything. They'll be too afraid of Fiske's retribution—dying on Ramin Five can be a particularly slow, painful process."

"Then how are we going to get the information?" Greyson was clearly getting frustrated.

"We'll trade for it."

"What? What will we trade?"

She grinned. "Me."

Chapter Nine

"*What?*" Greyson shouted.

"Don't worry." Shyanne laughed. "I'm not about to sell myself into slavery."

"Then what in all the blazing galaxies are you talking about?"

"Fiske has a thing for blue-green eyes. He's been after me for a long time to donate some genetic material for the clone he's creating."

"You'd let him clone you?" Greyson couldn't hide his revulsion. Because of the misuse of the technology and the resultant created abominations, centuries ago Earth had outlawed human cloning and DNA manipulation. Part of ASP's mandate was to prevent the trade of unlicensed DNA and illegal clones.

"No, he doesn't want to clone me; he just wants my eye color."

Looking into Shyanne's laughing eyes, Greyson could understand Fiske's fascination. Blue and gold flecks floated in green irises like moonlight on the sea. He shook his head at his fanciful thoughts and said, "I hope you know what you're doing."

"Fiske is harmless—mostly. Easy as riding a slipstream."

"Famous last words," Greyson muttered.

He reached over and took her hand in his. Her fingers felt cool and fragile, and his overwhelming need to protect this woman shook him. "What does Dempster want with you? Why's he doing this?"

She tried to tug away, but Greyson held on, forcing her to look at him.

"We have . . . history." She gave a weak smile.

Greyson kept quiet and waited to see if she'd continue. Unlike the open young girl he'd known so many years before, the girl who'd confided in him all her dreams, this woman held fast to her secrets. He mourned the demise of that girl, and though he knew he didn't deserve it, he longed to regain the woman's trust. .

She looked down at the console and began to speak, first in a halting whisper and then with more strength and volume. "When I was a child, I sensed Simon Dempster was jealous of me, that he wanted to be the only one Kedar loved. Odd, for a monster, eh? He hid his feelings from Kedar, so though I disliked and feared him, because Kedar held him in high regard I said nothing. As I grew older, Simon's interest in me shifted. Before I left for school, he tried courting me, but I couldn't stand him, and in my naiveté told him so in no uncertain terms. He didn't take my rejection very well. Now . . . now he just wants to *possess* me."

Greyson felt Shyanne shudder. He knew she'd left a lot out. Eldin had told him Dempster abducted Shyanne and held her for several days, and he could only imagine what she'd suffered at his hands. He'd read the reports and seen the vids of Dempster's attacks.

His grip tightened. When she flinched, he gentled his hold and said, "You're safe now."

She gave a short, humorless laugh. "I'll die before I let him get his hands on me again."

She yanked free of Greyson's grip and turned back to the controls, and he fell silent as she requested approach and docking permission from the tower. A few minutes later, they landed and stepped out on Ramin Five.

Warm rain poured over Greyson in never-ending sheets that turned the world around them into a watery gray blur. His gear diverted the rain, but in seconds his clothes felt soggy against his sweaty skin. One breath of the soaking, fetid air, and he slapped the OFU over his nose. The taste of decaying vegetation and moldy water remained in his mouth.

They moved across the tarmac toward the stone-block building that served as a transport terminal. Tendrils of vine crept along the edges of the landing zone, and through the veil of rain he saw flames. Pulling his pistol, he put himself between them and Shyanne.

She covered his hand with hers. "It's nothing. Plants on Ramin Five grow fast," she explained. "It takes constant attention to keep them from overrunning the place."

Feeling foolish, he blinked away the damp smoke of scorched foliage stinging his eyes and holstered his weapon.

Inside the building, the atmosphere was marginally dryer and cooler. Greyson shivered. A layer of greenish black mold decorated the stone walls and made the floor slick. The air tasted thick and sour. Both he and Shyanne kept their OFUs on. With a harsh grunt, a heavily armed and surly guard led them toward Fiske's office. All his skin not covered in grimy strips of cloth oozed a yellowish, foul-smelling pus. Shyanne's tension echoed Greyson's as they entered the dimly lit, humid room.

"Welcomes, Prettys Eyes," a hissing voice greeted them. "Fiske haves misses seeings yous."

Greyson peered through the thick steam. As his vision sharpened, he recoiled and swallowed back his meal. The man—if his genetically altered form could still be called that—floated in a tank of murky water. With no body hair, greenish gray skin, his nose reduced to mere slits, gills down to his shoulders from where his ears should have been and double eyelids, Fiske appeared more alien than even Silky.

Greyson knew, as did most Earth humans, that many Consortium member species bore little resemblance to humans, but owing to the restrictions of their probation, they rarely encountered any. Eons ago, to avoid xenophobic wars the Consortium's governing council had decreed that new member species would be introduced slowly and carefully to the myriad shapes intelligent life took. After his instinctive adverse reaction to Fiske, Greyson couldn't help agreeing. And Fiske was still human!

Shyanne showed no reaction to the man's appearance.

"Whats seeks yous froms Fiske?" The fish-man pulled his body half out of the tank and leaned toward them. Streamers of glistening green algae clung to him.

"A small bit of information," Shyanne said.

A long, grayish pink tongue snaked out of Fiske's slit of a mouth. "Informations iss expensives. Whats haves yous to trades?"

The covetous look in Fiske's eyes as he gazed at

Shyanne left Greyson with the urge to spatter the creature's probably green blood all over the room. He shook himself mentally.

"Credits," Shyanne suggested.

Fiske waved a web-fingered hand in the air. Droplets of water splashed Greyson's cheek. "I's nos needs of credits. Yous knows whats I's wants, yesss?"

Greyson saw her barely visible shudder, but Shyanne nodded. She held out a small vial. "I've prepared what you need."

"Takes its tos the doctors, Deek," Fiske directed a guard who stood by the door. After the guard left, Fiske looked at Shyanne. "Whats informations does yous wants, Prettys Eyes?"

Though they had the information they'd come for, the meeting with Fiske left Greyson feeling unsettled. The trade had gone too easily. Fiske had been almost too eager to comply, too eager to give them what they wanted. Too eager to see them leave.

As they walked through the rain toward their ship, the landing dock looked strangely empty. No other spacecraft rested on the pads. Apart from the constant roar of the rain, there was no sound. No engines idling. No clunk of metal against metal. No voices.

The hair on the back of Greyson's neck rose. Halfway to the ship, he stopped. Shyanne paused behind him.

"Something's wrong. Where is everyone?" Through her OFU, her voice sounded distant and hollow. "Able, come in."

As Shyanne tried to contact *Independence*, something moved off to his left. He struggled to see through the curtains of rain. Metal scraped against stone. He whirled and grabbed Shyanne's arm.

"It's a trap! Run!"

They dashed toward *Liberty*.

"Stop or we'll shoot!" a voice shouted.

The two of them ran up the ramp. Shyanne slammed her palm against the hatch control, trying to make it open. Heat from a laser blast sizzled through the watery air past Greyson's head and pinged off *Liberty*'s hull. He pushed Shyanne down. Another blast burned across his arm.

"Don't hit the woman! Boss wants her alive," someone yelled.

Before the hatch fully opened, Greyson and Shyanne squeezed through and closed it again. Gasping for air, he tore off his OFU, scrambled to his feet and pulled her upright. "Get us off this soggy rock!"

Discarding her OFU, she nodded and scrambled into the pilot's seat.

The initial thrust of the engine knocked him off his feet and pressed him flat to the deck. He staggered up, but a blast rocked the ship and threw him down again. Swearing under his breath, he pulled himself into his seat.

"You okay?" Shyanne glanced at him as she piloted *Liberty* at top speed away from the planet. Water dripped down her face and spiked her eyelashes.

He pulled open a rent in his rain gear and examined the burn on his arm. "Fine," he grumbled. "Let's hope the blast from the laser cauterized the wound against bacterial infection." The burn was painful but seemed minor. "Damn, I'm getting too old for this nonsense." Her laughter made him smile. "I'm glad you find this amusing. Looks like Fiske wants more than your eyes."

"Those weren't Fiske's men." Her voice was grim. "Fiske's people would never use laser pistols; their components start to rust after a few days. He uses water cannons. Blasts people off their feet and drowns them."

"Harmless, eh?"

She shrugged. "Like I said, it wasn't Fiske."

"Dempster?"

"He lured us into a trap. But where in the jerking stars is he?" She slapped her palm on the console. "We couldn't have missed his ship. It's too big to hide."

"He doesn't have to be here to rig a trap. He could have paid off Fiske. Or he could have a smaller ship than his usual battle cruiser—he's an expert at falsifying locator IDs, remember. Are we being pursued?"

She shook her head. "Nothing on the scope. *Independence* would call us if there was anything out there waiting."

The engine made a grinding noise, and the ship lurched, throwing Greyson onto his injured arm. Acrid smoke seeped out of the control console, filling the air with toxic fumes.

"Damn, navigation is out! Vent the cabin," Shyanne commanded.

Coughing, Greyson sealed off the leak and vented the cabin. "Ten minutes and we're out of air," he warned, seeing the gauges.

"Strap in. If we lose power before we break out of the gravitational pull, we'll crash long before we suffocate."

While she struggled to maintain control of *Liberty*, Greyson fastened their safety harnesses.

"Able, come in," she called, trying desperately to contact *Independence*.

". . . hear you . . . break . . . up. What's your . . . babe?" the man's voice crackled over the com.

"Navigation is gone! The engine is stalling! We won't be able to break out of the gravitational field! Five minutes to thruster failure. Mark our signal for pickup."

His voice was suddenly clear: "We're coming in for you, babe."

"No! You can't do a suborbital pickup. Not this close, in this soup. . . ." They hadn't broken out of the planet's thick cloud cover yet. "Abort! That's an order," she shouted.

"Can't hear you, babe. You're breaking up." Able's voice came through even louder and clearer.

"Able, damn your shiny bald head! If you crash my ship, I'll . . . I'll hold you down while Terle tattoos gray hair on it!"

"Hold her steady, babe. Two minutes to rendezvous," Able promised.

Greyson helped hold *Liberty* on course as her engines bucked and wheezed. Outside, heavy gray clouds swirled around them; then a dark shape loomed up out of nowhere: *Independence*. The docking bay doors slid open. Light spilled out into the gloom.

"Reverse thrusters are out!" Shy yelled over the grinding roar of the damaged engines. "We're coming in fast and hard!"

Without direction, Greyson cut the thrusters as Shyanne steered them toward the welcoming portal. Silence descended, but *Liberty* didn't slow.

"Force field web is up," Able answered.

"If it doesn't hold, we'll be coming out the other side!"

"It'll hold," Able assured them. "Twenty seconds to impact."

"It's going to be a bumpy landing."

Greyson reached for her hand. "Any landing you can walk away from is a good one." She gave him a wobbly grin in reply.

If he was going to die, he had to tell her how he felt. That he loved her. "Shyanne, if we don't make it, I want you to know—"

"Don't!" She pulled free.

Liberty plowed into the electronic webbing. The impact threw them forward into their harnesses, then back against their seats. For a moment Greyson's vision blurred. His teeth tore through his tongue. The pain kept him from blacking out, and the metallic taste of blood filled his mouth.

Before the ship could bounce back out and plummet to the planet's surface, Able erected another field behind them. In seconds, *Liberty* had shuddered to a stop. With a groan, Greyson turned to check on Shyanne. Eyes closed, her head lolled against the seat.

No! "Shyanne!"

He ripped off his harness and felt her neck. Beneath his fingers, her pulse beat strong and fast. She raised her head and blinked up at him.

"Any landing you can walk away from is a good one, right?"

Relief flooded his veins. He released her harness and lifted her in his arms.

"I can walk," she protested.

"You aren't doing any walking until Eldin checks you out."

"Your arm—"

"Is fine. Don't argue. Don't you dare argue."

Though being in Greyson's arms felt right, Shy knew it was wrong. Despite the fact that they'd made love, she couldn't trust him. The stakes were too high. If it were just her future, she'd take the risk, but she couldn't gamble with Rian's life. But . . . was it a gamble?

She knew Greyson would never harm a child. And if he knew about Rian, he'd do everything he could to protect the boy. But what would that mean? As the son of a known criminal, Rian had no rights under Earth law. On the other hand, he was also Greyson's son. Where did that put him? Would he be safer in Greyson's world and care than in hers? Not knowing ripped at her heart. Could she give him up if he were better off and Greyson wanted him? How could she not?

If they succeeded in capturing Dempster, she wouldn't have to. She'd have a pardon. She could take Rian and start a new life. Greyson would never have to know about his son. But if they failed, she knew she'd have to give Rian into Greyson's care and vanish.

She couldn't keep him in the dark forever about herself, though. Especially if she brought him with her, eventually the boy would learn who and what she really was. She couldn't bear to see the same pain in his eyes that she'd felt when she discovered the truth about her father. To spare Rian that, she'd do whatever it took.

Liberty's hatch opened. Light, along with fresh air,

spilled into the ship. That set her to coughing. Damon and Eldin rushed inside.

She could hear Able shouting over the com. "Babe! Answer me. Are you all right?" She tried to answer, but coughed instead.

Eldin leaned over her. "Get her to the med bay."

She wanted to tell him she was fine, but couldn't catch her breath. When she blacked out, she must have inhaled fumes. When he tried to put a portable oxygen mask over her face, she pushed it away.

She could feel *Independence*'s engines straining to break free of the planet's gravitational pull. She slipped out of Greyson's arms to stand upright. His unwillingness to let her go echoed her reluctance to leave. "There's no time," she told them. "It's going to take our help to get *Independence* out of Ramin Five's gravitational pull."

The ship rolled thirty degrees to port. Greyson caught her before she hit the wall. "Bear," she yelled into her com. "More power to the port thruster! Able, give her more juice!"

"If we do that, she'll go red," Able shouted back. "We'll lose an engine."

"We don't have a choice. Better one engine than a whole ship."

"Aye-aye, Captain."

Shy struggled to pull air into her raw lungs as she ran toward the bridge. Greyson followed. Eldin headed for the med bay to prepare for handling their injuries. Damon went to help Bear in the engine room.

Four long minutes later, she reached the bridge. Warning alarms wailed. Lights flashed and flickered.

Sparks jumped. Streamers of colored smoke curled in the air. Shy took the helm.

Able silenced the alarms, and the only sound was the shrill whine of the engines and the snap and crackle of small electrical fires burning around the room. Terle and Greyson smothered them while she and Able fought to keep *Independence* in the air. The ship was designed for space flight, not atmospheric travel, especially not across a water-laden atmosphere like Ramin Five. She closed down the ports that scooped the tiny specks of matter floating in the vacuum of space to supplement the fuel, but she could already feel the drag in the engine as oxygen and water clogged the works.

Shy read the gauges. Inch by inch, the ship was sinking. Another two hundred feet and they'd never be able to break free of the planet.

She rotated the ship until it pointed straight toward the stars, rerouted power from the stabilizers and artificial gravity to the thrusters. The move pushed Able and her into their seats and tossed Greyson and Terle against the back wall. She struggled to breathe against the pressure. At full power, the ship held its position but didn't pull out. Its own weight still tethered it to the planet.

Giving a low thump, an engine failed and Shy felt it. As gravity counteracted their thrust, the pressure on her chest eased, allowing her to breathe, but fear made her gasp. *Independence* was going down. If the remaining engine didn't burn out, she might be able to manage a controlled crash, but once they were down they'd never get up again. Surviving the crash might be possible. Surviving the planet? No. Crashing on Ramin Five was definitely not an option.

She rerouted the last bit of power from life support. It worked. They stopped falling. But for how long? And how long could they last without life support? The remaining engine groaned.

Greyson pulled himself up next to her. Blood trickled from a cut over his eye. "Terle's unconscious," he reported.

"Eject the bridge." Damon's voice sounded calm over the roar of the engine and the shrill shriek of metal against metal.

"Get up here and I will," she told him.

"There's no time. Do it now."

"We have five minutes until the second engine fails. Move your asses!"

"No can do, Captain. Lifts are out."

"Get to the docking bay. Launch one of the smaller ships. I'll hold her long enough for you to get away."

"Eldin's trapped in the med bay," Damon said. "And if Bear leaves the engines, you won't have five seconds. Eject. Now. It's your only chance."

Her hand hovered over the keypad. Physically, it would be easy to do. The mechanism functioned at the touch of one button. Emotionally, it would be the hardest thing she'd ever done. Pressing that button would save her, Able, Terle and Greyson but kill the others. Unless they could terminate it, ejecting the bridge set off a self-destruct command that would obliterate them. Then they'd have to survive the crash.

"Think of Rian. He needs you." Eldin's voice was soft and sad over the com.

Because of her, Kedar—her father—rotted in a Consortium prison. This close to dying, she let herself acknowledge his place in her heart. Could she live with the guilt of killing her companions, her friends, her family?

Do it. Bear's response appeared on her screen.

Tears of rage stung her eyes. She shouldn't have to choose. "Able?"

He shook his head. "It's your call."

She reached out to punch in the command. Greyson's fingers closed over hers, stopping her. Her head whipped around to meet his gaze.

"There's another option," he rasped. "Go to FTL."

"That's suicide!" Able said. "First we'll fall like a rock for twenty seconds. Then, when we engage the FTL, the oxygen around us will ignite and blow us apart before we escape."

"No, it won't," Greyson insisted. "The air's too thin and water-laden."

"Better to take our chances on the surface. After we land, we can use the smaller ships to get off planet," Able countered.

"If they survive. If we survive." His gaze locked with Shy's. "Trust me, it's our best option."

In that moment, Shy decided to trust him. "Sorry, Able, he's right. Hang on!"

She cut the thrusters. *Independence* went into free fall. Greyson grabbed hold of the edge of the console as he flew upward. Shy felt Terle's body thump against the back of her seat, then bounce away. For twenty long seconds, *Independence* tumbled toward the planet.

"Now!" Greyson shouted.

She hit the FTL control. In the vacuum of space, the shift from engine thrusters to FTL was a mere blip of spatial disturbance, but in a planet's gravity and atmosphere the effect was like being turned inside out. Space and time slowed and twisted. Shy's stomach turned. Her vision distorted. Colors flowed into piercing sounds that penetrated her brain. Sound crawled like spiders across her flesh. Her scream tasted of blood. Seconds stretched into agonizing hours.

Then it was over. *Independence* righted herself, flowing smoothly into the FTL slipstream.

Reality returned to normal, but Shy doubted she ever would. With each heavy beat of her heart, her head and body throbbed. She forced her eyes open and checked the controls. Except for being down one engine, *Independence* ran within normal parameters.

"Greyson?" Her fingers hovered over his head where it rested on her thigh.

He raised his head and grinned. "Told you it would work."

"Able?"

"I'm good, babe."

"Terle?"

"Here," came an answer with a low groan from behind her.

Shy twisted to look at him. Blood trickled down his unnaturally pale cheek, and he held his arm against his chest. "Get to med bay," she told him. "Eldin. Bear. Damon. Report." There'd been no time to warn them of the shift to FTL. She worried her lower lip as she waited to hear from each of her crew.

"Bear and I are a bit banged about but fine. What in the blazing stars did you do?" Damon asked.

"Later," she told him with a relieved laugh. "Eldin?"

"Still breathing," Eldin answered. "Brina's hurt."

Crap. She'd forgotten about the girl. "How bad?"

"She's unconscious. I've stabilized her, but I won't know until I run some tests. Can you keep this crate level for a bit?"

"Yes. Terle's coming to get checked out. Just so you know."

Terle started to argue, but at her sharp look swallowed, nodded and left the bridge.

Shy didn't bother to ask about Silky. That cat had more than nine lives and wouldn't answer the com anyway. "Greyson and I are okay," she told everyone.

Standing up, Greyson grimaced and muttered, "Speak for yourself."

Relief at his disgruntled look left her feeling weak and weepy. She tried to focus on *Independence*'s systems, fearing if she gave in and began to laugh, laughter would quickly turn to hysteria.

"Bear, how long before the engine's back online?" They'd need it when they dropped out of FTL. *Independence* could fly on one engine, but if attacked they would suffer a serious disadvantage. Dempster was out there somewhere, gunning for her.

Reading Bear's answer, she decided. For now they needed to go someplace safe to lick their wounds. She pulled a pistol from beneath her console and pointed it at Greyson. "Able, escort our guest to the brig."

Chapter Ten

"What's going on?" Greyson asked.

Shy didn't answer. She'd expected—could handle—his anger, but the look of hurt on his face left her feeling sick. She turned away.

Able looked confused but took her pistol and motioned for Greyson to precede him off the bridge. When Greyson hesitated, Able gave him a shove. She heard rather than saw Greyson stumble.

"Make sure Eldin takes a looks at his burn," she told Able without turning.

"Will do," Able said.

The door slid shut behind them, leaving Shy alone. As much as she wanted to trust Greyson, she couldn't risk him discovering the location of her safe harbor or learning of Rian's existence. She couldn't even trust him enough to let him know she needed to keep the location secret. No, he couldn't know where they were going at all, and the brig was the only place on *Independence* she could be sure he wouldn't have access to a computer console.

"Idiot!" Dempster backhanded the man held upright between two others. Greenish red blood spurted from his flattened nose; he whimpered and crumpled at Dempster's feet.

"You could have killed her. I told you I wanted her alive."

"I's s-sorrys. Misss-takes-s."

Through his rage Dempster barely heard the man's pathetically gurgled apologies. Man? He glared at the cowering creature, gills fluttering on each side of his throat, useless in the ship's dry air. Fiske was no man. He wasn't human anymore—not since his genetic manipulation. At that point he'd lost all such claim. In Dempster's eyes he was an abomination, a creature to be used and then disposed of. He was an *alien*. Dempster hated aliens.

When he was twelve, aliens had overrun his colony. After the attack that killed his family, the reptilian xenomorphs enslaved him. For six long years he'd toiled in an alien mine. Only by forgetting what it meant to be human was he able to survive while others around him perished. He'd grown tough and strong, taking control of the slave compound and using his limited power over the other slaves to stay alive. Still, in the end he would have died there like the others but for Stewart Kedar.

When Kedar raided the mining complex, he'd freed all the slaves. He'd given them credits to return to their old lives or build new lives. Dempster had chosen to become part of Kedar's crew, and his gratitude quickly grew into a possessive, obsessive love.

Through manipulation and deceit he'd become Kedar's second-in-command, the one Kedar looked to for advice, counsel and companionship. Those he couldn't control, he disposed of, including Kedar's faithless wife and young son. Then *she* came into the picture, and everything changed. The love and attention Kedar had given Dempster shifted to her. Oh, Dempster was still the second-in-command, but he was no longer heir to Kedar's empire. She was.

How he'd hated her, the little princess. Innocent. Unaware of who and what Kedar was, she lived a life free of the pain and suffering Dempster had known. She'd done nothing to earn Kedar's love. She didn't deserve it.

At first Dempster had wanted her dead, but after Kedar's wife and son disappeared, he kept the girl too well protected. Then, as the little girl blossomed into womanhood, Dempster's feelings shifted. Dead wasn't near enough punishment for her crime. Only owning her would do. Only by possessing her could he purge himself of his need for Kedar's love.

"Pleases," Fiske begged. "Nots kills Fiske. I's dos alls yous asks."

The fish groveled at Dempster's feet, getting his slimy blood all over the deck of the ship and Dempster's expensive leather boots. Anger and disgust churned Dempster's stomach.

"Gut this fish," he told his men. "And space the garbage."

"Nooooos-s-s!" Fiske wailed as the two men dragged him to his feet. One pulled a knife.

"Wait." Dempster's command halted the downward stroke of the blade.

"Thanks yous. Thanks yous," Fiske babbled, reaching out for mercy.

"I don't want fish guts all over my ship." Dempster evaded the fish-man's webbed fingers. "What's the closest planet?"

His crony sheathed his blade and grinned. "Dryden."

"Perfect. We'll drop him there. Until then put him in detention."

"Nos!" Fiske screamed as they dragged him away.

Dempster smiled. Dryden was perfect, an arid, barren rock, uninhabited, with a thin atmosphere. A fish like Fiske would last a day at most.

Too bad Dempster couldn't remain around to watch. He'd enjoy seeing the fish-man dry up and blow away. With his greenish gray skin and gills, Fiske reminded him more and more of the aliens who'd enslaved and abused him for so many years. Plus, it was good for his men to witness what happened to those who failed.

Sadly, Dempster didn't have the time to spare. She was still out there, waiting for him.

Greyson paced the brig. Able had let him get out of his rain gear and into some dry clothing, as well as helping him slap a bandage on his burn and clean up his disguise, but he couldn't sit still. What had happened to make Shyanne toss him here?

Just before Able escorted him off the bridge, Greyson had seen her start to enter coordinates into her navigation system. Where were they headed? And why didn't she want him to know?

And who was Rian—a husband or lover? Jealousy surged. He quashed it. He'd relinquished any claim on Shyanne when he betrayed her. Still . . .

He had too many questions. And locked in the brig, he had no way to get answers.

Time was running out. He had less than three standard weeks to locate and capture Dempster before the Consortium stepped in. In the meantime, every Earth, ELF and ASP agent was out hunting

Shyanne. Without the help he could provide with his access to ASP and ELF databases, she might fly right into them. Even if she managed to avoid those, Dempster was out there.

He could activate his UTD emergency beacon. Before she knew she'd been betrayed again, ASP ships would swoop in and capture *Independence*. Once in custody, she'd be safe from Dempster, but by the time he convinced his superiors she wasn't responsible for the attacks it would be too late to stop a Consortium action; if he was playing advocate for her, he couldn't be hunting down Dempster.

He plopped down on the bunk and rested his head in his hands. Even to save Shyanne, he couldn't allow the Consortium's plan to be implemented. For now he'd bide his time, but at some point he feared he'd have to choose between Earth and Shyanne.

Shy watched as Eldin finished stitching up and bandaging the gash on Brina's arm. The girl was lying pale, injured and unconscious, on the med-bay bunk—the same bunk she and Greyson had made love on. The memory aggravated Shy's guilt over Brina's injuries.

"Shy?" Eldin touched her arm. "She'll be fine. A small scratch."

"A scratch? It took fifteen stitches to close. I counted. And she's unconscious."

Eldin chuckled. "No. Asleep. I gave her something before you got here. She didn't want me to stitch up her arm."

"Why not?"

"I don't know. The blood and pain didn't seem to faze her, but the minute I brought out the laser needle, she turned white. So I gave her a light sedative before I started sewing."

"I should have left her back on that outpost with the others. She'd have been safe there."

"From what she told me, she didn't have anything to go home to. And her being a Regalian slave, ELF couldn't protect her from her owner. It was her choice: freedom or safety. Which would you choose?" He didn't wait for her answer. "Go get some rest. Doctor's orders."

"What university did you get your medical degree at?" she joked.

"I have one from the University of Life, another from Hard Knocks College. The practice I've had on this crew has made me a better surgeon than most on Earth."

Shy gave him a small smile of agreement. "What about Terle and Bear?"

"Bear's fine. Terle came in with some cuts and bruises and a sprained wrist. I patched him up and sent him to his cabin. Man's got a hard head."

"Have you seen Silky or her crew?" Shy asked, though she didn't doubt the cat was fine.

"Her fur is a bit ruffled, but she looked fine. The cats are hiding." He fussed with the already neat bandage on Brina's arm, then asked, "Is it really necessary to keep Greyson in the brig?"

Having her actions questioned by Eldin sent a pang of guilt through Shy. In the short time he'd been aboard *Independence*, Greyson had earned the respect of a man she truly admired. After Kedar's arrest and imprisonment, Eldin had been there for her. He'd protected her. Nursed her through a difficult pregnancy. And when she'd insisted on becoming a smuggler, he'd helped her assemble a reliable crew and taught her everything he knew.

She started to reach out for him but let her hand drop to her side. None of it mattered. "Yes, it's necessary. I can't risk him finding out where we're going."

"What are you really afraid of?" He turned to meet her gaze. "That Greyson'll find out about Rian, or that he won't?"

"You don't know what you're talking about. Why would I care if he knows about Rian?" She'd never told anyone who Rian's father was, not even Eldin. "I don't trust him to know the location of our base."

Eldin snorted. "I may be old. But I can see the similarity between them."

Shy felt the color drain out of her face. She'd thought she was the only one who saw the resemblance between Rian and Greyson. Now more than ever she had to keep them apart. She couldn't risk Greyson seeing Rian. If Greyson knew he had a son, life as she knew it would change in ways she didn't want to imagine. Part of her wanted to keep Rian at her side forever. Another more rational part knew she'd have to give him up eventually. She didn't want a life of running and hiding for her son. But not yet. Not this way. She needed more time with him.

To keep her knees from buckling, she leaned against the wall. Fear of losing the one person in her life who mattered most stiffened her spine. "Does everyone know?"

Eldin shrugged. "No one has said anything, but if they bother to look it's obvious. The minute Greyson sees the boy, he's going to know the truth."

Shy straightened. "No, he won't, because he's not

going to get the chance. Rian is staying with Matha and Tomas, so Greyson will never see him."

"Is that fair to either of them?"

She turned on Eldin. "What do I care about fair? Rian is my son. I won't give him up. You will not say anything."

He shook his head. "After all we've been through together, I thought you knew me better, trusted me." He turned and walked out of med bay. "If you need me I'll be in my quarters."

When two days later *Independence* slid out of the FTL slipstream into normal space around a small planet, Shy breathed a sigh of relief.

Because space in this sector, located just beyond Earth territory, tended to be unstable, more than a few ships had vanished without a trace, and past this point there was a void no one had yet crossed and returned. For that reason, few new travelers, legitimate or otherwise, bothered to come this way. Also, unless you were looking for it, hidden behind the glare of three suns, Uta was easy to miss. And if you didn't know the right coordinates to plot your course, chances were you'd find yourself swallowed by one of the area's many space anomalies. No one was quite sure what caused the anomalies or what they were, but they were dangerous and they made patrolling space around Uta difficult, capable of hiding an approaching threat as well as destroying it.

A young, primitive world, Uta had no intelligent native species. The largest animal was a foot-long, rodentlike creature called a snip, which lived in the dense jungle that covered most of the planet. Until Silky volunteered several of her cat crew, the grain-loving snips were becoming a major problem. Now they at least avoided the fields and granaries patrolled by Silky's feline guards, and the cats she left on the planet grew sleek and sassy.

Half land and half water, Uta was still in its infancy. Volcanoes dotted its surface, erupting frequently, constantly changing the planet's geography and weather. Shy had situated her home base at the southern tip of the planet's northern continent, far from any instability. In the last ten years the colony had grown from just herself, Rian and her crew to nearly a thousand residents, most rescued slaves who now worked hard to create lives and a community. But without the constant influx of supplies *Independence* provided, life on Uta would be short and hard.

Though she spent most of her time aboard *Independence*, Shy found Uta was as close to home as she had, and it was the only home Rian had ever known.

During the two-day trip here, Shy had spent her time working on the engines with Bear. Actually, she'd mostly hidden out in the engine room. Bear didn't need or want her assistance, but he was the only one who didn't question her about confining Greyson to the brig.

Even Silky had pointed out that confining the man didn't solve the problem. Once they landed, he'd be able to figure out their location. Even with the natural space difficulties keeping people away from Uta, eventually *someone* would find them here.

"What will you do with him if he discovers this place?" Silky had asked, sauntering away without waiting for an answer.

Shy didn't know. She couldn't keep him confined forever, neither aboard *Independence* nor on Uta.

While she'd hidden out and brooded in the engine room, her crew kept Greyson company in the brig. The day after she confined him, she'd stopped to check on him and found him playing cards with Damon and Terle through the cell bars. *Independence*'s cells didn't have standard force fields; they were old-style barred cages. Eldin had told her Kedar saw too many people desperate to escape a life of slavery commit suicide by pushing through those fields, so when he'd designed his brig he'd used old-fashioned metal doors and bars. Laughing and talking as if Greyson weren't the enemy and a prisoner, her crewmates never noticed her hovering in the shadows.

After that, she kept better track of his guests. Each and every one of her crew, even Silky—the traitors—as well as Brina visited with Greyson, and they never came empty-handed. By the time *Independence* settled into orbit around Uta, Greyson's cell sported a new bunk and bedding, a MAT unit, an entertainment vid unit (one not connected to the main computer grid, Shy made sure of that) along with fresh clothing.

Now she stood outside his cell. Damn, the cell looked more comfortable and appealing than her quarters. Or was it just the man inside?

For once, Greyson was alone. In the past two days he'd had barely a minute by himself. He'd played cards with Terle and Damon. Discussed politics with Eldin. Shared meals with Able and Brina. Even Silky and her ever-present entourage had come calling, though she hadn't deigned to enter into any conversations, lounging just close enough to keep an eye on him while appearing indifferent.

He liked this collection of outcasts and misfits that made up the crew of the *Independence*. Their company had kept him from dwelling on his predicament. And though they showed their disagreement with Shyanne's decision to lock him up by spending time with him, they were loyal to her. Now he rested on the bunk, an arm thrown over his eyes, and pretended to sleep.

He felt her presence outside the cell. The subtle scent of the vanilla lotion she used wafted over him, and the soft whisper of her rapid breathing told him of her agitation. Her clothing rustled, and then he heard the clank of metal as she unlocked and opened the door. He lifted his arm to look at her.

He wanted to be angry, but found only disappointment and regret over her lack of trust. But what had he expected? Why should she trust him? Since the moment they'd met, he'd done nothing but lie. And he knew to save Earth he'd continue to lie. He was, unquestionably, a practiced liar.

"We're here." Her voice sounded strained.

He swallowed a humorless laugh and sat up. "And just where is here?"

"Uta."

He shook his head. "Never heard of it." He stood. "So I can come out of solitary confinement now?"

"Hardly solitary. This place"—she waved her hand at his cell—"has been busier than Earth Central." She referred to Earth's largest spaceport.

"Didn't think you'd notice, busy as you were with the engines."

When she started to turn away, unwilling to end their conversation, he blurted, "Damon cheats at cards. I figured it would be Terle."

She laughed. "I'm surprised you noticed. Damon's good at cheating. He rarely gets caught."

"And when he does . . . Let me guess, he charms his way out the consequences." He couldn't help grinning.

The spark of anger in her eyes startled him.

"After a few short days you think you know us, know who we are, don't you? You think you know why we do what we do," she accused in a low voice that rose with each word. "You know nothing. Nothing."

A flush of angry red stained her cheeks and she glared at him. Her chest heaved, her fingers curled into fists at her side. This was the Shyanne he remembered: passionate in her beliefs, willing to take on anyone and anything to protect the ones she cared about, the woman who'd come alive in his arms. Not the reserved stranger, the smuggler who masked her fiery emotions beneath a pretense of indifference.

He wasn't sure why he wanted to shatter her facade. He knew her ability to maintain control was what allowed her to remain alive and free while engaging in the dangerous profession she chose, that if he succeeded in destroying her protection, she'd be left vulnerable in a perilous universe.

Needing to touch her, he caught her arm. "I missed you," he said softly, moving past her out of the cell. She shook off his hand and ignored his comment. He followed her to the docking bay.

"You'll go planet-side with me," she said in an even tone. Cool and collected, as if her passionate outburst had never happened, the stranger had regained control. "I'd ask you to stay aboard *Independence*," she continued with a sigh, "but then I'm afraid the crew would stay with you and they need some relaxation.

Independence's engines are back up and running, but she took a beating in Ramin Five's atmosphere. We need to shuttle up parts and supplies before we go anywhere else. I intend to refit a few things, especially since we'll be taking on Dempster."

"How long will it take? We're running short of time," Greyson reminded her. "This isn't a game."

"I know," she said. "A couple of days. Three at most. I want off Uta as quickly as possible. Still, there's no choice. Without repairs, *Independence* will be no match for Dempster if we find him."

"Don't worry. *He'll* find *us*." Greyson had come to that realization while sitting in the cell.

"That's what I'm afraid of," Shyanne replied.

They took Greyson's ship down to the surface. Watching Shyanne pilot the craft with effortless expertise reminded him of the hours he'd spent teaching her to fly. Though she'd known the basics, he'd helped her refine her raw talent until her ability actually rivaled his own. She'd loved flying, and he'd loved watching her fly. The exhilaration in her eyes. Her whoops of joy as she swooped through the air. The awe on her face as she broke out of the atmosphere and streaked through the endless void of space. Of course, after she'd escaped him by stealing an ASP shuttle, he'd had time to rethink the wisdom of teaching her to fly.

The tightening of her lips and the white knuckles told him she also remembered those lessons. Lessons that had continued on the ground. Lessons where the line between teacher and student blurred.

He stroked the ship's console. "Sweet little bird, isn't she?"

"Standard ASP-issue?"

"No." He leaned back in his seat. "But you already know that. You went over her for bugs and tracking devices—and to see how much you could get for her parts on the black market."

She nodded, smiling. "Where did you get her? I didn't know ASP deputy directors got paid so well."

"Hardly." He laughed. "She's a prototype under development for ASP." He didn't mention he'd taken her without permission. And though the knowledge was limited to a select few, the design was her father's. "But when they release the design to the public, I'll get one."

"That's right. I forgot you're heir to Chalmer Dane's fortune."

At her derisive tone, he squirmed. Dane Enterprises not only controlled the majority of transport in Earth space; it also designed and manufactured most of the ships—private, commercial and military.

"I never did understand what the son of one of the richest and most powerful men on Earth was doing working as an ASP agent," she continued. "Didn't like the taste of the silver spoon Daddy stuck in your mouth?"

He remembered her shock and disillusionment when she'd discovered not only that he wasn't a student, but that he worked for ASP and was the son of the man whose money and power were the reason ELF and ASP had spent their time and resources to track down and capture her father. He rubbed the scar hidden by the hair on his scalp and winced at the memory. Confused by his feelings for the target of his investigation, he'd handled the situation badly. When he'd tried to take her into custody that day, she'd bashed him over the head and escaped.

"Chalmer Dane is my foster father." He felt compelled to explain, to defend the man. "Chalmer took me in when I was ten, after an attack by your father's people killed my mother and Chalmer's four-year-old daughter. The Dane fortune isn't mine and will never be."

Though he loved and admired Chalmer, Greyson was ever aware he wasn't truly Chalmer's blood. He also recalled what he'd cost the man. Chalmer's wife had been unable to bear Greyson's presence, unable to handle the fact that he lived while her child had died. When Chalmer insisted on adopting Greyson, she'd left him. Until she'd died a few years later in an accident, Greyson knew Chalmer had always hoped she'd come back. Despite his wealth, good looks and charm, Chalmer had never remarried.

"Kedar wasn't responsible for that attack."

The lack of heat in Shyanne's voice told Greyson she defended her father out of loyalty, not certainty.

"Probably not," he admitted.

Eyebrows raised, she stared at him.

"Evidence points elsewhere—but that doesn't mean your father is innocent."

"Never said he was. Kedar has a lot of crimes to answer for." Shyanne sighed and looked away. "Just not that one."

"For what it's worth, Shyanne, I'm sorry." Greyson wasn't sure what he was apologizing for, the past, the present or the future.

He barely heard her whispered reply. "Me, too, Greyson. Me, too."

Chapter Eleven

Dempster's smile grew as he watched the information scroll across his monitor. He leaned back in his chair. Satisfaction tasted sweeter than the tea he sipped from a delicate porcelain cup. Things were going better than he'd planned. Perhaps he'd been too hasty with Fiske?

No. He'd done the correct thing. The creature had nearly gotten her killed. He couldn't tolerate such incompetence.

The matter resolved in his mind, he turned his attention back to his prey. Her ship damaged, with no idea she was being tracked and followed, Shyanne Kedar scurried back to her home base—the base he'd been hunting unsuccessfully for close to a decade.

Ten years. Dempster had intended to snatch Shyanne during Stewart Kedar's capture, but the clever little bitch had evaded both the authorities and him. When Shyanne first came into Kedar's life, he'd kept her with him aboard the *Independence*. How Dempster had instinctively hated the clingy little brat with her wispy blonde hair and big blue-green eyes that seemed to see deep into his soul and find him wanting. He couldn't endure what he'd seen reflected back at him in those guileless eyes. But her most serious crime was that she'd stolen what should have been his, what he deserved, what he'd earned: Kedar's love.

He doubted Kedar suspected him of orchestrating Shyanne's several near-fatal accidents—nearly being blown out an air lock, falling down a lift shaft and other events he no longer recalled. Kedar certainly hadn't realized his second-in-command's part in his wife being scared away. But the man had nonetheless removed his precious child to a safer location that, throughout the subsequent years, Dempster had never discovered. From then on, Dempster's contact with the child had been limited, and thus his opportunities to eliminate her.

Considering his hatred for the girl, it surprised him when she grew from an annoying child into a beautiful young woman and his feelings toward her changed. His unanticipated infatuation had been a shock, and remembering its onset made his fingers tighten on his spoon until it bent under the pressure. He sipped his now-bitter, cooling tea, grimaced, then stirred in more sugar.

Like some pimpled youth, he'd wanted her with a need that outweighed common sense. What enraged him more, he'd wanted *her* to want *him*. He abased himself by courting her with sweet words and gifts. Cruelly and without hesitation, she'd rejected him. Fury had killed his tentative tender feelings. If he couldn't have Kedar's love or his daughter's, he'd settle for their anguish and fear.

Recalling the few brief days she'd been in his possession filled Dempster with pleasure. Though he hadn't had the time to break her spirit, to make her his creature or to get word to Kedar about her capture, the memory of her screams was still delightful.

But she'd managed to slip out of his grasp, and that infuriated him. Those who'd helped her do so would also feel his wrath.

To calm himself, he took another sip of tea. The now oversweetened brew had a cloying taste. Jumping up, he threw the fragile cup across the room. It shattered, and sticky liquid dripped down the wall. Breathing hard, he stood motionless until he brought himself under control.

The road to reaching his goal had been long and hard, filled with roadblocks and detours, but now it neared its end. Each day and year she'd evaded him had only intensified his purpose. He was in a better position than ever. He'd watch in satisfaction as everything and everyone she loved was torn away from her. Then he'd own her body and soul.

"Captain, have the ships set a course for Uta." Growling the corresponding coordinates over the com, he waited for his orders to be carried out.

At the last moment, Shy diverted their trip in Greyson's ship to the landing pad nearest her old homestead rather than the one abutting her current home in the main compound. Hiding Rian's existence from Greyson there would be impossible. The young boy's photos and personal items filled the place.

Using *Spitfire*, Eldin, Terle and Damon were taking Brina into town. Terle and Damon would pick up the supplies needed to repair *Independence* while Eldin got Brina settled and talked with their local doctor—though not formally trained, Eldin was a skilled physician and a capable surgeon, and he was always checking up on current medical techniques. Able, Bear and Silky remained on board. None of the three felt comfortable on Uta.

Greyson's little ship handled sweet and smooth, settling on the pad with a small thump. If nothing else came out of her encounter with her old lover, possession of this ship put her ahead. Though she'd love to keep it intact, in the end she'd either have to sell it or strip it down for its tech.

Ever since the first time Kedar let her pilot a shuttle to the *Independence*, she'd loved the freedom and control flying gave her. That she'd learned most of what she knew from Greyson was something she didn't want to think about. She kept the memory of the hours she'd spent aloft with him locked deep in her heart. Resurrecting them served no purpose. That time and that girl were gone. The man she'd thought him to be had never existed.

As they disembarked, she watched Greyson's face. What would he think of the planet she called home? And why did his opinion matter? She turned and considered their surroundings, trying to see it through his eyes.

Aside from its geological instability, which didn't extend to this region, Uta was an idyllic little world. Its rich volcanic soil adapted easily to off-world crops. It had no particularly dangerous predators and few bugs or microbes harmful to humans. Its odd orbit circled three suns in a way that kept the temperature in this area a consistent seventy degrees Fahrenheit year-round. If Earth or any other Consortium world learned of its existence, they'd fight to claim it. Shy was determined not to let that happen. For the slaves she rescued with nowhere else to go, Uta provided a safe haven, a place to build new lives. It was her son's home. It was her home. It had been for a long time.

Closing her eyes, she breathed in Uta's unique fragrance: a blend of the smells coming from the profusion of plant life, a hint of the ever-present smoke from the distant volcanoes and of the briny sea a few miles away. She'd grown up here, sheltered not only from Earth and the Consortium, but also from the truth about Kedar.

Her earliest memories were of a safe and carefree if somewhat lonely childhood. Every few months Kedar came to stay for a few days. She'd loved him and enjoyed his visits, if the rest of the time she'd spent alone with her caretakers, the loving, childless couple who now watched over Rian in her absence. Though Matha and Tomas never spoke of their past, she knew Kedar had rescued them from slavery. But they stayed with her and now her son because of love, not gratitude. She owed them more than they'd ever owe her or her father. It was almost a perfect life Kedar had created for her here. Too bad it had all been a lie.

"What was a lie?" Greyson asked.

She hadn't realized she'd spoken aloud. "Nothing." The very childhood that had isolated and protected her for eighteen years had also left her easy prey to Greyson's charm and deceit—and along with the love she'd thought she felt for him, that naive girl had died. She shoved her memories where they belonged, in the past.

"The compound is just a few miles over that rise." Her old home was located apart from where the other people had settled. She, too, had since moved closer in.

He glanced around and frowned. His reaction made her bristle until she looked closer. Time and neglect had taken their toll. The old homestead was decidedly smaller and shabbier than she remembered.

She opened the door and froze in the doorway. Motes of dust danced and swirled in the sunlight that streamed in from behind them. The overstuffed floral furniture Matha favored still filled the rooms. Prints of badly painted landscapes hung on the walls. Faded, frilly curtains covered the windows. Memories of the happiness she'd experienced here rushed through and threatened to overwhelm her.

Watching Greyson move around the house's main room made her edgy, as if by seeing where she'd grown up he could somehow see into her soul, know who she was, find a way to reach her again. She shook away the delusion: Nothing had changed, but nothing of the Shyanne Kedar who'd grown up in this house remained. After Greyson's betrayal and learning the truth about Kedar, when she'd come back ten years ago she couldn't bear to stay in this house. In a storm of tears and rage, she'd torn through it and destroyed everything that reminded her of the lie she'd lived. Toys, clothing, journals, gifts, mementos of her life—all were consigned to the fire. She hadn't stepped foot inside this house again until now.

While waiting for Rian's birth, she'd lived aboard the *Independence*; then she'd built a new house—a huge one, one without any painful memories. In the following years, that compound had grown to a community of several thousand people. Though the residents looked to her as a leader, for the most part they governed themselves, since she was gone more than she was around.

"You'll stay here. I'll have supplies brought up for you." She stayed in the doorway, not moving. Being here weakened her resolve to remain apart and aloof from everyone but Rian. When he was born, she'd tried to cut herself out of his life, too, but had found the ties too strong to sever.

Greyson's question interrupted her memories. "Don't want me to meet any of the locals?"

She hesitated before she answered. If they stayed on Uta for more than a few days, it was inevitable he'd come in contact with someone from town. She couldn't risk having him ask the wrong questions. She'd have to tell him part of the truth and trust him to keep the secrets he learned. "Apart from my crew and a few others, no one here knows I'm Kedar's daughter or a smuggler."

That was a lie. Everyone but Rian and the other children knew the truth. She'd brought most of the people here. To keep Rian safe, she let him believe they were Matha and Tomas's daughter and grandson, that she was a legitimate space trader. He believed his father had died before he was born. Life had come full circle. She coughed to hide her bark of laughter at the irony. She'd created the same lie for her son as Kedar had created for her.

Eventually she'd have to tell Rian the truth, at least about what she did. The older he became and the larger the colony grew, the more likely someone would slip or he'd overhear something.

Greyson regarded her from where he'd settled in a chair next to the room's empty hearth. "What do they think you do for a living, the people here?"

She shrugged, continuing the lie. "Trading. They

have their suspicions, perhaps, but no one asks. They're just happy to be free."

"Then I'd bet most of them know exactly who and what you are but don't care."

"Maybe," she allowed, "but it's best if no one knows who you are. These people mistrust strangers and have little love for Earth or C.O.I.L."

"Best for who?" he asked.

She ignored that. "The house has been unoccupied for several years, so it's a bit dusty. If you promise not to interrogate them, I'll have someone come up and clean for you." Matha could be trusted not to reveal anything about Rian. And she would report if Greyson broke his word. The woman might not agree with all of Shy's choices, but her loyalty was beyond doubt.

"Cross my heart." He traced an *X* over his chest.

Shy's heart stuttered. How many times had he used that phrase and gesture, as they lay, bodies tangled together after sex, in affirmation to her questions about love? Why did he use it now?

She looked into his eyes but could find no answer in that hooded gaze.

Using a forged access pass and authorization, Chalmer Dane went to see Stewart Kedar. Sweat that owed nothing to the heat of the desert prison world dampened Chalmer's palms. After a lifetime spent safeguarding the rule of law, the laws he now broke could cost him more than credits or his freedom. He had no choice. His son Greyson's future—Greyson's *life*—was at stake. And Kedar was the only one who could help.

A churlish guard, clearly unhappy about his posting, led him to Kedar's open cell, informed him inmate SK-2560-15 would be returning from the day's last meal in ten minutes, then stomped away. The lax security didn't surprise Chalmer. A prisoner could easily walk away from this prison compound, but once outside stood no chance of survival in the dry hundred-plus-degree heat. Getting off the planet was impossible. While security on the ground might be lax, the sky above was well patrolled. In the planet's hundred years as a prison compound, not one prisoner had succeeded in escaping alive.

Chalmer looked around the ten-by-ten cell occupied by Kedar for the last ten years. Against one wall, a coarse brown blanket neatly covered the room's cot. A battered metal sink and commode sat in one corner. A drafting table along with a hard wooden chair occupied the other corner and took up what little open space remained. Though stuffed with books and papers, with sketches of spacecrafts covering almost every inch of wall space, a sense of order pervaded the crowded room.

Chalmer considered the detailed drawings. At Greyson's urging, over the years Chalmer had helped turn many of Kedar's designs into reality. The fact that the man created them using only a ruler, pencil, paper and his mind still amazed him. Not even the highly trained ELF and ASP engineers with all their C.O.I.L. technology could compete with this man's brilliant concepts and designs.

"Chalmer Dane. To what do I owe the honor of your visit?" came a low, even voice from behind him.

Chalmer turned. Familiar brown eyes met his.

This was going to be harder than he'd thought. He'd expected to find a man crushed and withered by incarceration. He should have known better. The man's designs were indicative of his zest for life.

The years had done little to change Kedar, Chalmer saw. He stood straight, his back unbowed by imprisonment. A mere sprinkle of gray touched his rich brown hair, unlike Chalmer's pale blond hair that had turned to silver years ago. At fifty-four Kedar looked young and fit, making Chalmer by comparison feel every one of his own fifty-three years.

"May I sit?"

"Make yourself comfortable. What's mine is yours."

Unable to detect any sarcasm, Chalmer perched on the edge of the cot and immediately realized his mistake. Kedar sat on the higher chair and loomed over him. Used to being in control, to running a multibillion-credit company, to commanding thousands of employees, coming to Kedar as a supplicant burned like acid in Chalmer's gut. But for Greyson he'd do more than ask; he'd beg. The boy meant more to him than pride. Pride had lost him his wife and daughter. No matter what it took, he wouldn't lose Greyson.

Chalmer cleared his throat and began. "Why did my son come to see you? I want to know what you told him and where he went."

Kedar didn't answer. He picked up a pencil and began to sketch.

Growing impatient, Chalmer demanded, "What did my son want with you?"

"Your son?" Kedar asked, his voice as cold and empty as space.

Chalmer's skin went clammy. Questions chased through his mind. What did the man know? *How* did he know?

Kedar stood and dropped his sketch in Chalmer's lap. With numb fingers Chalmer picked it up. The familiar face of a young boy looked back at him: Greyson.

"You know?" His words faltered. "When did you find out? How?" He'd lost his one bargaining chip.

"Ten years ago, at my daughter's school." Kedar took the sketch. The hard lines of his face softened as he studied the drawing. "My wife couldn't tolerate life with an outlaw. When she ran away, I didn't stop her. My son deserved a better life."

"When she died, why didn't you claim him?" As the woman died in Chalmer's arms, she'd revealed the truth of Greyson's parentage and begged him to care for her son. He'd agreed. First, as a way to gain revenge against the man who he believed had caused his daughter's murder. Later, because he'd come to love the boy as his own.

"I thought he died with her. By the time I realized he hadn't, you'd already adopted him. Besides, I found it poetic justice that the son of the most wanted man in the galaxy should become the son of the most powerful man on Earth. When Greyson arrested me ten years ago, I could see by his face he didn't know the truth. Who was I to shatter his world? He carries my blood, but he's your son."

Chalmer heard the pain and also something he couldn't identify in Kedar's voice. "Why did he come to see you?" he asked again.

"During the year between my arrest and trial he came many times. At first he came to interrogate me, seeking information about my business activities and associates. But even after he realized I'd give him nothing, he continued to visit. We became friends of a sort."

Chalmer could appreciate why Greyson was drawn to this man. Stewart Kedar projected an enticing air of command. Even incarcerated as he was, his presence seemed to promise well-being, protection and integrity. "Why did he come this time?"

"He wanted to know where to find my"—he hesitated a moment—"daughter."

"What did you tell him? Did you send him on a suicide mission?"

"I *sent* him nowhere. With or without my help, he'd have gone. Our son is his own man. He doesn't wait for permission to do what is right. He knows Shyanne is not the one Earth's forces should be hunting."

"How can you be sure?"

"I know my"—again the pause—"daughter. Murder, slave-trading and piracy are not in her nature. Greyson knows that as well."

Ten years ago, when the girl escaped, Chalmer had noticed Greyson's interest in her, an interest that couldn't be allowed to develop, considering their biological connection. It baffled him that Kedar seemed unconcerned. And there was also the fact that: "The evidence against her is damning."

"We both know evidence can be misleading." Kedar locked gazes with Chalmer.

Remorse made Chalmer look away first. His belief in Kedar's responsibility for the attack that killed his daughter as well as Greyson's mother had been part of what drove Greyson to join ASP. "Greyson told you what's happening? What's at stake?"

"Yes."

"Fujerking stars! The entire ELF fleet has been unable to stop this pirate. Now Greyson's out there on an impossible quest, without authorization, without backup, without hope. Alone."

"He's not alone. Shyanne is with him."

"That's part of what I'm afraid of," Chalmer muttered.

Kedar's laughter boomed through the cell.

"Are you mad?" Chalmer eyed the man with distaste. "Aside from the fact that if you're wrong about your daughter Greyson is throwing away not only his career but possibly his life, he and Shyanne can't be together. They're brother and sister!"

Kedar abruptly sobered. "Calm yourself, Chalmer. There's something you need to know about Shyanne."

Chapter Twelve

Shy sat in the shade of the porch, sipping the cool lemonade Matha brought out on a tray. The warmth of the day was draining her of ambition and energy. The house sat on the far side of town, just off the main road. Trees shaded the building from the sun. Flowers and Matha's herb garden, along with the fields of ripening wheat, perfumed the air.

She wondered what it would be like to stay here always, not to roam the dark depths of space, always looking over her shoulder, never knowing where the next attack would come from; to live free and safe. Then she laughed at her musings. Freedom and safety were illusions for children. Life would ever be a constant struggle.

Without asking, the older woman took a seat next to her. "If I'd known you were coming home, I wouldn't have let Rian go off hunting snips with Tomas. How long are you staying?" Matha asked. "They'll be back in four days."

Before they'd brought in goats, sheep, chickens and cattle, the wily little rodents had provided most of the colonists' meat. Some still favored the taste over the domesticated and more common Earth fare, but local cats were keeping the nearby population of snips low. Those that wished to hunt them had to travel out from the settled areas.

"I'll be gone by then," Shy admitted.

"I can signal Tomas to return—"

"No!" Shy spoke too sharply. She moderated her tone. "Don't ruin their trip."

"Rian will be crushed to have missed you. He misses you."

"He has you and Tomas, his friends and school. . . . Besides, I'll be back in a couple of weeks for a longer stay. We just came by to see to some repairs."

Matha lifted an eyebrow and looked ready to launch into one of her "You need to quit gallivanting all over the universe and stay home with your son" lectures. It was a sore point between them. Matha had no idea of what it took to maintain Uta's secrecy and continue to provide the goods that helped the colony survive. Even with the MAT units working at maximum efficiency, they couldn't provide everything the people of Uta needed. Someone had to obtain those extra things and bring them here. Who besides herself and her crew could she trust to do that and not expose the world?

"We also came to drop off Brina," Shy said, cutting the older woman off by changing the subject. "She's too young for the life of a smuggler."

"She's older than you were when you started."

"She's injured."

"You were pregnant."

Neither of them mentioned the emotional traumas both women had suffered.

"I didn't start smuggling until after Rian was born," Shy countered.

"True," Matha acknowledged. "What of your other passenger?"

Shy stiffened. She hadn't yet mentioned Greyson, and believed Matha would have had little time for gathering facts from other sources. "How did you . . . ?"

Matha laughed. "There's little that goes on that I don't know about."

"Eldin?"

"Actually, this time, no. Damon."

"Damon?" Though Matha and Tomas tried to care for Damon as they had her, at ten he'd been too old to accept their love. It had broken both Matha's and Shy's hearts when he'd chosen to ship out with Kedar rather than stay with them on this world. And that was before Shy knew her father was leading Damon into a life of crime.

"The boy's worried about you."

"Worried about me? Why?" She couldn't resolve the idea of Damon expressing worry about her to Matha. Damon kept his own counsel. He rarely revealed his feelings about anyone or anything; he hid them behind a smile and a carefree demeanor. "What did he say?"

Matha ignored the question and asked her own. "This man, Greyson Dane—he's Rian's father, isn't he?"

Shy let out a groan. "Does everyone know?" She'd hoped that aside from Eldin, her crew hadn't noticed the resemblance.

Matha laughed. "Stars, no. But from what Damon says, once people see him they will. Don't worry. No one will say anything. Everyone here is loyal to you."

"Maybe, but someone might slip." The sooner she got Greyson off Uta, the better.

What or who didn't Shyanne want him to discover? With time running short and a C.O.I.L. invasion looming, her secret shouldn't matter to Greyson, but it did. So despite her directive that he remain at the house, shortly after she left, he followed.

The three-mile trek into town took him through fertile farmland ripe with corn, wheat and grain. Plump livestock observed him placidly, grazing near fields already harvested. He didn't see any farmhouses, which were hidden by trees and the rolling landscape, but curls of smoke rose into the cloudless midafternoon sky.

A family working a field watched him pass. The woman clutched her children close. The man, his eyes hard and hostile, tightened his grip on an archaic hoe. Their fear and suspicion followed him. After he passed out of sight, Greyson's lungs expanded, but his body remained tense.

Thirty minutes later, he reached a town where modern technology collided with the more antiquated. A streamlined hover car sat next to a horse-drawn cart filled with bags of grain. Outside the town's general store, a digital sign flashed prices above a bin of fresh fruits and vegetables. The yeasty smell of baking bread and the sweet odor of fruit and flowers filled the air. Through the store's open doorway he saw a display of electronic household gadgets beside a rack of wooden-handled tools.

In the center of the square, where the town's two main roads intersected, surrounded by a broad grassy area, sat a gazebo. A group of young children played tag around the structure. As he approached, the buzz of conversation and commerce in the square died. One by one, people turned to regard him. Like tiny spiders, his awareness of their mistrust crawled in gooseflesh across his skin.

Impervious to the adults' regard of him, laughing and shouting the children raced past like a stream around a boulder. One little girl of about four stopped in front of him. Her thumb in her mouth, she regarded him curiously. She pulled out her thumb and said, "I Aimee. Who you?"

With her tousled brown hair and brown eyes, she looked nothing like the other little girl who haunted his nightmares, but decades-old pain held him rigid. He looked away. Since he'd failed to save Chalmer's daughter, Greyson avoided the company of young children, especially little girls. They reminded him of his failure. Reminded him of his guilt. Reminded him of his hesitation and what it cost his adopted father.

Around him, the other children ran to and fro, their laughter washing over him like a fresh breeze. The girl tugged insistently on his pant leg. Against his better judgment, he crouched down and met her gaze.

"Hello, Aimee. I'm Greyson."

Suddenly shy, she ducked her head and scuffed her bare toes against the grass. "You wanna play, Gaysin?"

Her innocent trust stabbed into him. When they'd saved the children from the slave auction, he'd held himself apart, shut down his memories, closed off his heart and refused to become emotionally involved beyond the rescue. Now, with a smile and a touch, this little girl battered down the carefully constructed wall around his heart.

He had started to reach out to tuck a strand of hair behind the girl's ear when a woman screamed the child's name in panic. "Aimee!"

Adrenaline jerked Greyson to his feet, looking around for the threat. He'd failed to save Anna; he wouldn't let Aimee down.

Unalarmed, the child cast him a sweet smile, then dashed away. At the shout, the other children scattered, leaving Greyson standing alone on the green. Soon a dozen men, their faces hard, circled around him. Armed as they were with everything from laser pistols to rocks, he didn't stand a chance of defending himself.

Holding up his hands in surrender, he backed toward the gazebo. Sweat trickled down his spine. "Easy, friends. I mean no harm." He spoke Standard. Unless they'd been slaves to an alien species, few out-worlders had TCs.

"Who are you?" asked an older man sporting a laser pistol.

"Greyson." As was the custom on outer worlds, he gave only his first name. Out-worlders preferred their family connections and places of origin to remain unidentified.

The other men pressed closer, and one asked, "What are you doing here?"

One wrong word and these men wouldn't hesitate to attack. Greyson prepared to fight or flee if he had to. He didn't have to; a new voice cut through the air.

"He's with me."

The men surrounding him fell back and parted,

leaving a path for Shyanne. She strode through their ranks. Greyson let his hands fall to his side.

"You should warn us before strangers come to town, Domina." The older man addressed her respectfully, but his tone was querulous. Apparently he held some position of authority and disliked being unaware of such important developments. Greyson understood.

Shyanne smiled and touched the man's shoulder. "You're right, Director Harmin. I apologize for my oversight." She frowned in Greyson's direction. "I should have known he wouldn't follow my instructions to stay away."

"Shall I take him into custody? Since your last visit, we finished building the jail." Now that his position and authority had been acknowledged, Director Harmin's tone held less overt aggressiveness, but he still looked eager and willing to take his anger out on Greyson.

"No need. Greyson is—"

Before she could finish, Greyson put his arm around Shyanne's waist, tugged her to his side and said the first thing that came to mind, "I'm her husband."

"Is this true, Domina?" Suspicion laced Director Harmin's question.

Cursing his impulsive action, Greyson held his breath. Would she go along with his hasty explanation of his presence? If he'd had more time or had been thinking clearly, maybe he could have come up with a better plan.

Beneath his fingers, he felt the tension in Shyanne's body. She gave a terse nod but didn't say more. He gave a brief sigh of relief.

Though Harmin still eyed him with distrust, at Shyanne's announcement the mood in the square shifted from hostility to congratulations. The women, who'd been listening, eagerly crowded close and their voices added to the din.

"Very well, Domina." Harmin gave Greyson one last look of warning, then strode off.

The other men went back to what they'd been doing before Greyson arrived. Tension drained out of him, leaving his knees feeling a bit like jelly. As an ASP agent he'd faced death before, but never by innocent people who were simply terrified he was some kind of threat. Shyanne remained rigid in his embrace.

Now that the men were satisfied Greyson didn't pose a threat, the women approached Shyanne to voice more of their good wishes. This went on for a bit, and then the conversation turned to other things.

"How long will you be here?" one of the females asked.

"Tomorrow starts the Festival of Plenty. Have you brought any trade goods?" asked another.

"Have you brought current news? Vids from Earth?"

Standing in the bright sunshine, Shyanne patiently answered each question, then chatted with the women, asking after their lives and families, listening and offering advice when asked. Though she ignored Greyson and appeared relaxed, he felt anger brewing beneath her calm facade. He'd weathered one crisis, but would soon face another.

Eventually, their questions answered, their concerns addressed, the women moved away. Shyanne shook off Greyson's arm and walked to the gazebo. He followed, remaining silent.

Out of earshot of the townspeople, she turned on him, her voice low. "Coming into town was stupid. They would have killed you."

"I know," he admitted. He hadn't thought about the reaction these people might have to a stranger in their midst. It had been a rookie mistake, and a particularly unforgivable one, considering that the two of them were Earth's last hope.

Shy clasped her hands together to stop them from trembling. Speaking with the townswomen had done nothing to soothe the anger and fear pulsing through her veins. But just whom was she angry with?

When she'd come into town and seen Greyson surrounded by an angry mob, her heart nearly stopped. A few minutes later and he'd have been dead—or at least seriously injured. If Matha hadn't noticed the commotion in the square and contacted her, she would have arrived too late. Her need to protect her secret had nearly cost Greyson his life.

"Why did you claim to be my husband?" The question popped out without premeditation.

"Fear?" His answer sounded more like a question.

Fear. Somehow, that didn't seem likely. He'd faced those men without a flicker of fear showing in his eyes. But, then, she knew him to be a consummate actor. He'd pretended to love her, hadn't he?

"With me posing as your husband, no one will question my presence."

That made more sense. A business partner or a new crew member for *Independence* could be regarded with suspicion for a long time. But if it was an emotional bond such as marriage . . . well, the people regarded her as their patron. They trusted her. If she claimed Greyson as her beloved, they'd likely accept him without question.

Her beloved. A bitter taste filled her mouth. "What happens when they discover the lie?"

He shrugged. "We'll deal with the questions when they arise. But will they?"

Probably not. There was little communication between her crew and the people of Uta. They admired Eldin for his wisdom and allowed him to treat them in supplementary service to the colony doctor. Damon charmed them. But Able, Terle and Bear were merely tolerated, their rough looks and ways too reminiscent of the slavers who'd abused them. Silky had only come planet-side once. Her surly and alien nature, sharp claws and teeth had made her less than popular. She'd stayed just long enough to settle a few cats and never returned.

"Why did you come into town?" she asked.

"I got hungry?" he teased. Before she could respond to his ill-timed humor, he took her hands in his. "Relax. Nothing happened."

The warmth of his hands tempted her to move closer. Instead, she jerked free and turned her back to him, afraid he might see what was in her heart. "Are you really as calm as you seem?" Anger at the lingering fear for what might have happened ate holes in her gut.

His hands settled on her shoulders. "Of course not, but what good would panicking do?"

Against her will, his voice soothed her rattled nerves. His calm was what had always attracted her to him, the way he stood rock solid, steady and sure, when all around him the universe seemed to be spinning madly out of control.

Though she'd adored Kedar, he'd rarely been there when she wanted or needed him. Matha and Tomas loved her and made a home for her, but they had never given her the sense of security she craved as a child. Away from home for the first time at eighteen, she'd felt lost and alone. Then Greyson was there, the anchor she needed to keep from drifting away, the bright star she could circle.

Being with him, loving him—it had given her purpose, direction, sanctuary. Even when their relationship exploded, casting her out into the blackness of space, alone again, he'd been calm—though that time she'd loathed him for it. He'd stood there as her father was arrested and in an emotionless voice told her who he was and what he'd done. In her rage, she hadn't listened to the rest of his explanation. She'd hated him for his composure. When he'd turned away, she'd bashed him over the head and run. For a long time she didn't know if she'd killed him, and she'd lived with a confused mixture of satisfaction, guilt and grief. When she'd learned how he had survived and prospered, relief and anger took over.

"It's over. No harm done," he said.

"It's far from over," she whispered. And there'd been plenty of harm.

The warm weight of his hands eased the tension from her muscles. He moved closer until his chest pressed against her back, then leaned forward until his cheek touched hers. She caught her breath. The smell of sun-warmed male rising on his body heat filled her lungs. She fought the urge to lean into him, to allow him to assume her burdens, to drink from his fount of tranquility.

Self-preservation stiffened her spine. She no longer needed an anchor to keep her steady or a star to circle. She had her own strength now. Others looked to her for security and protection.

Then, why did it take all her will power to step out of his hold?

Lost in her thoughts, she needed a moment to realize a host of curious eyes were watching their exchange. Afraid of what Greyson might read in her face, she kept her back to him and suggested, "Since you're my husband, you can come into town." She just had to keep him away from the house, at least until she had Matha clear away any evidence of Rian.

Let him think he'd won this battle. Rian was out of town.

Chapter Thirteen

When the evening meal was over, Matha chased them both out of the kitchen. Greyson followed Shyanne onto the porch, relieved and grateful. After they'd told the older woman about their matrimonial deception, conversation had become strained. Though she didn't comment or argue, the woman's sharp searching glances made him uncomfortable; the sweet-faced, plump matron made him feel as if he were ten years old again, caught stealing cookies from the pantry before dinner.

Shyanne seemed unaffected by the woman's censure. Before dinner, under Matha's disapproving glare Shyanne had helped him get settled into a spare room. Now, as she leaned against the porch railing and crossed her arms over her chest, Greyson settled in a chair.

In the distance, past waving fields of ripening wheat, the last rays of the remaining sun disappeared below the horizon, throwing the world into a dusty shadow. Insects chirped. Birds twittered as they settled down for the night. An evening breeze, bringing with it the scent of salt water, cooled the air but didn't lessen the tension between him and Shyanne.

If not for the brewing confrontation, replete with

Matha's delicious cooking as he was, Greyson would have enjoyed the peace of the evening. Shyanne was right to keep Uta's location hidden. Even with its unstable topography, this world held small bits of paradise. Without protection, Uta would stand little chance against an invading force bent on stealing her riches.

When the strain of waiting for her to speak grew too great, he asked, "Why did you tell Matha the truth?"

"I can't lie to her!" Shyanne replied. "She and her husband, Tomas, practically raised me. Up until my crew and I started bringing refugees to settle here, the three of us lived alone on this planet."

"It must have been hard growing up so isolated."

"Until I got older and Kedar brought Damon home, I never realized I was alone. Children accept their lives as a given. You don't miss what you've never known. But when Damon turned sixteen and left to join Kedar's crew, I went crazy with loneliness. Easy pickings for a handsome, charming ASP agent."

Her tone was teasing, but he could hear the pain hidden beneath. Guilt hit him anew. Ten years ago he'd been so focused on bringing down Kedar and building his career, he hadn't bothered to learn about the woman with whom he was falling in love. These were things he should have known about her.

"What happened to your mother?"

Her face hidden by shadows, Greyson couldn't read her expression, but he heard Shyanne sigh. "I have only faint memories of her. I was four when she died, and Kedar found Matha and Tomas to care for me. Though at the time I didn't agree, apparently he didn't feel a smuggling ship was the proper place to raise a child." She seemed to be thinking out loud. "After that, in a way he was more a beloved uncle than a father. He visited every few months, but Matha and Tomas acted as my parents. Still, I adored Kedar. I used to cry and beg him to stay whenever he was leaving. Matha and Tomas did their best to comfort me, but I think I needed more than they could give."

Greyson wanted to comfort the child she'd been, console the woman she'd become, but afraid of ending her commentary he stayed silent.

"As I got older, I enjoyed Kedar's visits differently. I learned how to manipulate his guilt about not being with me to my advantage. Every time he visited, he showered me with gifts . . . but they never really filled the void in me. Things never take the place of personal attention."

Her revelations made his heart ache. What a lonely little girl she'd been, what abandonment she'd suffered. Though he'd lost his mother at a young age, his memories of her were clear.

"Every child needs the security of a parent's unconditional love," he agreed. "I don't remember my father. He died when I was very young. My mother rarely spoke of him. When she died, my life shattered. Without Chalmer Dane I might have turned out a different person. I love him and owe him, but . . ." He hesitated to put into words his conflicted feelings about the man who'd raised him.

Shyanne didn't say anything, so he found the courage to continue. Maybe by revealing his past doubts and insecurities, when the time came she'd understand his current deception.

"I'm always aware I'm not his blood kin. As a result,

I've always worked harder to earn his respect. The only thing I ever did that he didn't approve of was joining ASP." Had his success in the agency always been intended to earn Chalmer's approval for a choice with which he didn't agree?

"Why?" Shyanne asked.

It surprised him that the inferno of rage in his heart he'd fed all these years at the death of his mother and little Anna no longer burned so hot or bright. "I vowed vengeance against the man I believed killed my mother." He couldn't bring himself to mention Anna. That pain was his alone to bear. Though logic told him there was nothing he could have done to save her, he still bore the guilt of her death. He always would.

"Kedar," Shyanne guessed.

"Yes. That was what I believed. Working as an ASP agent gave me the opportunity to get to him."

"And now that you know he didn't do it?"

He'd known the truth for years, since his first interview with the incarcerated Kedar. "I'd like to see the man responsible brought to justice. Of course, I learned the hard way that vengeance cuts both ways. I captured Kedar, but it cost me."

She didn't press to see what he meant. Instead she asked, "What convinced you he wasn't responsible for the attack that killed your mother?"

Greyson sighed. "After he was in custody, ASP officials realized they didn't have enough evidence to convict him of all the charges they'd been planning. Some of the testimonies didn't add up, and they began talking to him about a deal. They were open to one all the way through the trial. He represented himself, you know."

"No, I wasn't aware of that. After his arrest, I was on the run. I didn't exactly have an easy way to keep up with what was going on." Shyanne glanced away. He heard bitterness creep into her voice.

"He did quite well. If he hadn't struck a deal, he might have even walked."

"What kind of deal did he make?"

"A full pardon for you, in return for his confession to select charges." Though ELF hadn't had any real evidence against Shyanne, Kedar had struck the deal anyways to spare her the ordeal of a trial. Neither the authorities nor Greyson had seen fit to inform him she wasn't in custory. They'd used his love for his daughter against him.

She gave a small gasp. "I didn't know. Why wasn't I told?"

"No one could find you. And by the time you resurfaced, you'd racked up a whole new list of crimes that nullified your father's sacrifice."

Shyanne was silent for a long moment. Finally she said, "That still doesn't explain why you believe him innocent of causing your mother's death."

"When he agreed to the terms of the deal, for some reason of his own he refused to give any further testimony to anyone but me." Greyson suspected it had been because of his personal connection to Shyanne, but the man had never explained. "I spent months talking with him. It didn't take me long to realize that this pirate—"

"Smuggler," she interrupted.

He laughed. "Some of your father's activities eventually went beyond smuggling. But either way, I realized he was no slaver or murderer. And all evidence was absent regarding those charges. Against my will,

I came to admire him. If his life had taken another track, he would have been an important man on Earth. In fact, in some ways he still is. While I was taking his testimony, I discovered some of his drawings of spaceship designs. With his permission, I showed them to Chalmer. Over the years Kedar's designed dozens of ships for Dane Enterprises. When he gets out of prison he'll be a wealthy man. In fact, my prototype ship is your father's design along with some C.O.I.L. technology."

Shyanne looked annoyed. "Then you knew all along who designed *Independence*."

"I had a good idea," he admitted. "She's older, but her lines bear his mark."

"It seems you know Kedar better than I ever did."

She looked sad, so he rushed to reassure her. "No, not better. Different. You knew him as a child knows a parent. I know him as a man."

"I never got that chance."

"Well, when he's released in a few years you'll have plenty of time to get reacquainted." At least, Greyson hoped they would.

"Maybe. First we'll have to find a way to forgive each other. He lied to me—betrayed my trust. And my stupidity got him captured and sent to prison. He didn't want me to go to that school, but I insisted. It's one of the best business schools in Earth space. I was determined to study hard so I could help him in his business ventures, so I could be with him. Ironic, no?" She gave a short, humorless laugh.

"You really had no idea what your father did?"

"I was a blithering idiot. All the evidence was there. How could I have missed it?"

Hearing the pain in her voice, Greyson went to

stand next to her. The last remaining glow from the setting sun illuminated her face. Unable to resist the urge to touch her, he stroked a finger down her cheek. The satin softness of her skin was temptation itself. He knew he should pull his hand away, but couldn't bring himself to do so.

"Isolated here, how could you have known? You were an eighteen-year-old innocent. I was the idiot. I should have known from the moment I met you that you weren't involved in Kedar's illegal activities. But I believed the bullshit my superiors fed me. I wanted—*needed*—to believe. To do otherwise risked everything I'd worked for, everything I was."

She tilted her head so his palm cupped her cheek. Heat streaked through him, blurring his vision. Of its own accord his hand slid through her hair to hold the back of her head. Their faces were inches apart.

"Was it all a lie between us?" Her breath feathered across his lips. The soft plea in her voice tugged at his heart. Could they find a way back to each other? Could she forgive his betrayal? Could he see past crimes she'd committed as a result, even if they were all well intentioned? And what about his current fraud? Would she forgive him that as well?

Suddenly aware of what he was doing, he jerked away and stuffed his hands into his pockets. Until he knew the answers to those questions, he had no right to touch her. Though he'd made love to her, it had been at her instigation, a mere physical connection, a way to affirm life after facing death. He found himself wanting more, but doubted he deserved it.

To avoid explanations, or seeing the pain of rejection in her eyes, he turned away. He would at least tell her this much: "I told myself I was just acting a part, that I seduced and used you to further my career, but deep down I knew different." He took a breath and continued. "You scared the hell out of me. In the end I wanted you so bad I broke every code of ethics I thought I possessed in order to have you."

The sound of her rich laughter startled him. "Who seduced who?" she asked. "I seem to remember chasing you around campus for weeks before you finally succumbed to my dubious charms. You weren't the only one with needs. I knew what I wanted, and I wasn't a bit shy about going after it."

He chuckled at the memory of her determined pursuit. "It came as a big surprise when I discovered you'd never been with another man." Some of his humor fled. "You might have mentioned it to me first."

"And have you play the gallant and turn me down out of some misguided sense of honor? I thought not. Virginity really wasn't my choice. There just wasn't anyone around that I cared to have relieve me of it. Until I went off to school, the only men I came in contact with were Kedar, his crew and Damon. At eighteen, all but Damon seemed ancient, and Damon was more a brother than a possible lover."

"What about the boys at school? I couldn't help but notice their interest in you."

"I wasn't interested in them. They were . . . boys. Sons of privilege. Spoiled. Vain."

"As far as you knew, so was I."

She shook her head. "From the first there was something that set you apart from the others. You carried yourself differently. I sensed the strength, both physical and mental, in you. That alone should have warned me you weren't what you appeared."

"I was older than most of them, twenty-four to their eighteen."

She cocked her head to study him. "What set you apart didn't have a thing to do with age. Your appeal for me had to do with experience. Understanding. Wisdom."

At her careful perusal, he shifted in discomfort. "Well, I was older. I don't know about wiser."

Rising moonlight washed the color from her skin and hair, leaving behind an alabaster statue, cold and remote. Despite the mild night air, a chill invaded his heart. He shuddered.

"Back then we were both young and terribly foolish." She took a step toward him.

As the warmth radiating off her body flowed around him, the image of stone melted. She was no sculpture. Shyanne was a courageous, warm, vibrant woman. A woman who deserved better than Greyson Dane.

She lifted her hand. Her fingers trailed fire across his cheek. "Can we find a way to forgive the people we were? To live in the here and now?"

He had no right to take what she offered. And yet, though the stars might damn him to burn in a supernova, he couldn't resist her plea. With a groan of surrender he reached out and folded her against his chest.

Without saying a word they moved into his room.

Shy knew the accord couldn't last. Too much time and history, along with the lies, past and present, lay between them. She nonetheless went willingly, eagerly, into Greyson's arms. For this brief moment in time he was hers. Someday he'd forgive himself for his betrayal of her and come to her without her asking, but for now she'd take what she could get.

His solid frame gave her something to cling to, a secure shelter from the storm she knew would soon rage around them. The heat of him pressed against her, melted the ice in her veins and sent her blood swirling through her body like liquid fire.

Aside from a tic in his jaw, he stood motionless as she leaned away and began to undress him. His shirt slid off his broad shoulders to reveal his muscled chest. A few scattered chest hairs tickled her cheek as she kissed her way across his collarbone, then dipped lower. His skin felt smooth and warm. She pressed her mouth to first one flat brown nipple, then the other, delighted as they hardened under her lips. She felt his breath hitch and his pulse race.

When she reached for the fastener of his trousers, he groaned and caught her hands in his. Trapped there, she felt the length of him pressing against her palm.

He pulled away. She swallowed her moan of disappointment. With swift, efficient motions he stripped off the remainder of his clothing.

"My turn."

At his promising grin she quivered in expectation. A cool night breeze caressed her skin as he peeled away her garments. She shivered. His arms came around her, blocking the evening chill, stoking her internal fire. Limbs entwined, together they sank to the bed. He bathed her body with kisses. With his mouth, teeth and tongue he kissed, nipped and laved his way from her throat to her knees, never staying in one spot long enough to grant her release from the tension spiraling out of control inside her.

She squirmed in dissatisfaction. She wanted more. Now! Impatient, she gripped his head in her hands and pulled it to hers. Wild with need, she used her tongue to show him what she desired, thrusting it past his willing lips. He met it with his own, starting a duel where neither asked or gave any quarter.

She shifted her hips to grant him access, but when he finally entered her, he moved with excruciating slowness.

She glared up at him. "I didn't know you were a tease."

"What's the rush? We have all night."

The chuckle of satisfaction in his voice drove her over the edge. With a feral growl she wrapped her legs tight around his hips and surged upward. She only had a second to enjoy the startled look in his eyes before a climax claimed her. Afterward, neither spoke or talked for a long time.

The smell of night-blooming flowers wafted through the open window, but it was Shyanne's sweet scent that filled Greyson's lungs. He never wanted to move. Limp with pleasure, he forced himself to shift his weight off her. At the loss of his warmth, she muttered a rude protest, then curled against his side.

Moonlight leeched her skin of color. A cool night wind swept over them. Goose bumps rose on her bare skin, and he ran his fingers along the bumpy texture, savoring being able to touch her.

"Sleepy?" he asked.

She nuzzled his chest. "I'm not tired. Are you?"

To her laugh of amusement, his body answered the question.

Hours later, limbs entangled, the air filled with the smell of love, Greyson watched as Shyanne slid into blameless slumber. Sleep eluded him, however. With his passion drained, doubt and guilt resurfaced.

The twitter of birds outside the window woke him, and Greyson blinked against the bright morning light streaming in around the curtains. A sense of completion filled him. What had passed between Shyanne and him went beyond the physical. For the first time in years he felt at peace.

Though she hadn't said a word about what had gone before, he knew the hurt and anger from that time was gone, for both of them. Secrets still existed on both sides. He sensed that, like him, she held something back, hid some piece of the puzzle that would determine their future. But at that moment he felt confident they could find their way around whatever separated them. Once Dempster was captured and the threat of C.O.I.L. intervention eliminated, he and Shyanne would have time. Time to forgive. Time to live. Time to . . . He blocked his last thought from being born.

Stretching, he reached for her. His hand met nothing. She was gone, the sheets cold and empty. After what they'd shared, she left without a word?

Confidence faded, replaced by hard reality. She didn't really trust him. Nothing had changed. He groaned, admitting ruefully she *shouldn't* trust him. Nothing he'd said or done in the night negated his lies, his deceit, his betrayal. Nothing was different than it had ever been.

A soft tap on the door kept him from descending into a bout of useless self-castigation. What was done was done. He couldn't change it; he could only make sure the end justified the means. That his bargain with Shyanne was kept by success.

"Come in," he called, hoping it was her.

Matha poked her head through the opening. "Are you up?" She didn't wait for an answer. Instead, she strode into the room carrying a tray. The rich smells of coffee, bacon and eggs made him momentarily forget he was naked in Shyanne's bed.

The woman tsked as she set the tray on the bedside table. "Though it's near lunch already, I've brought you breakfast."

Eager for a jolt of caffeine to wipe the fuzz from his brain, he sat up and reached for the steaming mug she proferred. The covers fell away, exposing him. Matha's frown sent a flood of heat into his cheeks.

He snatched back his hand and tugged the cover over his lap. "I'm s-sorry," he stammered.

"No need to blush, young man." But Matha's tone was as cold as the air on his damp crotch. She handed him the mug. "You haven't a thing I haven't seen before. Eat. When you're finished, bring the tray to the kitchen. Then Shyanne said to meet her at the shuttle port." She turned to leave.

"Matha."

"Yes?" The woman paused at the door but didn't turn back to face him. Though her tone was neutral, Greyson could read disapproval in the stiff set of her shoulders.

He wasn't sure what to say. "I didn't intend . . ."

Matha whirled around. "Intentions don't mean squat, boy. It's actions that count." Her hands were planted on her plump hips, her eyes blazing with protective anger. "Tomas and I have raised that girl since she was four years old. She's as much our daughter as she is Kedar's. Hurt her, and there won't be a corner of the galaxy where you can hide. She's seen too much pain and suffering already."

"I didn't mean to end up in her bed. It just happened!"

"Bah." She waved one hand in dismissal. "You think I care who she beds down with? I'm no prig. You're young, healthy and attractive. Plus, you have"—she paused, some of her steam dissipating, then hurried on—"history together. I'd have been amazed if you hadn't. But the hurt you can do her goes deeper."

"I . . . care for Shyanne." He couldn't bring himself to say the word *love*. If and when he admitted to loving Shyanne, it wouldn't be to a third party.

Matha studied him for a minute, then sighed. "Perhaps you do. But that doesn't mean you can't hurt her." She shook her head and her tone softened. "Pay me no mind. What happens between you and Shyanne is between you. My loving her doesn't give me the right to interfere in her choices. She's long since grown, though at times I'm hard pressed to see it. Eat your breakfast before it gets cold."

Appetite gone, Greyson ate and dressed quickly. The need to see Shyanne grew with each beat of his heart.

Chapter Fourteen

Dempster strode onto the bridge of his newest ship, the *Vanquish*. He was tired of constantly switching from one ship to another to elude ELF patrols. Now that he had a class-one Regulan battle cruiser, he could stand against anything ELF sent after him. Pride of ownership swelled inside him. She'd cost him a fortune but was well worth the expense. Top of the line, sleek and modern, fast and powerful, well armed and dangerous. His confidence soared. Nothing in space could match her—and therefore nothing could match him.

His crew acknowledged his presence with averted gazes and tightened jaw muscles. He knew each treacherous man who served him aboard the *Vanquish*, and all of them hated him. At the slightest hint of weakness they'd turn and tear out his throat like the two-legged dogs they were. But for now they feared him more than they hated him, and so long as he filled their pockets with credits he would keep their loyalty.

It rankled that he had to employ scum. And though meting out swift punishment to those who failed to obey and please provided him with pleasure, it took time and effort he could ill afford. Stewart Kedar's men had followed him out of respect and even love. Still, Simon had been one of those and what had it gained either of them? Better to control through fear and intimidation. He'd learned through hard lessons love was a useless, profitless emotion.

Near his command chair, he paused. A dark, oily odor invaded his lungs and his nose wrinkled in distaste. Though he'd had the air purged and replaced days ago, the stench of the fish lingered, smelling of terror and feces. A dark spot where the fish had soiled himself and the floor caught his eye. Damn the creature! If he weren't already a dry husk, Dempster would take great delight in gutting the fish-man again. The carpeting would have to be replaced.

"We're approaching radar range," said Gerhan, his second-in-command.

Dempster studied the screen. Through the glare of the three-star system, he could discern nothing. "There's a planet in there?"

"Don't know. We'd have to get within scanning range to be sure. But our tracking beacon is definitely broadcasting from orbit around something, and I don't think it's one of the suns."

"Clever little bitch. She's found a nice little hidey-hole, hasn't she?"

"Yes. Flying through the suns' solar fields and finding the planet will be tricky and risky."

"But not impossible for the *Vanquish*."

"No. She can handle the fields and we have the equipment to pinpoint the planet quickly once we're in range. But the minute we enter the system we'll be spotted."

"By then it'll be too late."

"I'm not sure this is a wise plan, sir. *Independence*

may be old, but she's well built and well armed. And Shyanne Kedar is a crafty, capable captain. Is capturing one woman worth the possible cost?"

Gerhan's prissy warnings and fears enraged Dempster. Nothing and no one was keeping him from his goal. He'd worked too hard. Waited too long. Given up too much to hesitate now that he was so close.

The violence that was ever a breath from the surface of his personality now erupted. Without warning, he backhanded the man out of his chair. Before Gerhan could react, Dempster pointed his laser pistol at the man's head. "Are you questioning my command? Are any of you?" He glared around the bridge.

Blood dripped from Gerhan's split lip, adding another stain on the carpet. Eyes wisely averted, he wiped his mouth with his sleeve. "No," he said.

"Then get back to work. Signal me when we have a lock on *Independence*."

As Gerhan crawled back into his seat, Dempster holstered his pistol and strode off the bridge; the smell had grown too thick to tolerate. As he passed, none of the other crewmen met his gaze. He used fear, pain and intimidation to control these stupid but useful dogs. He only wished the same had worked on Shyanne Kedar.

He hadn't had her in his possession for long enough, he reminded himself. But he would get another chance. Over the years he'd honed and refined his appetite for pain, learned to appreciate the pleasure of inflicting it on others. Anticipation of having her again thrummed like a drug through his veins, anticipation of the things he would do to her.

This time, there'd be no escape for her.

* * *

Wary gazes followed Greyson through town. He knew without Shyanne's protection these people would give him no leniency. Heck, if they knew he was an ASP agent, even she might not be able to save him. Though life on Uta appeared peaceful, its existence had been born of desperate need, and its survival remained fraught with peril. If these people believed him a threat, they'd do what they must to protect their homes and families.

When the last building and person disappeared from view, he let out a sigh of relief. Sunshine warmed his skin and eased the tension from his muscles.

A few miles out of town he reached the shuttle port. Surrounded by older, battered, space-weary crafts, his own ship's sleek lines and smooth silver skin gleamed in the midday sun, a precious jewel among corroded rocks. The smells of fuel and sun-warmed tarmac mingled with the scent of cut hay from a distant field and the tinge of salt wafting on the sea breeze.

He found Shyanne in the control tower, speaking over the com with Able on board *Independence*. He took pleasure in watching her. Dressed in tight trousers, short boots and a man's shirt, the tails tied at her waist, she looked both vulnerable and competent. The three men manning the tower regarded her with a mixture of affection and awe.

When he came in, she glanced up at him. Her gaze revealed nothing of her feelings about the previous night.

He heard Able's voice over the com. "Bear's got the engine back online and the shields are operating at ninety percent, but there's a problem with weapons control. Every time we run a test, something knocks them off-line. Targeting's screwed, too. Right now we couldn't hit a supernova at ten paces. Terle's down checking it out."

Her brow furrowed, Shyanne rested one hand on the com unit and leaned in. "I thought Terle was still in med bay."

"Yeah, he was, but Eldin couldn't keep him there. Besides, he's the weapons expert. We need him."

Greyson saw her nod.

"How long for repairs?"

"Not sure." Able paused and spoke off-mike. Greyson couldn't make out his words. "Twenty-four hours, minimum," Able finally reported. "Then at least another ten to test the system."

"We've got forty-eight. Then, fixed or not, we're out of here. I'll be up in an hour to help."

"Relax, babe, we've got it covered." Able chuckled. "Enjoy your shore leave."

"But—"

"No buts," Able countered. "There's nothing for you to do up here 'cept get in our way. Eldin and Damon are bringing Brina down to check out the place. Then you can try and convince her to stay. Say hi to Rian for us."

Annoyed at being unable to think of an argument, Shy smacked the com link closed. She needed to get off planet, away from Greyson. But Able was right: She was a good captain. A great pilot. Handy in a fight. But she was no mechanic or weapons expert. A good part of her success as a smuggler was due to the men who crewed with her. They didn't need or want her hovering over their shoulders.

She spent a few minutes touching base with the

tower crew and learned all was quiet in the space around Uta. Thinking about the colony's various needs made her head ache, and dwelling on thoughts of her night in Greyson's arms played havoc with her concentration.

When she'd woken this morning, the sight of him sprawled next to her, his body relaxed in sleep, left her weak with longing for what could never be. Too much stood between them. Too many lies. Too many years. Too much pain. Her head might accept the truth, but her heart kept insisting she try.

They'd shared physical passion, and even a sense of communion, but no words of understanding or forgiveness had passed between them. Their conflicts went deeper, were more personal than his career with ASP and her criminal activities. Could she tell him about Rian? Would he accept her decision to keep his son from him? Could she risk his anger about that?

As questions churned in her head, her stomach roiled. She whirled around, eager to flee the curious eyes of the men stationed in the tower—and ran straight into Greyson.

"Oof!" Air burst out of her. He staggered slightly at the impact. His hands clamped onto her upper arms to steady himself and keep her upright. Her face pressed against his shoulder. The smell of sunshine and coffee filled her nostrils. Her bones went liquid and she sagged into him.

He rested his cheek against her head. "Are you hurt?"

Startled at her urge to remain wrapped securely in his embrace, she jerked free and looked up at him. For a second he held her gaze. She couldn't read the expression in his dark, hooded eyes. Then abruptly he released his hold on her arms and took a step back. Cool air replaced the heat of his body. She shivered.

He glanced at the other men, eyeing them with a combination of suspicion and amusement. "Let's walk."

She nodded and led the way out of the tower and across the tarmac. Two of Uta's three suns shone in the sky, one straight overhead, the other already near setting as Uta made her way along her odd orbital pattern. Heat radiated in waves off the blacktopped landing field, but it didn't ease the chill growing inside Shy. Greyson walked behind her. She could feel his gaze on her, but couldn't determine his mood or intentions.

They walked away from the shuttle port and town, along a hard-packed dirt path through the jungle, down the mountainside toward the sea. Birdsong and the hum and buzz of insects filled the silence between them. A warm, humid breeze carried the scent of brine. Shy let the heat soak into her weary bones and melt away the tension.

Despite the leaden feeling in her body from the increased gravity, after an extended stay aboard *Independence* she appreciated her return to solid ground. Like being on an ocean ship, months of lower artificial gravity in space changed a person's sense of balance. When they returned planet-side, space-farers often staggered as they adjusted to the unaccustomed pull on their muscles. Shy was no exception. Regular exercise aboard ship helped, but only time planet-side cured the problem.

"What are Uta's defensive capabilities? The colony, I mean."

Startled by Greyson's question, she turned abruptly and stumbled over a small rise of dirt. As she fell, Greyson caught her. Her sudden urge to rest in his embrace angered her. She jerked free and snapped, "Why do you care?"

He reached out a hand to steady her. "I care about you."

"Do you?" She couldn't keep the pleading note from her voice. To hide her weakness, she stepped back and answered his question. Since he'd never know Uta's actual coordinates, she supposed it didn't matter what he knew about the colony's defenses.

"Uta is well hidden and protected by the space anomalies and star fields surrounding her. If you don't know the safe paths through them, it's . . . well, it's a dangerous trip. We have monitoring beacons to warn us of any ships that do slip through, and also a dozen surface-to-air defense systems to take out anyone who poses a threat."

Greyson frowned. "No battle cruisers?"

Shyanne almost rolled her eyes. This was a small colony; where would they be getting battle cruisers? The safety of the colony was based on its secrecy. "We have several small scout ships that patrol the area around the planet. Those have laser cannons . . . but they're built for speed and maneuverability, not combat. They wouldn't stand a chance in a full-fledged battle."

"Without at least one or two battle cruisers, an attacker could easily maneuver to take out your surface defenses." Greyson was shaking his head. "Leaving the *Independence* in orbit would go a long way toward beefing up your defences."

"I know, but we need her for our operation. I'm

working on getting a couple battle cruisers, but if you're not affiliated with ELF they're difficult to find and, when you do, expensive to purchase. Until things change, secrecy is our main defense."

"That's why you confined me to the brig."

At her nod, his mouth tightened. "Don't you know I would *never* expose Uta's location?"

She wanted to trust him but couldn't take the risk. The safety of these people depended on her. "Why should I trust you? You betrayed me before."

Pain flickered in his eyes and then the stiffness went out of him and he looked away. "You're right, you shouldn't."

A surge of anger replaced her guilt. Why should she care about his feelings?

Because you love him. The answer left her confused. What she felt for this man couldn't be love. She wouldn't allow it to be.

He started moving again. Unsure of what to say, she followed. After fifteen minutes of uncomfortable silence, they broke out of the jungle onto an open stretch of ground overlooking the sea. Knee-high grass waved in a warm, salt-scented breeze. The edge of the field fell away to the sea, which spread out before them in a shimmering expanse of blue-green water.

One sun sank toward the horizon, casting its golden reflection across the whitecapped waves. The other followed more slowly, its brighter light dancing over the water like scattered amber beads.

Several yards below them, the sea crashed onto a rock-strewn beach. Offshore, massive boulders, remnants of the extinct volcano that formed this bay, rose from the water. Waves crashed and broke all around these large, dark sentinels.

Silvery white seabirds swooped through the sky, their keening calls joining the cacophony of sea noises. The breeze was a constant, cool mist, which dried into fine white powder across their skin.

To break the growing silence between them, Shy sat, her legs dangling over the edge of the cliff, and started to speak. "Most of Uta's people are former slaves from mining and agricultural worlds, but a few flew supply ships. There's even some ex-military. The latter put their technical skills and military experience to use by serving as Uta's eyes and ears on the ground and in space. If we're attacked, we'll manage. Somehow."

She glanced up as Greyson sat next to her. Neither anger nor hurt showed on his features; though she sensed his emotions were as tumultuous as hers, he looked relaxed and untroubled.

At first meeting, she recalled, people often assumed Greyson was little more than he appeared, an attractive man with no depths, a crystal-clear pool of water. She'd made the same mistake. In fact, after her having lived with Kedar's secrecy, part of Greyson's appeal for her had been his seeming openness. In her innocent first rush of attraction, she hadn't realized he was a chameleon, adapting himself to his surroundings, blending in by reflecting back whatever the viewer expected to see. In truth, nothing about his character was simple or easy to discern. He hid his true self beneath myriad disguises.

Which of the men she'd known—the simple college student who courted her with charm, the hard-edged ASP agent who betrayed her with ease or the sincere man who sought her help in saving Earth—

was the real Greyson? Or had she yet to meet the real one?

Perhaps as a girl she'd sensed he wasn't what he seemed. A one-dimensional man would never have captivated her as Greyson had from the first moment they met. At the same time that she was confused by the complexities and contrasts she discovered in his personality, they kept him endlessly fascinating.

As the two of them sat in silence, one of Uta's suns sank fully below the horizon, dying in a burst of color. The sunrays set the clouds on fire, a conflagration of red, orange, pink and purple.

As the first sun disappeared, the second sun took over the death scene, splashing an even more impressive display of colors across the sky in its final throes of luminescence. The wind shifted inland. After the heat of two suns Shy shivered as a cool, misty breeze ruffled her hair. Under her long-sleeve shirt, goose bumps rose on her arms.

"Lovely," Greyson whispered.

"One of the perks of living on Uta. Her volcanic activity throws continuous clouds of dust into the air, and the atmosphere is particularly refractive. This is my favorite place to be at sunset."

"I wasn't referring to the sunset."

His voice husky with an unspoken need, his words tugged at something deep inside her. Afraid to see what was in his eyes but unable to resist, she raised her face until their eyes met. The last of the second sun's rays cast a reddish gold glow across him, turning his hair to burnished bronze and his eyes to melted chocolate.

When he stretched out his hand to her, she met it

with her own and entwined her cool fingers with his warm ones. With his other hand he traced a finger down her cheek.

"Soft," he murmured.

A bolt of heat raced through her chilled flesh. Like the green flash of the setting sun, her hunger flared to meet his.

He slipped his hand around her neck to cup the back of her head and tugged her body to him. Smelling of mint and coffee, his breath sighed over her lips. Warmth slid down her spine. She no longer felt the chill of the coming night.

"Make love with me," he said.

"We shouldn't," she breathed in response.

"Shouldn't we?"

She didn't reply, and as his lips closed over hers, reason melted. Right or wrong, she wanted these moments. She wanted the physical release he offered. Soon enough, circumstances and secrets would tear them apart. She trusted him with her body, even if she was yet hesitant to trust him with her heart.

Greyson's arms trembled with his need to lay Shyanne down on the grass and bury himself deep in her body. She molded herself to him. Her belly pressed against his erection. He tried to force himself to stop, to pull back. He had no right to take what she offered. His lies and betrayal stood between them. Instead, he held her close and drank in her flavor, warm and sweet with a hint of salt from the sea.

She leaned away and opened his shirt. A cool, damp breeze swirled across his chest. He shivered. When her warm hands slid over his bare skin, his blood turned molten. Heat coursed through his veins. Restraint snapped. Soon enough she'd discover his lies, soon enough she'd hate him. Until then, he'd take whatever part of her she offered. He wasn't strong enough to resist.

With a low growl, he stripped away his clothing and hers before they erupted in the flames that threatened to burst up between them. He pulled her down atop him on a makeshift bed of rumpled clothing. Back arched, her breasts thrust upward, she straddled his hips. Moonlight bathed her in a pearly glow, turned her hair to spun gold and her skin to alabaster. Lost in the vision of Shyanne, he barely noticed the sharp stabbing of the sea grass pressing into his spine.

Moisture dampened the crisp curls at her center, teasing his erection, which strained toward her in the same manner as his soul. The pounding of his heart kept rhythm with the endless crash and whoosh of the waves against the rocky shore. Wind rustled through the grass and carried the smell of brine to mingle with the heady aroma of arousal, both his and hers.

Eyes alight with suppressed laughter, she leaned back, her hands braced above his knees, and she hovered above him, touching but out of reach. The position opened her to his view. She rocked back and forth, dragging the petals of her nether lips across the head of his penis. The sight and feel sent lightning bolts through him. With each motion he tried to slip inside her, but she easily avoided him.

Fabric and grass clumped in his fists. "Please," he groaned.

She tilted her head forward to meet his gaze. "In a hurry, are you?"

His eagerness to be inside her warred with his need to savor her. Impatience won. He'd savor her later. He couldn't wait.

With a feral growl, he gripped her hips and surged upward into her. Her mouth opened in an O of surprise. Letting go, he lost himself inside her. The world dissolved from consciousness. Yesterday and tomorrow, past and future—it all no longer mattered. In that moment, the heated friction between them was Greyson's only reality.

Chapter Fifteen

A cool night breeze played over Shy's damp, naked flesh. She shivered and curled against Greyson's enticing warmth. He pulled her against him and draped his shirt over her shoulders. The rest of their clothes lay beneath them, little protection from the sharp edges of the trampled sea grass that formed their bed. Satisfaction left her body boneless, her mind at ease. She couldn't find the energy to care or to move.

The scent of the sea and crushed grass mingled with the tang of sweat and sex. She breathed deep. Never again would she be able to smell the brine of the sea and not remember Greyson. The cry of a lone seabird as it sought its roost drifted across the water. Above, stars struggled to shine in the bright glow of Uta's moons. Orbiting around three suns left Uta with long days and short nights.

Lifting her head, she studied Greyson's face in the reflected light. He was so distinct. Through the years, even when she'd tried to forget him, she couldn't—with shaggy brown hair that always seemed too long, always hanging in his warm brown eyes, Rian was a miniature version of his father. It seemed he'd inherited none of his mother's physical appearance.

Tall and lean for his age, Rian was a natural athlete.

Curious at times to the point of foolhardiness, he managed to get into trouble on a distressingly regular basis. But when caught in some bit of mischief his lopsided grin and wicked sense of humor made it difficult for her or anyone to remain angry with him.

At that moment, Shy's heart ached to see her son. With Greyson here she wouldn't be able to, however. She couldn't take the risk. And yet how could she not? If things went badly with Dempster, she might never again have the chance to see him.

She tried to get back to Uta every week or so, but of late the days between her visits had stretched into weeks and then months. Though he never complained, she knew her son missed her as much as she missed him.

Rian was a happy little boy, secure in his world, secure in his place in it, secure in her love. He was well cared for by Matha and Tomas, who saw him as their grandson if not by blood. It pained Shy to admit that since she'd gone into space as a smuggler, they, more than she, had raised the boy. At nearly ten, he was past babyhood—had passed it years ago—and she was missing most of his childhood.

As well adjusted as he was, however, he needed his mother. Just as she needed him. She remembered how much she'd longed for Kedar when she was a child. The thought of Rian suffering in the same manner tore chunks out of her heart. Had Kedar felt even a portion of what she now felt? But she couldn't see any other way to live her life.

Liar. Tell Greyson. He'll help you find a way. He'll protect Rian.

The confession trembled on her lips, the admission of their child and all the things she'd kept from him. He'd hate her, though. Could she live with that?

"Why do you do it?"

The restrained anger in Greyson's voice answered her question. No. Blast her for the selfish coward she was. She couldn't tell him. She couldn't risk losing what little time they might have together.

She looked up. "Do what?"

He didn't look at her as he spoke. His gaze remained fixed on the sky, but she felt his body tense. "Smuggle. Run blockades. Rescue slaves. Risk your freedom, your life, all in criminal activity."

Despite his clear frustration, despite the fact that he was asking questions, which long ago would have infuriated her, she was unwilling to leave the warmth of his side. She rested her head on his chest. The feel of his arm around her, his fingers stroking the bare skin of her neck and shoulder and the steady thud of his heart against her cheek eased her disquiet. "Without the money I make, and without the goods and supplies *Independence* can smuggle here, Uta wouldn't survive."

"You have MAT units. They would supply the basics."

Shy shook her head. "Not enough. Have you ever run a colony of a thousand people? And don't just say to get more. Even three times as many units couldn't supply all the needs of Uta's growing community. Like battle cruisers, MAT units are difficult to come by and expensive to maintain. No, we need to be self-rcliant."

She felt his hesitation, then a nod of agreement. "Okay, but why not stay on Uta? Retire from smuggling. Let someone else captain *Independence*. Build a life for yourself—a life that doesn't involve the danger and criminal activity. The people here obviously love you. Perhaps you could take a less . . . criminal role."

She'd thought of it often. Could she give over control of *Independence* to her crew, let them smuggle the goods Uta needed? Let them make the runs? Let them take the risks? Let them make the choices that decided Uta's fate? Her fate? Rian's fate? Would that be the right thing to do?

Knowing the answer was no, that she couldn't turn those responsibilities over to anyone else, she avoided his question. "Every year Uta becomes more self-sufficient. Eventually I'll retire from smuggling, but that day is still years away." By then Rian would be grown and no longer need her. The pain and guilt of that bit into her. Plus there was another consideration: "Even when Uta is self-sufficient, however, she'll still need the protection *Independence* provides."

"Do *you* have to provide it?" His question echoed the one she asked herself.

"She needs a captain."

"That's not an answer. Able could captain her. Hell, even Terle could."

"*Independence* is my ship. I'm her captain. Why do you care, anyway? Uta is outside Earth space. She's not ELF or ASP's concern."

"As long as she harbors smugglers, she's ASP's concern."

"But when Uta is self-supporting she won't be harboring smugglers, so what's your point?"

"Because, damn it, I care about what happens to you! Why is that ship more important than your life? You stick to it, to flying it, to smuggling. . . ." The growing frustration in his voice softened her resentment at his comments.

She teased the crisp hair on his chest and felt his sex swell against her hip. "*Independence* is the only tangible thing I have left of Kedar—of my *father*." It was the first time in years she'd admitted her sense of loss. "Giving her up would feel like severing the last link between us." Tears burned her eyes. She tried to blink them away, but they trickled down her cheeks to dampen his chest.

The mood between them shifted. All tension dissolved. Rolling to his side so they lay face-to-face, he cupped her cheek in one hand and stroked the tears away with his thumb. "Letting someone else captain her isn't the same as giving her up," he pointed out.

"I know, but when I'm aboard her I feel like he's still with me. I m-miss him." A dam broke inside her and more words spilled out. "Some of my earliest memories are of being aboard *Independence*. With him."

"I can imagine it." Greyson grinned. "You'd flash your big blue eyes at his crew and run roughshod over the entire group. A girl in charge of pirates."

"Smugglers," she corrected without heat.

"Right, smugglers."

Staring at Shyanne, Greyson couldn't help imagining her so many years ago, traveling with her father's crew. Tiny, adorable. She would have been the same age as Anna when the pirates attacked. The memory wiped away his grin.

Shyanne continued talking. "For me, *Independence* was like one big playground. At first nothing was off-limits. Kedar or one of his crew allowed me to explore every inch of her."

Greyson pulled his attention back to Shyanne. Anna was long dead. Nothing he did could bring her back. But he could make sure Shyanne didn't suffer the same fate. "How old were you when Kedar first left you here?" he asked.

"When I was almost five, Kedar decided a spaceship was no place to raise a child, so he found Matha and Tomas and set us up on Uta."

"Why?"

"I guess I was a bit too independent. Sometimes I managed to slip away from my caretakers. There were a couple of accidents that almost killed me."

The thought of Shyanne dead put a knot in Greyson's belly. "What happened?"

"I don't remember most of them. One time I tumbled down an access tube. I must have been a disaster waiting to happen. Another time I nearly managed to put myself out an air lock."

Her wry chuckles turned the knot inside him to an icy shard of dread. No child of four could operate the controls necessary to accidentally open an air lock. "Was Simon Dempster part of your father's crew back then?" he wondered aloud.

She shivered in his arms. "Yes. He was Kedar's second-in-command."

"Are you sure those incidents were accidents?"

"Yes . . . Well, probably. What are you saying?" She lifted her head.

"Dempster's been leaving your locator ID at the scene of his attacks. Why would he do that?"

"I don't know. To divert suspicion from himself. Doesn't that make sense? He's got to blame someone."

"What if his motives are more personal?"

Shyanne sat up, turned her back to him and hugged her knees to her chest. He missed her warmth, but the chill that slid down his spine had nothing to do with the breeze that touched where she'd rested against him. Sensing her reluctance to talk about her relationship with Dempster, he chose his next words carefully.

"Eldin said a while back that Dempster held you prisoner."

"So?" Her tone was guarded. "What's your point?"

Moonlight painted the smooth curve of her back a pearly white. The sight sent a bolt of fire to Greyson's groin. "Well, he could use any locator ID to throw off ASPs scent. Do you think his goal is to draw you out and capture you?"

Her body trembled. "Maybe. I suppose so. When I was a child, I knew he hated me. The feeling was mutual. He wanted what I had—Kedar's love, such as it was. For all the good it did me.

"When I got older, his attitude changed. The fu-jerking slime tried to *court* me." She gave an indelicate snort. "His feelings toward me had changed—at least his physical feelings. And maybe he believed if he had me, he'd also have Kedar's love. But my dislike of him didn't change. In my eyes he was and is lower than bilge scum. What he wants now I don't know or care. But he'll never have me the way he wants." She curled her head close to her knees, muffling her last words. "I'll die before I let him touch me again."

Wanting to comfort her but afraid to touch her, Greyson reached out. His hand hovered a hairbreadth above her shoulder. "Did he . . . ?" He needed to see her face, needed to know the answer, yet he couldn't bring himself to finish the question.

"No." She shook her head, then continued in a harsh whisper. "Not physically, anyways. He didn't have time. Eldin and the others got me out before that happened."

She shot to her feet. As she stood with her back to him, her voice strengthened. "I don't want to talk about Dempster anymore. Whatever his plan, our job is to see he doesn't succeed. To see he's destroyed. To try to understand him . . . that's just a waste of energy and emotion. It's time to go back, anyway. Morning dawns early on Uta."

Greyson stood. The wind picked up, bringing with it a spray of seawater. Teeth chattering, Shyanne swore and wrapped her arms around herself. She didn't hesitate when he handed her clothes to her; clutching them to her chest, she strode away. Unmindful of the bits of sea grass stuck to his damp skin, to ward off the chilly air, Greyson dressed quickly and followed.

Despite the comparative warmth of the night air away from the sea, Shy shivered. She should have told Greyson about Rian just then, but the words hadn't come. If he knew the truth, what feelings he had for her would die. He'd hate her for lying to him, for keeping him from his son. And he'd be right.

Though he moved quietly, she knew when Greyson caught up with her. She'd pulled on her wrinkled clothes, but wisps of grass were stuck in her tousled hair and her feet were bare and dusty. With his shirt hanging open over his bare chest, anyone seeing them would know what they'd been up to. She didn't care, though. Their future together was cloudy, so she intended to grab whatever time fate granted the two of them. Once Dempster was stopped and Earth was safe, she'd tell Greyson about Rian and that time would end.

When he reached her side, he held out his hand in a silent question. Without hesitation, she slipped her fingers into his. The warmth of his strong clasp eased the chill in her heart.

Together, they hurried back to the house. Once they were inside, she followed him into his room, into his bed, into his heart. Clothes were shed. Greyson warmed her heart and body.

"Let's take a ride," Shyanne suggested.

Greyson looked up from the breakfast he'd been regarding, poking it with his fork. Thoughts of the pending C.O.I.L. invasion had dulled his appetite. They had to get back to their pursuit of Dempster.

Shyanne gave him a considering look, then grinned. The quiet, determined woman from the night before was gone. Looking at her now, smiling, eyes clear, Greyson wouldn't believe her capable of running a smuggling operation or harboring the secrets he knew she did. Which was the real Shyanne? The bright, carefree girl from his past? The dangerous, intense criminal? The warm, caring woman gazing at him across the table?

"There's not much we can do while we wait for *Independence* to be repaired, so let's take your sweet little bird out for a jaunt," she suggested.

She had a point: They could only move as fast as her crew got her ship refitted. "Anything's better than sitting around here waiting." He pushed aside his plate and stood, and the two of them headed for the spaceport.

Though he itched to be out tracking Dempster, Greyson couldn't regret the hours subsequently spent with Shyanne. That time sped by. The two of them flew for hours, over prairies, mountains, rivers, lakes and seas of both water and lava. As she flew, he explained his ship's features: her stealth mode, how she could fly undetected by any known radar. He delighted in watching Shyanne's excitement as she tested the ship's maneuverability and speed, implementing stomach-lurching dives and rolls and trying out her weapons against innocent boulders.

At her insistence, he showed her the intricacies of flying in stealth. In that mode, the pilot of this craft needed to sense, adjust and adapt to stimuli using pure instinct. It had taken him months in a simulator to manage not to crash three out of five times. She accomplished the first task he set her with amazing ease—on her first attempt. He prayed he'd never have to outfly her.

Thcy also talked as they flew, about their lives, past and present. He told her about his mother. About his life working with her aboard various cargo and cruise ships, and how it had all changed when she died and Chalmer Dane adopted him. He talked about his position with ASP, the satisfactions and frustrations of trying to police and protect the vast areas of Earth's space. He refrained from mentioning the corruption and mismanagement under the current director. If all went well, soon enough he'd reach his goal and things in the agency would change for the better. And if things went wrong . . . Well, little would matter then.

She recounted stories of her smuggling operations, at times making him laugh but mostly making him want to berate her for the risks she took. Time seemed to roll back as they repeated age-old arguments about the politics of C.O.I.L., ELF and ASP. Despite all the time that had passed, neither could completely sway the other.

When hunger overtook them, Shyanne landed on a broad mountain plateau and brought out a picnic lunch she'd had Matha prepare. They ate and talked some more, and a short while later, they were replete with crispy fried chicken, honey-slathered rolls, creamy potato salad and a sweet, mellow wine.

Greyson groaned and leaned back on his elbows while Shyanne packed up what little remained of the food. Uta's two visible suns stood high in the sky, bathing them in light and in warmth despite their high altitude. A smattering of fluffy clouds drifted through a powder-blue sky. Birds twittered in the trees.

He gazed out over the view. Mountains rose all around them. Some were still scarred by volcanic activity; others were green and covered with lush vegetation. A thin grayish blue ribbon of a river ran a twisted path through a deep canyon below. If he strained, he could hear the rush of water over rocks above the steady drone of insects.

Two predatory birds circled the canyon, likely keeping their eyes peeled for any movement. Greyson watched as one wheeled around and dove out of sight. A minute later, it rose back up, a much larger but limp form clutched in its talons. The other bird let out a keening cry, and together they disappeared into the trees.

"Mountain hawks." Shyanne answered his unasked question. "Mates."

"What did it catch? That thing in its talons looked twice its size!"

"They live on snips, fish and insects. They're fast, strong, smart little birds. Though the male is larger, the female does most of the hunting. Unless you're a cat or a mountain hawk, snips are tough to catch. Rian's been trying to find a hawk nestling to raise and train for that very purpose."

Greyson jumped on the name. He'd heard it before. "Who's Rian?"

At his question, Shyanne froze. The color drained from her face. "No one. Just a friend," she mumbled. Before he could ask anything more, she snatched up the food and shot to her feet. "Bring the blanket. Time to get back."

Shyanne responded to his questions and comments during the return flight with curt replies and grunts, and finally Greyson fell quiet, taking the message. They settled into an uncomfortable silence for the rest of the trip. He missed the easy camaraderie of the morning, but he wanted to press her about this Rian. He also knew she wasn't about to reveal more. Who was the man? He must live on Uta, but he couldn't be her husband. No one had objected when he claimed that honor. So, was Rian her lover? Maybe. But if so, why was she keeping him a secret? And if she loved this Rian, why make love with him?

A possible answer to that question ripped a hole in Greyson's heart.

Now's your chance, Shy's conscience urged. *Tell him about Rian.* She knew she had to tell Greyson eventually, but she couldn't force the words past her dry lips.

Even if they captured Dempster and she was pardoned, once Greyson learned the truth, he'd never forgive her. She'd lose him.

He knew something was wrong. As hard as she tried, she couldn't recapture the easy flow of conversation between them. She answered his questions about Uta with one-word answers and grunts until he fell quiet.

By the time they reached town, she'd regained control and made a decision: She'd tell Greyson about Rian tomorrow. He deserved to know his son, and Rian deserved to know his father. However, even though she didn't deserve it, she wanted one more day, just a few more hours with Greyson before her hopeless dream came to an end.

The ship touched down on the landing pad with an almost imperceptible thump. Shy patted the console with a shaking hand. "Don't you think this little bird deserves a name?" She was proud of how even she kept her voice.

Greyson shot her a puzzled frown, but he responded in an equally measured tone. "Why don't you name her?"

"Really?" She couldn't keep the eagerness out of her voice. Naming a thing made it yours, if only in spirit.

The scowl on Greyson's face eased, and he nodded.

"Hawk. Her name is Hawk. She's small and fast and smart. Like the hawk we saw on the way back here."

"No," Greyson responded.

She swiveled in her seat to glare at him. "What do you mean, no? You said I could name her!"

"Hawk isn't quite right. She's more a *Lady* Hawk. The hunter."

"Lady Hawk she is, then."

Shy's grin had started in her heart and spread across her face. Greyson smiled back, and the truce between them was reestablished, at least for a bit. But the look in his eyes promised that soon enough he'd demand some explanations.

Uta's setting first sun splashed pinkish color across the horizon, and her second sun was beginning its own slow descent as the two of them left the small spaceport and headed back toward town. Greyson kept pace with Shyanne. After their brief discussion on naming his ship, conversation had died away again, but now the silence was companionable.

Her thoughts were clearly distracted, for she stumbled over a rough patch of pavement. Greyson slipped his arm around her waist to steady her. She didn't object to his nearness.

The smell of her sun-warmed body tantalized Greyson. He glanced down at her. Despite her relaxed facade, a tiny frown marred the serenity of her composed features. Against his side he felt the subtle tension coursing through her. All he wanted was to ease away her pain.

How he loved this woman. Whatever her crimes, whatever her secrets, whatever the future might bring, he loved her. He'd loved her since the first moment he saw her, running across campus, young, beautiful and innocent, laughing, her long hair flying behind her, the object of his investigation. He'd loved her when he'd believed her a party to her father's crimes, loved her even as he betrayed her trust. He'd loved her through the years, jeopardized his career by directing interest away from her criminal activities, loved her enough to risk his life to save her. The knowledge stopped him in his tracks.

She turned toward him, her mouth opening to question his abrupt stop. Before she could speak, he gripped her arms, jerked her hard against him and pressed his mouth over hers in a kiss of possession. Instead of objecting and trying to pull free, she molded her body to his. Her lips softened and parted.

Sweetness exploded on his tongue, the sweetness of desire fulfilled. With a groan of surrender he ravaged her mouth, feeding his need for her. She answered with demands of her own. Her hands slipped up under his shirt to stroke his back. He shuddered. He wanted to touch her, to taste her, but couldn't while pressed together from shoulders to hips.

"Shyanne!" a familiar voice called. Greyson couldn't imagine worse timing.

Reason returned to Shy's muzzy brain as if she'd been doused by a bucket of icy water, and she jerked free of Greyson's hold. Part of her mourned the loss of his warmth, part thanked the unknown caller. Another few minutes and they'd have been naked.

"Shyanne, I—" Greyson started.

She cut him off. "Don't say anything. Straighten your clothes. Try to look like we're being respectable. Please." She smoothed her hair and tucked in her shirt, but couldn't do anything about her swollen lips or the heat burning in her cheeks.

Matha, her face twisted in distress, hurried down the path toward them. Shy touched her arm. "What's wrong?"

"I tried to stop them," Matha wheezed.

"Stop who? From what?" Sudden fear curled inside Shy. "Is Rian all right?" She felt Greyson stiffen.

"He's fine. Still out with Tomas."

"But it's the others." Matha gasped between every word, trying to catch her breath. "What they've done. The tower told me you landed. I wanted to warn you before—"

"What's going on? What have they done? Spit it out!" Shy urged.

Greyson stood behind her, and she could feel his tension growing along with hers. Had the townspeople discovered his true identity? If so, she had to get him off planet immediately. Their regard for her might not be enough to save an ASP agent.

Matha clutched her palms to her ample chest. "A moment. Let me catch my breath. Please."

"Warn me of *what*?" Shy gave the woman a small shake.

Matha inhaled deeply and sighed. "A party. They've planned a party for you and"—she shot a disapproving glance at Greyson—"your new husband. To celebrate your nuptials."

Greyson gave a shout of laughter.

Shy's heart rate slowed. Relief washed through her. "A party? That's all?" She let go of Matha's arm. "You scared the stars out of me. I thought we were under attack."

"Well, forgive me for being concerned." Matha took a step back and sniffed. "I thought you might like to know before you walked in unprepared. Everyone brought food. They even decorated the square." Her head high, back stiff, the woman turned and stomped toward town.

"Matha, wait! I'm sorry," Shy called after her.

The woman didn't stop, but she did wave her hand over her head, a gesture Shy knew from experience indicated she accepted the apology.

When Greyson gave a chuckle, she whirled on him. "Don't laugh. It's not funny!"

"Of course it is." He held out his arms.

She stepped into his embrace with a groan and leaned her head against his shoulder. "I should have known something like this would happen. Life on Uta is good but hard. They don't need much excuse to celebrate." Under her cheek, his chest rumbled with laughter.

As she spoke, his hands stroked the length of her back, melting the icy fear Matha's warning had engendered, replacing it with a different kind of tension. Heat curled low in her belly. She nuzzled the hollow of his throat. Her tongue traced its way up his neck, tasting the salt on his skin. His laughter stilled.

With a suddenness that left her wobbling, he gripped her shoulders and stepped back. She looked at him in surprise. He said, "We'd better go get cleaned up and join the party, before someone else comes looking for us."

If not for the tremor in his voice and the heated look in his eyes, she would have thought him unaffected. Still, his rejection, no matter how appropriate to the moment, stung. She straightened and said, "Of course."

As she started to walk away, he swung her back into his arms and kissed her. His kiss offered everything she wanted, and when he let her go, she staggered.

"Later," he promised, and strode off.

Chapter Sixteen

Greyson stood by the window, staring off into the dark night. The moon had set and it was hours from sunrise. Only the twinkle of stars lit the blackness. Though short in duration, the night seemed to drag. Many things weighed on his mind.

A soft breeze stirred the hair on his arms, and he breathed deep. The sweet smell of night-blooming flowers carried on the wind couldn't compete with the heady aroma of sex that lingered in the warm room. He turned to eye the woman sprawled across the bed in slumber. As with everything in her life, Shyanne dominated that space, made it hers. She was always in charge, and yet she was adaptable, too. He knew if he joined her she'd adjust, make room for him in her bed, in her life. The question was: Could he give up his goal of directing ASP? Could he alter *his* life for *her*?

He gave a humorless laugh. What life? After his mother and Anna's murders, he'd built no life. Working for ASP filled his time, took his energy and left his heart empty. He hadn't started truly living until he met Shyanne. She'd given him her love and her trust, illuminated the darkness in his soul. And what had he done? He'd betrayed her. His life had ended once more.

But . . . now she offered him a second chance. As before, he was betraying her. Even if they succeeded in bringing down Dempster, even if he convinced ASP to grant her the pardon he'd promised, she could have no place on Earth, in Earth space or in his life as an ASP agent. Assuming he could convince her to live under C.O.I.L. rule, which was doubtful, her presence in his life would end his career.

She stirred in her sleep, rolling onto her back. Her eyes flickered half open and she smiled. "Come back to bed," she called. Her drowsy voice seduced him.

Could he turn his back on everything he'd worked and strived for? Abandon ASP? Join her merry band of smugglers and live out the rest of his life as an outlaw? His heart knew the answer, but his mind rebelled. He started toward the bed.

Her eyelids dropped shut and she murmured, "Rian."

Greyson stopped. Anger heated his blood. He wanted to grab and shake the truth of the other man from her, but he knew unless she was willing she'd tell him nothing. With an oath, he stalked out of the room.

He'd never believed himself to be a jealous man, but he had to admit he hated the sound of another man's name on Shyanne's lips. Though he lacked the courage to claim her for himself, at least for good, the thought of her in another man's arms brought him close to rage. He was the worst kind of bastard.

He paced down the hall into the house's front parlor and stopped short. Someone sat in a chair by the window.

"Well, don't just stand there, boy."

"Matha?" He moved closer.

"Who else? I do live here, too, you know." She chuckled. "What are you doing up? After all that dancing and . . . whatnot, I would think you'd be needing some sleep." Her chuckle was pronounced. Greyson was thankful for the darkness that hid both his bare chest and the heat flooding his cheeks.

"I could say the same of you—the dancing, anyways."

By anyone's standards the party had been a rousing success. He'd enjoyed being with Shyanne and found he liked the people of Uta. Their love for her was obvious in their acceptance of him. People talked, laughed, ate and danced long into the short night. To his relief, none of the *Independence* crew had stayed for it. Damon, Terle and Eldin—though he liked the men, they knew the truth and their suspicious looks made him uncomfortable. Brina had opted to remain. He'd seen her laughing and dancing with a besotted young suitor. The resilience of youth amazed him. It also made him feel old.

"I do love to dance," Matha admitted. "Though I'm sorry Tomas missed the party."

Unable to settle, Greyson wandered about the homey room, peering through the gloom at the smattering of pictures. Perhaps Rian was one of the people. He stared at each, wondering how he would know. Bare spots on the walls and tables led him to believe some pictures had been removed. He picked up a picture of a much younger Matha and a man. The two were laughing at something not pictured.

"That's my Tomas. Handsome devil, isn't he?" Matha came to stand beside Greyson and turned on a lamp. "Shyanne took that when she was just ten. She always had a good eye."

Though the picture was an old-style still shot, the composition, color and lighting were excellent. She'd certainly captured the dynamics between the couple and whatever they saw.

Matha waved her hand at the pictures decorating the room. "In fact, she took almost all of these." The woman moved with Greyson, identified each subject and added little stories. He absorbed every detail, a portrait of Shyanne's childhood taking shape in his mind.

He studied each picture, as if by doing so he could understand the woman behind the camera. It helped some. He could see her humor, her passion, her love reflected in each picture, but they didn't reveal any more about who she was. Not as much as he needed to know.

He paused in his perusal of the gallery. "You've been with Shyanne since she was a child. What was she like as a little girl?"

"She was five when we came into her life," Matha told him. "Bold. Fearless. It was all me and Tomas could do to keep up, bless her heart. We never thought we'd have children. Before Stewart rescued us, we were slaves. Our master sterilized us. Mine-fodder and pleasure slaves don't need to breed."

Her matter-of-fact words about the horror of slavery sent a shudder through Greyson. The evil of pirates and slavers was one of the reasons why he'd worked so tirelessly in ASP. Too many people still suffered the fate Kedar had saved this couple from, or died like his mother and little Anna.

"So when Stewart asked us to foster Shyanne, we were thrilled. She may not be the child of our bodies, but she's the child of our hearts," the old woman admitted.

Greyson picked up the last picture, a shot of a family group, a man, a woman and a child of about five. He didn't really see it, though. Instead, he looked at Matha and asked, "Who's Rian?"

Her plump features reflected her surprise; then a wary look replaced it. She shook her head. "That's not for me to say. Ask Shyanne."

"I did. She wouldn't tell me."

"Then, there's your answer. When she's ready, she'll tell you. The question is, are you ready to know?"

To hide his frustration he studied the picture in his hand. The shot was old, but the features of the people were clear. His breath stilled as he recognized each person, the man, the woman and the child.

"Who are these people?" He forced the question through frozen lips.

Seemingly unaware of his distress, Matha peered at the picture. "That's Stewart, his wife and his son. Sad story. I don't know all the details. Tomas and I weren't here then. She ran off with the boy shortly after that shot was taken. Rumor has it she couldn't handle life as the wife of a smuggler."

"What happened to them?" he rasped.

"I'm not sure. I always thought it strange she'd leave her baby girl behind, but it's fortunate she did. A few years later she died during a pirate attack on the cruise ship she was working on. I assume the boy was with her. Stewart never spoke of them. He had Shyanne to console him."

The first hint of dawn was touching the sky, but nothing could light the dark well of blackness growing inside Greyson. He barely noticed as Matha said good night and headed for her room. He sank into the chair by the window and ran his fingers over the familiar images staring up at him, as if by doing so he could change what he knew to be true. His hands shook with rage, horror and disgust.

His mother had lied to him. Chalmer had lied to him. Kedar had lied to him. All these years they'd known the truth.

With an anguished groan he gripped the frame in his fist until the glass snapped.

He was Stewart Kedar's son. Which meant . . . he was Shyanne's brother.

Shy woke smiling. Sunlight streamed through the open window, bathing her in warmth. The twitter of birds sounded like music. Hours of dancing and love-making had left her body aching in a pleasant way. She stretched and rose.

Greyson was nowhere in the room, but she could hear Matha moving around the kitchen. The smell of frying bacon and fresh rolls wafted into the bedroom. Despite the quantity of food and wine she'd consumed the night before, her stomach growled in response. The aroma had probably drawn Greyson as well.

A twinge of anxiety threatened her burgeoning happiness. Today she'd tell Greyson about Rian. How would he react? Surely, she reassured herself, after last night he'd understand and forgive her. Maybe before they left to chase after Dempster he could even meet his son. Rian, she knew, would be thrilled with Greyson. Though the boy had never mentioned it—he loved Tomas too much to suggest such a thing—Shy knew he longed for a real father. How could he not?

Greyson couldn't help being pleased with Rian, either. He was a great kid, the kind of son any man would be proud to claim. Thoughts of their reunion filled her mind as she dressed.

"Good morning, sleepyhead," Matha greeted her as she entered the large, airy kitchen.

"Morning," Shy answered. She plopped down at the table and reached for the coffeepot. "Smells good!"

His back to her, Greyson stood at the window, a steaming cup of coffee held immobile in his hand. Something about the rigid set of his shoulders gave her pause.

"Food's on the table. Serve yourself," Matha said. "I'm off. I promised to help clear the square this morning." Then, with a cheery wave, the older woman bustled out the door, leaving Shy and Greyson alone.

He didn't respond or turn. Hunger forgotten, Shy stood.

"Greyson? What's wrong?" She walked to his side and reached out to touch his arm. He sidestepped, avoiding her touch, then turned to face her. His gaze gave her frostbite.

"Nothing's wrong. What could possibly be wrong? I talked to Able. In a few hours they'll have the weapons system up and we'll be off this rock."

She stumbled back in recognition, realizing that all along she'd been waiting for this man to reappear. His features rigid and cold, he looked at her as if she were less than human. He gave her the same look he'd given her so many years ago when he'd arrested her father.

She tried to resurrect the anger she'd felt then, but all she felt now was pain. Somehow, he knew about Rian. "Greyson, please. I wanted to tell you about . . ." She reached out for him.

He jerked back. Hot coffee splashed across his hand, but he didn't seem to notice. His skin reddened and puckered, but she could see a deeper, emotional pain churning in his eyes.

"You knew?"

"Of course I knew."

"How . . . how could you?"

His questions and reaction confused her. She'd expected his anger, but not this cold disinterest. Why didn't he ask about his son? Somehow she had to explain, had to make him understand why she'd kept Rian a secret.

He turned away and slammed the cup down on the table. Coffee sloshed. His shoulders shook with emotion.

Abandoning the pride that made her want to confront him with his own sins, she went to his side. "Look at me." She cupped his cheek in her palm and turned his face to her. His tortured expression sliced at her heart. She'd caused this pain. Only she could heal it. If she had to she'd beg.

"Let me explain. I was afraid I'd lose you," she pleaded.

"Well, you were right. We're over."

"Can't you find it in your heart to forgive me?"

He straightened and shoved her away. She grunted in pain as she stumbled back and the small of her back slammed into the hard edge of the table. For a second, regret flickered in his eyes. He started to reach for her but pulled his hand back. All expression drained from his face. His eyes looked like unpolished ironwood, cold and dull. His tone was flat.

"Forgiveness won't change the facts. Once Dempster is caught, I never want to see you again."

"What about Rian?"

"You're welcome to him." He stalked toward the door.

This was wrong! Of all the reactions she'd imagined from him, she couldn't believe he would turn his back on his son. "Greyson, wait! We can't leave things like this." She started after him.

An explosion shook the house. Glass shattered. Plaster rained down on her head. She stumbled and fell to her knees. Her ears rang. Dimly she heard and felt other more distant explosions. She blinked away the grit. Greyson lay on his back in the doorway. Motionless.

Oblivious of the glass biting into her palms, she crawled to his side. Blood trickled down his forehead. Heart racing, she felt his throat for a pulse. It beat slow and steady beneath her fingertips. Relief left her weak. She used a stray dish towel to wipe the blood from his head. The cut appeared minor, but he sported a large lump.

"Greyson, wake up." She dampened the towel and patted his cheeks.

Outside, she could hear the wail of the town's sirens. Voices yelled instructions. The ground trembled with more explosions.

Greyson groaned. His eyelids flickered open. He struggled to sit up. "What happened?"

"We're under attack." Another explosion rattled the house. "We have to get out of here. Can you get up? Are you hurt anywhere else?"

He touched the lump on his head and winced. "I'm dizzy and my vision is blurry, but I don't think so. Help me up."

"Come on." She braced her shoulder under his arm. They staggered out of the house into chaos.

Houses lay in rubble. Fires burned everywhere. Bodies were strewn in the streets. People screamed.

Shy wanted to go to them, to help them. She knew she couldn't stop, though, couldn't give in to the horror, couldn't surrender to the rage burning in her gut. She attempted to contact *Independence*, but her internal com link gave back nothing but static.

"I've got to get to the tower and contact *Independence*. She's our only hope. Can you make it?"

Greyson straightened and stepped away from her. He was all business. "I'm fine. Let's go."

Distantly she registered her hurt at the chill in his voice, but was relieved when his weight left her shoulders.

She stopped briefly to give instructions to the men in town. She told them to take everyone to the caves. They'd be safe there for now, as long ago she'd stocked them for just such an occasion. There was canned food and provisions in there for at least a month, and the underground network was safe from all aerial attack. She hadn't told Greyson about it because she'd hoped it would never be used.

A moment later, she and Greyson were running through town toward the landing area. She didn't wait to see her orders carried out, because if she didn't stop the attack, no one would survive to be evacuated. She closed her mind to the cries of the injured. Was Matha one of them? She praised the stars Rian was away from town; Tomas would see to the boy's safety.

She broke out from the tree line and skidded to a halt. The landing area lay in ruins. Almost every ship was destroyed or damaged, but the tower still stood. How had the attacker missed it? Men scurried among the ships assessing the damage. As she watched, one lifted off, a patrol ship with modest weaponry. Burns and dents marred its normally pristine hull, but it still flew. It wobbled in the air, then streaked off into the sky.

Halfway out of the atmosphere it was blasted into oblivion. Fiery debris rained down.

"No!" Shy screamed, bolting forward. She didn't wait to see if Greyson followed.

Men called out to her as she charged up into the tower. She ignored them. The tower com was alive with chatter. The attacker had clearly left the tower intact for a reason. She wanted to discover what that was.

"How many patrol ships are still up?" she demanded without preamble.

"Five," the controller answered.

"Can they engage?"

"No. This ship's too large and well armed. They're staying out of range. You saw what happened to the *Infinity.*"

"Yes. What about *Independence*?"

"Here." Able's gravelly voice came over the com.

Relief made Shy sag against the console. "Is everyone all right?"

"A bit shook-up but fine. This ship came out of a blind spot created by the space anomalies in this area. They hit us before we even knew they were there."

Shy nodded. "How bad's the damage? Can you engage?"

"A few dings. Force field is holding. But the weapons system is still down. We can't return fire. Even if we get them online, it'll be a close fight. They have a class-one battle cruiser! Regulan design!"

"Damn!" Though older, the *Independence* had weapons that matched any cruiser's when they were online. Kedar had designed and built her well. Nothing he'd done since could match her for power or endurance—probably one of the reasons she'd never been caught or destroyed. But without her weapons she was no use in protecting Uta.

Shy felt Greyson behind her. Despite the conflict between them, his presence gave her strength. "Can you make out who's attacking?"

"Dempster," Greyson answered before Able could speak. "Somehow he tracked us here."

"The attack on Verus. I knew we slipped away too easy. He must have tagged *Liberty* with a homing device. That's how he found us at Ramin Five," Shy guessed.

"Took you long enough to figure it out," a strange but familiar voice said over the com.

Shy froze. "Dempster."

"You can call me Simon."

"I'll call you dead, you fujerking bastard." She wanted to reach through the com and wrap her fingers around his neck.

Dempster's chuckle sent a chill of foreboding down her spine. "Tsk-tsk. Such language from a lady. I'll have you know my parents were legally wed."

"What do you want?" She forced the question through clenched teeth. Greyson rested a hand on her shoulder. His warmth helped her maintain composure when all she wanted was to rage at her enemy and smother him with insults.

His easy tone grated on Shyanne's ragged nerves. "You know what I want."

She sneered. "I can't give you Kedar's love."

Dempster's rasp of laughter chilled her blood. "I stopped chasing that illusion a long time ago."

"You're like a stray dog with his nose pressed against the window of a butcher's shop, longing for what he knows will never be his." She was thankful the vid portion of the com was malfunctioning and he couldn't see the terror reflected in her eyes. "A sad, mangy, pathetic, little dog."

"Your tongue hasn't grown any less sharp since last we spoke." Dempster's tone was now hard and low with menace. "Guard it well, lest someone sees fit to remove it," he growled. When he spoke again, it was softly. "What I want now is infinitely more valuable and . . . obtainable."

Though Shy knew the answer, she played his game and asked, "And that is?" Greyson's fingers tightened on her shoulder in unspoken support.

"Why, the pleasure of your company, my dear. Of course." His voice oozed false charm. "That can save everyone down there."

"No!" Greyson's and Able's shouts echoed her own inaudible whisper. Her stomach rolled in protest. Her knees went weak and only her grip on the console kept her upright.

"I didn't hear your answer over the shouts, my dear. Think carefully before you reject my offer. The lives of your friends and comrades rest in my hands—or in yours, really. I have the firepower and time to obliterate your little planet. Come to me and I'll leave them in peace. I'll give you an hour to decide." Without another word, Dempster terminated the link.

Greyson watched, helpless, as Shyanne sank into a console chair. Her lips looked marble blue against the stark white of her skin. She closed her eyes.

"You can't turn yourself over to him, Shyanne. It's suicide," Able commanded over the com.

"Suicide would be easier," Shyanne whispered. "He doesn't want me dead. He just wants me to wish I were."

"There's no guarantee once he has you he'll keep his word and leave Uta alone," Greyson added. He couldn't let her sacrifice herself. Despite her deception and their blood bond, he couldn't turn off his emotions: He loved her. There had to be another way to save the innocents.

If they could stall for time, he could activate his UTD and call for help. It was a thin hope. He doubted Dempster would wait the thirty-six to forty-eight hours it would take for the nearest base to respond. But even if Dempster would agree to wait, how could he convince her to stall without revealing its existence?

"Are any of our ships on the ground operable?" she asked the controller.

"Two. *Liberty* and the new ship. Dane's."

Dempster had left one ship for Shyanne to use. It seemed that, because of *Lady Hawk*'s stealth ability, his targeting system hadn't even seen her on the ground. That was a lucky break.

"Get them both ready to fly," Shyanne ordered. "Evacuate the rest of the personnel to the caves."

The tower controller hurried to do her bidding.

Greyson grabbed her arm. "You're not going up there."

"You have no say in the matter," she snapped, and tried to jerk free of his hold. The sharp motion sent a shaft of pain behind his eyes. His head throbbed. He swayed, but didn't let go. Shyanne went still and added in a softer tone, "But I'm not giving in to his demand. We've a few tricks up our sleeves yet. Sit down before you fall." She tugged free of his hand and turned back to the com. "Able?"

"Yes, Captain."

Greyson remained standing, afraid if he sat down he wouldn't get up again. Apparently during the explosions he'd hit his head harder than he thought. He heard the relief in Able's voice.

"How long can you hold *Independence* between Dempster's ship and the planet?"

"As long as you need, babe."

She gave a small laugh. "Good. In fifty minutes, move into position. In the meantime see what you can do to block their planet scans. No sense letting them know what we're up to down here. And get that blasted weapons system back online!"

"Aye-aye, Captain."

Shyanne turned to Greyson. "Come on. Now's your chance to show me just what *Lady Hawk* can do."

"What have you got in mind?" He swallowed the bile in his throat as he followed her out of the tower and across the tarmac to his ship.

She stopped next to *Lady Hawk*, which had been knocked off the pad by a laser blast. The ship sat at an angle, but aside from some dings didn't look damaged. "You snuck up on *Independence* undetected. Can you do the same to Dempster's ship?"

"Possibly, but then what? *Lady Hawk* doesn't have the weaponry to take down a class-one battle cruiser."

"No, but if we get close enough we can take out her shields, maybe even her weapons system. Once those are disabled, the crew can use *Independence* herself to blow Dempster to hell." She quickly laid out her plan to detach the bridge and ram Dempster's ship with the bulk of *Independence* set to self-destruct. Her colorless lips were tight with determination.

He remembered her lecture on *Independence*'s self-destruct option. "It's a risky move. The explosion might not destroy Dempster's ship."

She shrugged. "What other choice do we have? Even if *Independence* gets her weapons back online, she's fairly evenly matched with Dempster's ship. There's no guarantee she'll be the victor."

He nodded, then wished he hadn't. Every movement made his stomach roll and his vision blur. To keep from falling, he leaned against the side of *Lady Hawk*.

Shyanne lifted his chin with her fingertips and studied his face. The feel of her cool fingers on his skin soothed the pounding in his head.

"You're in no condition to fly. Go to the caves with the others."

He blinked away the blurring, swallowed heavily and pulled himself straight. "There's no way you're going alone. I'm fine."

Concern warred with need in her eyes. Then she nodded and reached for the hatch. "Let's go."

"Shyanne!" Matha's frantic call stopped her. The

older woman charged across the buckled tarmac, her hair in wild disarray, blood streaking her face and clothing.

Shyanne caught the woman as she stumbled. "Are you hurt?"

"No, no. Not me." Matha's voice slurred with her sobs. "*Rian.*"

What little color remained in Shyanne's face drained away. Whoever Rian was, it was clear he meant everything to her. A pang of jealousy stabbed Greyson.

"He can't be. He's out with Tomas!"

"I'm sorry," Matha cried. "I called Tomas to bring him home. He needed to see you, and you needed to see him before you left." She glanced over at him. "And he needed to meet Greyson."

"Where is he? How bad?"

Though Shyanne's voice was low and controlled, Greyson sensed the turbulent emotions brewing inside her.

"In town." Matha took Shyanne's face in her hands. "It's bad. Really bad."

"No!" Shyanne's control shattered. She took off at a run.

Chapter Seventeen

Greyson started after Shyanne, but Matha's hand on his arm stopped him. "Let her go."

"I need to be with her. I need to help her." Seeing Shyanne's pain negated all his anger. No matter what she'd done, he couldn't wish this on her.

"The only way you can help her is to save her boy."

"Her boy? Rian is her *son*?" The information rocked him. "He's a child?"

"Of course. What did you think he was?"

"How old is he? Who's his father?"

"Nearly ten. And I think you know." Matha gave him a searching look.

"He's mine?" Distaste soured his brief joy. He'd fathered a son with his sister. "Why didn't she tell me?" But when had he given her the chance?

"There's no time for this," Matha said. "He has a head injury. He needs surgery, but our doctor was killed when the hospital was hit. Eldin and the *Independence*'s med bay are his only chance. Can you get him there?"

Greyson thought of their plan to destroy the *Independence* along with Dempster's ship. If they carried it out, Shyanne's son would die. If they didn't, the boy along with everyone on Uta would be killed. It was a devil's choice.

Rian lay on a makeshift cot in the dim cave. Shy knelt at his side. Amid the cries and whimpers of the other injured, he was still and quiet. His normally tan skin looked pale and waxy. His thin, boyish chest rose and fell erratically.

The smell of blood and antiseptic stung her nostrils. Through the years she'd seen the aftermath of many attacks; her mind had registered the pain and anguish of the survivors, but she'd never let it seep into her heart, to make her feel what they felt. To do so would have left her helpless to act. This time she was powerless to prevent the agony from paralyzing her. If Rian died, nothing else mattered.

For a while Brina sat with her, then left to help care for the others. The girl's unspoken sympathy nearly shattered Shy's thinly held control.

Crying loudly, a little girl sat next to an injured woman. Through her pain, the woman murmured soft assurances, and the girl's sobs quieted.

Memories of another child drifted through Shy's mind, one laughing and playing hide-and-seek with a serious, dark-eyed boy much like Rian. Loud noises. Screaming. Hard hands grabbing her. Crying out for her mother. A woman falling, blood blossoming across her chest. The flash of fire. Acrid smoke filling her lungs . . .

She shook her head. These memories meant nothing, were mere remnants of her childhood nightmares. She cradled Rian's hand in hers. His fingers felt cold and fragile, unlike his warm, strong grip when he was awake.

The medic had explained what Rian needed—brain surgery to relieve the pressure—or he'd die. It was a surgery no one on Uta could perform. She had to get him aboard *Independence*, to Eldin. How could she do that? She didn't know. But whatever the cost to her, Rian must survive.

She sensed Greyson's presence before she saw him. Her skin went cold and clammy. She turned her head. He stood behind her, looking down at Rian. This close together, no one could mistake the connection between man and boy. The pain in his eyes echoed that in her heart.

"Why didn't you tell me I had a son?" he asked.

In a spurt of anger she said, "Would it have mattered?"

His silence was an answer. The pain in his eyes made her flinch with guilt. She'd stolen ten years of his son's life from him. The warmth generated by her rage drained away, leaving her icy cold.

His shoulders sagged. "You're going to do it—surrender yourself to Dempster, aren't you?"

"There's no other way." Shuddering with the knowledge of what she was about to do, she tore herself from Rian's side and stood. "I need your help."

"On one condition."

She bristled. "My son's life lies in the balance and you want to make deals? No more deals. With or without you, I'm getting Rian aboard *Independence*. If you won't take him, I'll find someone who will."

As she turned to leave, he caught her arm in a punishing grip. There'd be bruises. She welcomed the pain.

"You're the only other pilot capable of flying *Lady Hawk* in stealth mode. And you have another destination." His grip and tone gentled. "I'm not turning you down. Rian is my son, too. Help me help you."

She nodded. Time was running short. In less than thirty minutes Dempster would demand her answer. Without Greyson's help, Rian would die. Whatever he wanted from her she'd give. "What condition?"

"Wait one minute." He went over to a medic, one of the few trained personnel remaining from the hospital. After a brief argument, the medic looked at Rian, then nodded and handed over a small bag. Greyson returned to her.

"Come with me," he said. "What I have to tell you, no one else can hear." When she hesitated, he added, "They'll bring Rian to the *Lady Hawk*."

With one last look at Rian, she followed Greyson out of the cave.

Neither Shyanne nor Greyson spoke until they reached the landing port. As she'd ordered, both *Lady Hawk* and *Liberty* were prepped and ready to fly. What was left of the tarmac and the tower were both deserted.

When they reached *Lady Hawk*'s hatch, Shyanne started toward *Liberty*. Greyson stopped her. Years of training and mental conditioning had made it difficult, painful even, but to save his son and the woman he loved, he found the strength to tell her about his UTD. Her face remained impassive as she listened. She had no idea what it cost him to reveal ASP's most carefully guarded secret.

"Once it's removed," he told her, "I'll use this injector to plant it inside you. When you reach Dempster's ship, activate it and I'll track you. Do you understand?"

"Yes. Do what you have to. But make it quick."

He could tell she was using every fiber of her being to maintain her self-control.

She stuck out her arm but her whole body strained toward *Liberty*, standing ready. "First, you make sure Rian is safe."

He placed the scalpel in her palm and lifted his shirt to expose his chest and stomach. "You'll have to take the UTD out. Make a cut just below my rib cage. Here. *Not too deep.* Reach in with your fingers. It'll feel like a grain of rice. Grab it and pull it out."

Horror flickered across her face as her fingers gripped the handle of the scalpel. "I can't cut you!"

"There's no one else and no time. Ten minutes until Dempster wants his answer." He leaned back against *Lady Hawk*'s hull and gritted his teeth. "Do it quick. But seriously, don't cut too deep. Just about a centimeter beneath the muscle."

He didn't tell her that removing the UTD without an extractor put his life at risk. One slip with the scalpel posed horrible consequences, the worst of which was he could bleed to death internally. He just had to pray she didn't nick the artery that ran just beneath.

Icy hot pain flared under his ribs, but he didn't flinch. Her fingers pushed inside him. Cold sweat beaded on his brow. He swallowed a groan.

"I can't feel it," she murmured. Tears spiked her lashes as she looked up at him.

"Cut a little deeper. You haven't pierced far enough through the muscle." His voice came out as a strained rasp.

Blood smeared her hands and dripped down his belly. She staggered back a step. "I . . . I can't."

He gripped her hand with the scalpel and pulled it against him. "You have to."

Sweat beaded on her upper lip. She nodded and pushed the scalpel deeper. He felt something give, and his vision blurred. Her fingers delved deeper, pushing him nearer the brink of unconsciousness—

"I got it!" she cried in triumph, holding up bloody fingers.

Struggling against the urge to close his eyes and let the darkness overtake him, he snatched the UTD. It took only moments to implant under Shyanne's skin at the base of her skull. That was the best place, as her hair would hide any scar the UTD's internal mechanisms left as it healed the implantation incision.

"Remember, when you're aboard Dempster's ship, press the UTD until you feel it snap." He took her hand in his and pressed her fingers against the invisible lump under her skin and hair. "That'll activate it, and I'll be able to track you." Ignoring a pain under his rib cage that made breathing difficult, and the blood trickling down his belly, he cupped her cheek in his hand. Her skin felt cold against his. "Do you understand?"

"Yes. Just take care of Rian first." Her bloody fingers clutched his shirt in a white-knuckled grip. "Save him."

"I promise."

Though he knew it was wrong, unable to stop himself, he tilted his head to hers. As their lips met, her rigid control snapped and she returned his kiss with breath-stealing passion. Heat flared between them. Pain retreated. In that moment, nothing existed beyond the two of them.

A pair of men carrying a stretcher approached, and Shyanne jerked free. Without looking at the still figure being carried, she turned and ran toward *Liberty*.

Greyson went to the pair with the stretcher. Taking a bandage from them, he applied it to the small wound on his chest and then went to help load Rian onto the *Lady Hawk*. He couldn't bring himself to watch as *Liberty* lifted off. Cold, oily tendrils of reality slithered into his mind. Shyanne had sworn she'd die before she let Dempster touch her again. Yet to save her child, *their* child, she was headed willingly into her worst nightmare. He both admired and cursed her courage.

As brother and sister, he and Shyanne could never be together. Even if no one else knew, he couldn't live with the guilt of breaking that taboo. The future stretched out long and lonely before him.

Suddenly, he laughed. The odds were against either of them surviving. He doubted Dempster would honor his word to leave Uta alone once he had Shyanne, and either way the problem of C.O.I.L. intervention loomed if Dempster wasn't brought to justice. The burgeoning pain in his gut reminded him he was almost out of time.

Sitting on the hard metal floor, Shy shivered and hugged her chest to her knees. To keep from thinking about what was happening to Rian, she focused on her physical misery.

The cell where Dempster now confined her was cold, dark and damp. Her bones ached. Despite the discomfort, she preferred it to the luxurious cabin he'd held her in for the first two days. While there, she'd refused to bathe away the dirt and blood crusting her face, hands and arms, to wear the clothing he provided, eat his food or drink his wine. She did this because the man wouldn't hesitate to drug her. He'd done so the last time. But it was her refusal to speak or look at him that pushed him past the limit of his meager control.

She touched the base of her skull and lightly stroked the almost imperceptible bump, her stiff lips curling upward. When she'd docked on Dempster's ship he'd scanned her ship and her for tracking devices and hadn't found anything. Greyson's UTD worked.

Her fingers itched to activate the UTD, but she snatched her hand away. Not yet. Not until they reached Dempster's stronghold. That way, when Greyson found her—and she refused to believe he wouldn't—Dempster's reign of terror would come to an end. Uta would be safe, and Earth would have the proof they needed to prevent a C.O.I.L. invasion.

Her stomach growled. When had she last eaten? Four days ago. At the party. If she'd had any spit left, her mouth would have watered at the memory of pork and beef roasted slowly over that open pit, the tantalizing smells saturating the balmy night air. Steamed vegetables drizzled with fresh butter. Greyson laughing as he stuffed rich chocolate-frosted cake into her mouth to the partygoers' delight. Then the fruit, cheese, chocolate and wine they'd shared. And the delights of the bedroom she'd tasted right after.

Memories flowed like melted chocolate through her, sweet and rich. Kissing, stroking, loving . . . they'd continued until the world dissolved into heated bliss. Of course, the next morning he'd provided only cold anger. That dead, bleak look deep in his eyes had been worse than almost anything else she'd ever seen.

Shy forced her thoughts from his emotional betrayal and focused on her current misery. Physical pain was somehow easier to deal with than mental anguish, and she had plenty of that, as Dempster had given her no water for the past few days. She had no idea if he ever would. To alleviate her thirst, she forced herself to lick the moisture condensing on the upper metal walls of her cell. She gagged at the foul, oily taste.

Hours crept by. The door finally swung open. She blinked at the glare of light spilling into the room. Hands gripped her arms and jerked her upright. Without a word, Dempster dragged her out of the cell.

He led her to a shuttle ship, clearly intending to take her planet-side. Which planet, she had no idea. She hoped it was his lair.

Dazed and weak, she staggered when he shoved her toward a seat. "Strap yourself in. You're a mess and you stink." He wrinkled his nose. The scar on his cheek pulled his lip upward in a mockery of a smile. "I'll have no more of your silly games. In my home you'll bathe and eat or I'll have you cleaned and force fed."

During the trip down, Shy's stubborn silence seemed to feed Dempster's darkening mood. Though she sensed he wanted to speak, he said nothing more. She ignored his irate glances and focused on the ship's controls and the coordinates for the planet. If she didn't feel so dizzy, she might even have tried to wrest control of the shuttle from him.

When they landed, he escorted her to another luxurious suite of rooms, ones like the first she'd been offered aboard his battle cruiser. She stood in the middle of the biggest while he paced.

"Why do you persist in fighting me? You can't win." He stopped in front of her.

She lifted her hand to the back of her neck but didn't lift her gaze. Her fingers rubbed the UTD, wondering if they were at their final destination.

He grabbed her chin and forced her face up to his. "You'll look at me when I speak, bitch."

Yes. It was time. She could no longer wait. But as she pushed hard against the lump, sharp pain stabbed back at her. She hoped it had worked. "You're insane."

"Perhaps." He chuckled, and the obsession in his eyes as he looked at her sent a shiver down her spine. She took a step back.

"Ever Kedar's little princess," he went on. "So strong. So secure in his love. So sure of her place. The place you stole from me!" Dempster paced once more in front of her.

"I never wanted your place in Kedar's life," Shy snapped. "I never knew about his activities until he was captured. I was no threat to you."

"But you were, my dear. Your very existence threatened everything I'd worked for. You distracted Kedar from the business. Made him think about going legit. If he'd done that, what would have been left for me?"

"What are you talking about?" Shy hissed.

"Until his son was born, Kedar looked on *me* as his son. And then—"

"What's that got to do with me?" Shy interrupted. "My brother died years ago."

Dempster looked furious. "Died? No, he didn't. Despite all my efforts, he still lives. And you—"

"My brother is alive?" She couldn't stop herself from asking. Other questions flooded her mind, too. To keep from babbling, she bit her tongue. Asking Dempster anything further would gain her nothing but pain.

The man burst into laughter, the maniacal sound of which chilled her to her soul. "It took me five years to poison her against Kedar," he said. "To get her to leave him."

Shy blinked. Who the hell was he talking about?

"But even after she was gone, taking her brat with her, Kedar didn't turn back to me. For five long years he spent all his time and energy searching for those two. When he located them, I knew what I had to do. Once the boy was dead, your father would be mine again."

She pressed her back against the wall. The man was totally deranged.

He shoved his face close to hers. Saliva sprayed her cheeks as he hissed, "The incompetents I sent to do the job failed. The bitch died, but Greyson survived. Out of Kedar's reach and mine, which was fine—but then you arrived."

Knowledge punched her in the gut. "Wh-what are you saying?" Greyson was Stewart Kedar's son, her brother? Bile choked her. Had Greyson known all along? No. He couldn't have! Now she understood his rejection. Somehow he'd just learned the truth—a truth he believed she'd known. His reaction to this news made more sense than his rejecting their son. "He's my brother?"

Dempster's rage faded. He giggled. The high-pitched and girlish sound warned Shy he teetered on the brink of something more terrifying than mere insanity. "You *are* dense, girl. You have no brother," he answered. "Greyson is Kedar's son, but he's not your brother because you are not Kedar's daughter."

"I'm not?" Shy's head spun in confusion.

Still, when she thought about it . . . the news that she wasn't Kedar's daughter held no horror for her. It didn't even surprise her very much. Despite her love for the man, and despite his affection for her, deep inside she'd always felt distanced from him. And they looked nothing alike. When she was younger the gap between them had made her strive harder to earn his love and respect. After his arrest and Greyson's betrayal, she'd celebrated the difference, deciding to make her own way, determined never again to give her heart to another.

Of course, she'd failed. Despite her efforts she couldn't totally evict Kedar from her memory, and now Rian held her heart. As did her crew and the people of Uta. And Greyson. Most of all Greyson.

As Dempster moved away and began to pace again, she straightened. "Whose daughter am I?" she dared to ask.

He paused and turned to face her. The look of satisfaction in his cold eyes warned her of what was coming. "Your parentage doesn't matter. You're mine now."

"I'll never be yours. My crew will come for me. They'll save me like they did the last time, and you'll be destroyed like the space scum you are." Even to her own ears, her words sounded like false bravado. Only the faint sting at the back of her neck gave her any hope at all.

Dempster laughed. "No, this time no one will be coming to rescue you." He stalked closer, triumph gleaming in his eyes. "The battle is lost. Your crew is defeated, destroyed. *Independence* and Uta are no more. As soon as you landed on my ship, I blew them apart. There's nothing left, and as the victor I claim the spoils. You're mine."

The pain at the back of her head disappeared beneath the agony exploding in Shy's heart. Pain and rage darkened her vision. Rian. Greyson. Everyone she knew, everyone she loved was gone? Dead?

"No!" Her fingers curled into claws and she launched herself at Dempster.

Chapter Eighteen

Greyson used his ship's stealth mode to dock *Lady Hawk* unnoticed at Carter's ELF outpost; what he was about to ask from his onetime friend went well beyond taking care of rescued slaves, and if he and Carter were caught, what little was left of the man's career and possibly his life could be forfeit. Also, with or without Carter's cooperation, Greyson was determined to succeed. He had to patch in to ASP's UTD tracking system. Shyanne's life depended on that.

Once Shyanne docked the *Liberty* with Dempster's ship, the man had made one aborted attempt to destroy the *Independence*. But Bear had gotten *Independence*'s weapons system back online and returned fire, attempting merely to disable the cruiser and not cause any damage that might harm Shyanne. At *Independence*'s attack, apparently unwilling to engage in a two-sided battle and satisfied with his prize, Shyanne, Dempster quickly turned tail and left Uta's orbit.

Because of Rian they couldn't risk going to FTL to follow. Doing so during surgery would have killed him.

Greyson had waited aboard *Independence*, torn

between wanting to follow Shyanne and needing to make sure Rian made it through surgery. Eldin had exited the OR fairly quickly with a smile on his face, however, so Greyson didn't lose much time. He'd taken off with a plan to report back soon.

Yes, as soon as he reached the outpost and tapped in to the tracking system, he'd notify *Independence* of the coordinates so they could follow. Even if Dempster hadn't captured Shyanne, the bastard now knew Uta's location. He needed to be destroyed. With her weapons system back online, *Independence* was the best chance at accomplishing that task.

Greyson slipped out of *Lady Hawk* and melted into the shadows of the ELF outpost's cavernous docking port. Even though the station's radar equipment couldn't detect his ship, by now the opening and closing of the main air lock would have triggered alarms. And while *Lady Hawk* might be invisible to scans, the human eye could easily see her. He had only minutes to get past the guards and reach Carter's quarters.

The stomping of feet against the metal deck alerted him. He ducked out of sight and waited until the guards moved by.

He pressed a palm against his rib cage in a futile attempt to ease the burning. Swallowing the nonstop nausea, he forced himself to move quicker. Sweat dripped into his eyes. Pain stabbed through him as he paused to catch his breath. In the four days he'd been traveling, his condition had grown steadily worse. He was bleeding internally; he was sure of it. Without surgery to repair the damage, he feared he'd soon collapse.

He gripped his laser pistol and eased the door to Carter's office open. Carter sat at his desk with his back to him. It surprised Greyson the man hadn't gone with his men to investigate the intrusion.

"Either shoot me or put the damn pistol away," Carter said as he swung around.

Greyson shook his head.

Carter sat forward. His eyes narrowed as he took in Greyson's pale, sweaty skin and blood-soaked shirt. "You look like shit, man. Come in and sit down before you fall down."

"I need you to hack me in to ASP's UTD system," Greyson said without preamble.

Shock widened Carter's eyes. Ignoring the pistol still pointed at him, he stood. "You don't ask for much, do you, old friend?" He studied Greyson's face, then tapped the com.

"Don't!" Greyson pressed the barrel of his pistol against Carter's chest.

His old friend ignored him and continued. "Doc, send up a dozen Drexel-five hypos."

Greyson sagged in defeat. He couldn't bring himself to shoot.

"That's highly irregular, Captain Kincaid," the doctor objected. "Drexel five is a regulated narcotic. If you're having pain or weakness, you need to come in for a checkup, not self-medicate."

"Doc, I don't have time to argue. Send it up now. That's an order."

"Very well." The doctor huffed, and closed the connection with a snap.

"Doc's a bit touchy about handing out prescription drugs, but it looks like you can use it. D-five should take the edge off whatever's ailing you. At least for a bit. But I'm with Doc—you need to get it looked at soon."

Relief lent Greyson strength. Carter hadn't betrayed him. "There's no time. Get me into the UTD system."

"Tell me what's going on first; then I'll decide."

"Dempster's taken Shyanne. . . ." Greyson quickly explained the particulars. With each word, Carter's face reflected more surprise and concern. He sank back into his chair and stared up at Greyson as if he'd never seen him before.

The com gave a shrill whistle.

"Ignore it," Greyson pleaded.

"Priority-one message from headquarters coming through, Commander Kincaid," a voice said.

Carter glanced up at Greyson, shrugged, then answered, "Put it through."

"Commander Kincaid, this is Chalmer Dane."

Shock rippled through Greyson. His pistol muzzle dropped and he sagged against the door.

Without waiting for Carter's response, Chalmer went on. Though the man's voice was even, Greyson could hear the strain. "Greyson's emergency locator has been activated. ELF and ASP forces are en route to his location as we speak, but your outpost is closer. President Sinclair has authorized you to mount a rescue operation and—"

"Mr. Dane," Carter interrupted. "Greyson is standing right in front of me." He swung the vid screen around to prove his words.

"Greyson? What's going on?" Relief and bewilderment showed on his foster father's face. The man had aged greatly in the weeks since Greyson had last seen him. All trace of blond was gone from his hair.

Lines of pain and tension radiated around his eyes and pulled his mouth downward.

"Long story. Is there anyone one else with you? Is this a secure line?" No sense involving Chalmer in his crimes.

"No, I'm alone. And the line is secure. I still have quite a bit of clout in both ASP and ELF."

Greyson quickly laid out the situation. To his credit, Chalmer listened without comment, but with each word he aged more. When Greyson finished, Chalmer shook his head.

"What have you done, son?"

He didn't try to justify his actions with excuses. "What I needed to do. When this is over I'll live with the consequences." If he lived. Nausea left him woozy. Cold sweat trickled into his eyes and he couldn't stop himself from asking, "Why didn't you tell me I was Kedar's natural son?"

He heard Carter suck in his breath, surprised.

Chalmer ran a hand across his weary face, then gazed at Greyson. "With her dying breath, your mother made me promise not to tell you."

"Why?"

"She wanted you to have a better life. To be a member of society, not an outlaw, an outcast."

"And what about Shyanne, her daughter?" Greyson spat out the question. "How could she leave her behind to that life?" He left his other issues, such as his horror regarding his relationship with Shyanne, unaddressed.

Chalmer hesitated for a moment, then met Greyson's gaze. "Shyanne isn't your mother's or Kedar's daughter."

Against reason, hope and relief blossomed in Greyson's heart. "What? Then whose daughter is she?"

Chalmer met Greyson's accusing glare without flinching. "Mine."

Greyson swayed. He didn't object as Carter grabbed his arm and pushed him into a chair. He listened in numb shock as Chalmer continued his story.

"After years of searching, Kedar learned your mother was working aboard a space cruise ship. He was going to attempt contacting you and her. Unbeknownst to Kedar, Dempster planned an attack to kill you. He wanted no rival to his place at Kedar's side. But things went wrong. The ship's crew drove the attackers back. During their escape, one of Dempster's men grabbed Anna as a shield. When your mother tried to stop him from getting away with the child, he shot her." Chalmer's voice cracked. "We assumed Anna died along with her abductor in the following explosion. We were wrong."

"Why didn't Kedar ransom her back to you?" Carter asked.

"If only he had! I would have paid anything to have her back. Kedar decided to keep her for himself. He figured a daughter for a son was a fair trade." Anger sparked in Chalmer's eyes. His words came out harsh and full of pain as he stared at Greyson. "You remember my sweet little Anna? During the trip, despite the age difference between you, the two of you were inseparable.

"Forgive me, Greyson, I didn't learn about Shy—about Anna—until a few days ago when I went to see Kedar. *He* told me."

Chalmer's words faded as memories flitted through

Greyson's mind. The image of little Anna's innocent blue eyes staring up at him with adoration melded with Shyanne's look of love; then that faded to her look of betrayal. How could he not have recognized her? Anger at both Chalmer and Kedar burned in his gut. Pain blurred his vision. Why, during all the time they'd spent together, hadn't Kedar told him the truth?

Honesty forced him to ask: If he'd known the truth, would it have changed his life? Perhaps if he'd learned when he was young, but after he'd chosen a career with ASP, no, knowing the truth wouldn't have swayed him from his path. But it might have altered his course with Shyanne. When they first met, if he'd believed her to be his sister, things would have gone down entirely differently. He would never have let himself fall in love with her. Never made love with her. Never fathered Rian. Which was totally unacceptable. Despite the pain Kedar's and Chalmer's lies of omission had cost him and Shyanne, he wouldn't trade his experiences with her.

"I'm in." Carter broke the silence, clicking away on the keyboard. "Got him. Let's go." He read off the coordinates of Dempster's location.

While Greyson was coordinating timing with his foster father and the *Independence*, Carter had been busy hacking in to the UTD system. It was a reminder of what he'd known all along: He had to get to Dempster's stronghold before those other troops, and before Dempster did anything irreparable. Greyson would deal with his fathers later, if there was a later for him. First he had to rescue Shyanne.

Shy shivered and blinked as consciousness returned. When she lifted her head from the hard pallet where she lay, pain jolted through her. With a groan, she swallowed the rising nausea, then gasped as memory rushed in.

Dead! All dead. Everyone she knew and loved. Dead. Uta's people. Her crew. Her friends. Matha. Tomas.

Rian.

Greyson.

There was nothing, no one left for her. Dempster had destroyed them all. Emotion drained away, leaving her numb but resolved. She wanted to die. When ELF forces arrived to destroy Dempster's stronghold, she would die. But she would die killing Dempster.

She sat and waited. When the door to her cell finally opened, light spilled into the room. She looked up at the two men silhouetted in the opening and smiled.

"You don't have to do this," Greyson told Carter as he settled into *Lady Hawk*'s pilot seat. "You don't have to risk your career. Your life. I can do this alone. Stay here. Stay safe. Or come with your troops."

"And miss all the fun? Hell, no! Besides, you need me, man. You can barely stand." Carter slipped into the copilot's seat.

Reluctantly Greyson agreed with Carter's assessment. His hands shook as he powered up *Lady Hawk* and entered the coordinates of Dempster's stronghold. After each shot of D-5, he felt the boost to his strength fading more quickly. He didn't have time or energy to talk the man out of joining this suicide mission.

Triggering a UTD emergency beacon was almost always a doomsday code, indicating the sender was dead or as good as, and that the enemy needed to be taken out. ELF and ASP would come in, guns blazing, set on destruction. He and Carter had to get in and get Shyanne out before the troops arrived and leveled the place.

Based on the outpost's location, they would arrive about about thirty minutes ahead of the authorities, assuming ELF and ASP launched from the expected bases. Carter's troops would follow, but Greyson decided to use *Lady Hawk*. She was faster and could sneak past Dempster's defenses undetected, giving him one chance to rescue Shyanne. *Independence* would arrive soon thereafter, based on the information Terle had given Greyson in their recent conversation. If nothing went wrong, they could be in and out before the authorities arrived, leaving the beacon behind so the base remained the target. But all this could only happen if nothing went wrong.

The hours of travel passed in a blur of pain.

"Greyson, wake up. We're coming into range."

Carter's voice roused him from a half dream. He gratefully blinked away the distressing images of Shyanne lying dead, Shyanne screaming in pain over the broken body of their son, Shyanne looking at him with hate in her eyes for the destruction of those she loved.

He switched the ship into stealth mode. Each motion it took to fly the damn thing sent shards of pain through his gut. He felt as if he swam through mud, his movements sluggish and clumsy, his limbs stiff and uncoordinated. He fumbled with the last D-5 hypo. The drug entered his system in a rush, deadening the pain and giving him a burst of energy. It wouldn't last, but for the moment he felt invincible.

Their destination was a wholly inhospitable planet. One devoid of life. Stark mountains strewn with sharp, jagged peaks and deep, dark crevices covered the orb's surface; violent winds and storms swept across through the thin, barely breathable atmosphere, scouring away any life foolish enough to try and take root. Dempster had chosen his stronghold well. In this place, the one who controlled water, food and shelter controlled all life. Here none of the scum he surrounded himself with through promises of wealth and power as well as fear and intimidation would dare cross him.

Lady Hawk glided unseen passed Dempster's battle cruiser and land-based watch posts. Despite Greyson's rough handling, she settled featherlight on a narrow ridge just out of sight of what was clearly Dempster's stronghold. The bleak stone fortress rose three stories into the cold, thin air and covered over an acre. Greyson groaned. This last shot of D-5 would wear off in less than an hour. Would he have the time to locate and free Shyanne before Earth's troops arrived? Their attack would be merciless, focused more on destruction than rescue.

"Twenty-eight minutes until Earth's troops arrive. Mine will be here in fifteen, but they won't come in guns blazing, they'll wait for my orders," Carter answered his unspoken thought. "I've pinpointed Shyanne's location. Let's get moving." He started to rise.

Greyson clamped a hand on Carter's arm. "No. You need to stay with the ship. If Shyanne and I aren't back in twenty-five minutes, get the hell out of here. No reason for you to risk your life needlessly. Coming along was gesture enough."

"But—"

"There's no time to debate this. I'm going. You're staying." Greyson grabbed the portable tracking unit. His UTD still broadcast its emergency signal. Without waiting for Carter's agreement he strode out the hatch.

"Keep your com open, so I can track you," Carter shouted after him.

Greyson nodded, but he didn't look back. With his first breath of the thin, frigid air, his lungs clenched. He quickened his pace. Deprived of oxygen as he would be, the D-5 would burn itself out even quicker.

Shy raised no objection as her guards led her to a nicely appointed chamber and told her to bathe and change into the clothing provided. The continued luxury made no impact on her. Considering the icy rage in her heart, she barely felt the warmth of the fire blazing in the room's large hearth or noticed the rich wall hangings that kept it free of any drafts. The elegant furnishings, the soft fur rugs beneath her feet and the lavish spread of food on the table were equally ignored.

Impervious to her guards' leering and crude comments, she stripped and washed away the sweat, blood and grime of the last few days and forced herself to don the revealing dress Dempster had provided. When the guards left, she fought to suppress her true thoughts, to smother the grief threatening to swamp her, and to harden her determination.

For what was to come she needed her strength. Because of the hunger gnawing her belly, she compelled herself to eat a bit of cheese and bread, but only that, and had difficulty swallowing past the knot in her dry throat. Afraid the wine might be drugged, she ignored her intense thirst. Before she lay down on the room's big bed to rest and wait, she scoured the room for a weapon. There was nothing, not even a butter knife.

Time crept by as she waited for Simon Dempster's arrival. It was time enough for her numbness to wear off. Time to think. Time for the pain and grief to sink deep into her soul. She wanted to cry. To scream. To rage. But she knew if she succumbed to those needs, she'd lose her chance to avenge the deaths of her loved ones.

Finally she heard the click of a lock and the door swung open. She rose from the bed and waited as Dempster strode into the room.

The man carried his years well. Tight black trousers and a white silk shirt emphasized his lean build and complemented his pale complexion and black hair. Aside from the scar twisting the side of his face, a mark she'd given him the last time they'd met, Dempster would be considered an attractive man, if perhaps an effeminate one. But she knew well enough the strength in that trim body. And his mind was brilliant though deranged.

Perhaps he'd been a human being once, a boy who loved and was loved. Now nothing but evil burned in those black, soulless eyes. Her gaze homed in on the sidearm he wore, a laser pistol.

When he glanced at the barely touched food and still corked wine he raised an eyebrow. "Not hungry? Thirsty?"

She kept her face impassive and made no response.

He chuckled. The sound made her legs tremble, and regret at her foolishness stabbed her. She should have eaten more, built up more strength. After four days of no food and little water, she had no stamina, no reserves to call on. Hatred alone kept her upright.

His cool, calculating gaze sent a new sliver of fear rippling through her—fear for not what might happen to her, but that through weakness she might not succeed in her goal. She *would* kill him before ELF forces arrived. The pleasure of his death must be hers alone.

"Let me pour you a drink," he said.

She watched him uncork the wine, pour a glass and hold it out. She didn't take it, and he sighed.

"I assure you it's not poisoned or drugged." He took a sip. He held it out again.

As if hypnotized, she accepted the fragile stemware and its tempting elixir. Sparkling red liquid sloshed in the glass as she lifted it in shaking hands to dry lips. Sweet and crisp, the wine flowed into her parched mouth. She fought to keep from gulping.

Like lightning, energy sizzled through her, but like lightning the burst faded as fast as it arrived, leaving her weaker than before.

"As I said, no drugs." He leaned closer. "I want you completely aware when I take you to my bed."

She choked on the image. "Never!" She tossed the wine at him. It splattered like blood across his face and shirt, and his features twisted into rage.

"Bitch!"

She lunged for his pistol, but as her fingers touched the grip, his fist hit the side of her head. Staggering beneath the dizzying pain and blurred vision, she tried to remain upright, to protect herself as he continued to rain blows down upon her. She had no strength left of body or of mind. She'd failed. Fight drained away as she accepted, even welcomed the inevitability of death. If there was an afterlife, she'd soon be with those she loved. If not, at least the pain would end. She crumbled and lay gasping for breath.

He knelt above her. She flinched as he ripped her dress from neckline to hem, leaving her exposed. Anticipation gleamed in his eyes. With no strength to struggle, she closed her eyes and attempted to shut her mind to the coming horror.

His weight lifted off her. Cool air swirled over her naked flesh. She shivered. His clothing rustled. She tried to summon her strength to fight or flee, but her limbs felt heavy and unresponsive, her mind disconnected from her body.

Then he was over her. Like burning brands, his hands gripped her breasts. Her eyes flew open. She tried to claw his face. Smiling, he grabbed her flailing arms and pinned them above her head. He forced apart her thighs and lowered himself onto her. Bile rose in the back of her throat. She gagged and bucked, but couldn't dislodge his weight.

"Relax," he crooned into her ear. The ice in his voice froze her blood. "Enjoy. I will. I've waited a long time for this, to have you in this room, at my mercy, though I find my mercy along with my patience has long since gone. But have you I will. Again and again."

An explosion rocked the room. Plaster and stone rained down upon them. Dempster shrieked in pain as a large chunk hit his shoulder. Blood splattered everywhere.

He jumped to his feet. Free of his weight, Shy sat upright. Her head spun as she tried to stand. She crouched on the floor, shaking her head to clear it.

Amid a series of explosions that shook the room

and filled it with a cloud of plaster dust, the door burst open. She looked up as Greyson barreled in. He was alive! Her heart soared in joy. Why had she believed Dempster's lies? The man was the prince of falsehoods.

His gaze reflecting her own relief, Greyson headed directly toward her. His expression changed as he saw the state of her attire, becoming one of rage, and he didn't see Dempster sneaking up behind him, a rock clutched in his bloody hands as he appeared out of the cloud of plaster.

"Look out!" Shy screamed.

Too late, Greyson whirled. Dempster brought the rock down. It grazed Greyson's temple and impacted against his shoulder with an ominous crack. His arm went limp. His pistol flew out of his hand and he staggered to his knees. Over the sound of explosions and distant laser fire, Dempster's laughter rang out. He raised the rock again, this time to smash Greyson's head. It descended and—

Sizzle! Pop!

Dempster's eyes widened. He looked down at the blackened hole in his chest, then at Shy in disbelief. Holding Greyson's laser pistol, which she'd snatched up, she watched the bastard's eyes lose focus. The rock slipped from his hands. Dempster crumpled to the floor, dead.

Dropping the pistol, Shy crawled across the rubble-strewn floor to where Greyson lay motionless. The pallor of his skin frightened her. Surely Dempster's blow hadn't killed him! She pulled his head into her lap and stroked his cheek with trembling fingers.

"Greyson? Talk to me."

His eyes opened and he smiled, looking dazed. "Shy. Did he hurt you?"

She shook her head, surprised to find tears streaming down her cheeks. "No. He's dead."

Greyson lifted his uninjured arm to wipe them away. "I'm sorry I hurt you. I said terrible things. I thought—"

She stopped him. "I know. Dempster told me the truth. Funny, I think deep down I always knew Kedar wasn't my father. As a child I had strange memories of another man and woman, as well as horrible nightmares of abandonment, death and destruction." She gave a slightly pained laugh.

"I never forgot you, Anna," he replied.

Shock rippled through her at the sound of her real name. Everything fell into place. And yet . . . "No, I'm no longer Anna. In all the ways that count, Anna died. I'm Shyanne."

Eyes solemn in understanding, Greyson nodded. "Anna, Shyanne, it doesn't matter. You're the woman I love, the only woman I've ever loved or ever will love."

"I love you, too, Greyson. I've loved you since I was that child we both mourn." She leaned down and pressed her mouth to his. Though his lips were cold and dry, warmth flooded through her, banishing the frigid emptiness inside Dempster's lies had created.

The room shook, the explosions continuing everywhere. She bent over Greyson to protect him from the plaster and stone that rained down. She could hear shouting, screams and laser fire growing closer. Somewhere nearby, they heard the beginnings of an inferno. Dust and smoke clogged her lungs. She coughed.

He gripped her hand. "You have to get out of here.

Lady Hawk is close. You have to get to her." He gave her the coordinates and shoved a small tracking unit into her hand.

She helped him sit upright and brace his back against the wall. "I can't leave you."

"You have to get to *Independence*. Get her out of here. Earth troops will arrive in minutes, if they haven't already. They'll blast her out of the sky. Rian is aboard."

"Is he . . . ?" She couldn't finish the question.

"Good as new." He gave her a crooked grin. "He's tough like his old man. But you have to get him out of here."

She took in Greyson's drawn, pale features and cold, damp skin. Blood matted his hair. Through the tear in his shirt she could see a bruise darkening his colorless skin. But it was the dark crimson stain spreading below his rib cage that frightened her. "You don't look so tough right now."

"I'm fine. Earth troops will expect to find me here. It's my UTD that's broadcasting. If I . . ." He paused, then continued. "But you'll be considered a hostile. It might be months before I can get you released. Go. Our son needs you. I'll follow as soon as I can."

Something was wrong. She hesitated. The need to see her son fought with her need to remain with Greyson. "I can't leave you. We brought down Dempster and his operation. What about the pardons for me and my crew? Can't we just contact your friends and let them know what's going on . . . ?"

Before he spoke she saw the truth and the guilt in his eyes. "There are no pardons. There never were, were there?" He'd lied to her. Again.

He shook his head. "Shyanne, I'm sorry for everything. I love you." He reached out to touch her face.

She jerked back. His hand dropped, and the look on his face tore at her resolve. Somehow his hurt at her rejection pained her more than his betrayal. All along she'd known in her heart something was wrong, but she'd desperately wanted to believe in him, to trust him, to have his love again.

She felt him take a deep breath. He touched her hand where it rested in her lap, and his fingers felt icy against her skin. "I know I've broken your trust in me, but I will do everything I can to honor my promise of pardons for you and your crew. It wasn't something I could give you before or I would have. I really do love you. I always have."

Her shoulders sagged. "I know." She did know. His actions were consistent with the man she knew him to be. He'd lied to her, but she'd lied to herself. He loved her, but he loved duty and honor more. As before, his foremost loyalty lay with Earth, with ASP. In that, he'd never lied to her. Of course, that truth didn't ease the hurt of never coming first in anyone's life.

"Can you forgive me for lying to you, for not trusting you with the truth?" he asked. "I could have told you everything, should have trusted you, but I was afraid you wouldn't help. It had been ten years since I saw you. You could have changed from the idealistic young girl I fell in love with. With you being a smuggler, always working against the law . . . I just didn't know how you'd react. I should have."

The sorrow in his eyes nearly undid her. She loved and understood him, but could she forgive him? Her jumbled emotions kept her answer locked in her throat. "I don't know." He'd played with her life and the lives of her crewmates, not trusting them to do the right thing. Of course, she hadn't trusted him to do the right thing with Rian, either. What was fair?

"There's one last thing you need to know," he continued, his voice losing strength. "If something happens, if I . . . if you're picked up by any Earth troops, contact my foster father, Chalmer Dane. He'll help you."

"Why should he?" She looked at him in confusion. Because of her, Greyson was dy—was badly injured.

Greyson held her gaze. "Because he's your father."

Shock held her rigid. "My father?"

Someone cleared his throat. Shy froze and looked up to find a man in the doorway. She started to dive for Greyson's pistol, but he grabbed her arm.

"Easy. It's just Carter—Carter Kincaid, commander of the outpost where we left the children." Greyson eyed the man and coughed. "Thought I told you to wait."

Carter shrugged. "Never was much good at taking orders. Good thing, too. Looks like you could use a bit of help."

He gave Shyanne an assessing look. She scowled in return. He grinned.

"Take out the UTD and get her out of here. Back to the *Independence*," Greyson told him. This time when he cupped her cheek in his palm, she didn't pull away. "Please, Shyanne." His voice rasped with the effort of speaking. "Carter'll see you safely away, then bring *Lady Hawk* back. That way, there's no proof you've been here. Remember what I told you. Leave now while there's still time. For Uta. For *Inde-*

pendence and her crew. For Rian. My people will take care of me." He sagged. His hand dropped and his eyelids fell shut.

With her arms empty of his meager warmth, a chill went through her. Shy leaned forward and kissed him. His lips felt cold and lifeless. Carter leaned over and put his fingertips to Greyson's throat, then straightened and shook his head.

Icy pain froze Shy's tears. "I forgive you for your lies, but I'll never forgive you for dying. Damn you!" That was the ultimate betrayal: his dying. He'd betrayed them both.

She didn't object as Carter tugged her to her feet. "One last thing," the man said. He pulled his dagger and before she knew what he planned she felt a sharp prick at the nape of her neck.

"Sorry, but Greyson was right. As long as you had this thing, ASP would continue to track you." He dropped the bloody UTD into Greyson's limp palm.

The man's cold attitude over Greyson's death made Shy want to scream and rage. She wanted to shrug off his hold and drop back next to Greyson. She wanted to hold him close and stay with him forever; instead she headed toward the door, toward an empty future. She had no choice. She had to protect Rian and her crew.

At the door she paused and looked back. Across the chasm made up of lies and guilt she whispered, "I forgive you." She couldn't leave without having said it.

Over the objections of Commander Jonas of the ELF fleet, Chalmer entered Dempster's fortress along with the first wave of soldiers. Money and political clout had their benefits. It had cost him dearly in both credit and favors, but he had to find Greyson and his daughter.

The fighting was intense. ELF orders were to give no quarter. Any hostiles who didn't immediately surrender were to be eliminated.

Because Greyson's emergency beacon had been activated, no one at ASP or ELF expected to find him alive. Though Chalmer knew more, he'd told no one of his conversation with Greyson or of his daughter. If Anna-Shyanne were still there, he had to find a way to protect her. Favors could only carry him so far, and he feared he'd used up most of his already.

"Hold." The squad leader raised his hand and looked at the beacon tracker. "I've got the signal. This way."

None of the other soldiers objected as Chalmer worked his way toward the front of the squad, just behind the leader. Dust and rubble filled the halls. In places, the walls had been blown out. Cold wind whistled through these openings. Broken bodies lay buried beneath rock, wooden beams and plaster. He checked each face and breathed in relief each time it wasn't Greyson's.

The fighting wound down; the explosions ceased. The sounds of laser fire and men screaming grew farther apart.

"Here." The squad leader stopped in front of an open doorway. Chalmer rushed forward but was stopped before he could actually see into the room. "Check it out," the squad leader said, motioning a soldier forward.

Laser rifle held ready, the soldier moved cautiously into the room. Seconds later he cried, "All clear."

Chalmer glared until the leader released his punishing grip. They moved into the room together.

With the chimney blocked, the fire burning fitfully in the room's hearth belched gray smoke that mingled with the lingering dust from the crumbling plaster and stone. In the center of the room, a man lay amid the rubble on his back, eyes wide and lifeless. Blackened edges surrounded the hole in his chest. A laser wound.

But this wasn't Greyson. It was Dempster. His heart pounding, Chalmer felt air rush back into his lungs. He scanned the room and saw there, sitting against the wall, another man. An ELF soldier knelt next to him, his body blocking Chalmer's view.

The soldier shifted and Chalmer saw him: Greyson, his son. Though Greyson was not of his blood, Chalmer had never felt the bond between them so strongly. His brave boy. He looked so still. He couldn't be dead.

He rushed forward and dropped to his knees. "Greyson?"

His son's eyes opened in his pale face. "Chalmer?"

"I'm here, son. Don't try to talk. You're safe."

"Sh-Shy-anne?"

Chalmer strained to hear Greyson's ragged whisper. "Not here. No sign of her."

"G-good. S-safe." Greyson's eyelids closed as he slipped back into unconsciousness.

"Move aside, sir." The soldier pushed Chalmer out of the way and began emergency aid. "Call the med vacs! I'm losing him!"

Chapter Nineteen

"You have a visitor."

Greyson looked up in surprise. These were the first words the little-seen but ever-present, ever-silent guard had spoken to him, the first human voice he'd heard since he'd woken up thirty-nine days ago in this detention cell. He wasn't even sure if his guard was human. What had happened? What was going on? Why had no one interrogated him? Questions without the possibility of answers multiplied in his head.

He remembered nothing of what had happened after Chalmer found him dying in Dempster's fortress. How long he'd been out of it from his injuries he didn't know. Physically, he felt fine. When he'd woken up his wounds were healed, so it could have been days, months or years. Before that, his last memory was of Shyanne's face as he slipped into unconsciousness. He feared she believed him dead and he had no way of letting her know otherwise. And what had happened to Chalmer?

His captors, whoever they were—ASP, ELF or C.O.I.L.—provided for his basic bodily needs: food, water, bedding and toilet facilities. Only his mind, heart and soul remained neglected. Those were shredded beyond repair.

For the first week he'd argued, screamed and pleaded for answers until he was hoarse. No one responded. They'd left him alone. He'd sat with nothing but his thoughts, his imagination, his fear.

The cell door creaked as it opened for the first time. He rose in anticipation. Whatever came next had to be better than the boredom of waiting, though for what he had no idea.

Light spilled into the dimly lit cell. A man stood silhouetted in the doorway. The door shut with a clank behind him. The man flinched, then stepped forward.

"Chalmer?" Greyson let out the breath he hadn't realized he was holding. His foster father looked tired, his features drawn, but excitement glinted in his eyes.

"What's going on?" Greyson demanded with a gasp of relief. If Chalmer was here, he was obviously in Earth custody. "Why haven't I been debriefed? Is the Consortium aware of Dempster's death? Have they forgone their plans to purge the outer worlds?" Questions spilled out of him, but he didn't dare voice the one he most wanted answered: Was Shyanne safe?

Agitation drove Greyson to pace the small cell, three steps one direction, three steps back. "I've been going out of my mind. No one will tell me anything. I have no idea what's happening." He stopped in front of Chalmer. "Tell me everything."

"Sit. There's much to tell." Chalmer pushed him down on the bed and sat next to him.

"I don't know if my cell is bugged," Greyson cautioned in a whisper. Though, since no one would talk to him, he didn't know what anyone expected to overhear. He supposed he might talk in his sleep . . . ?

"No one is listening."

Greyson grunted in disbelief. "Why am I being held? Why wasn't I allowed to speak with counsel? What have I been charged with?"

"During the threat of C.O.I.L. intervention, the Earth Council suspended a few civil liberties with directly related personnel. One of these rights was that of independent counsel. The ASP director represented you against about a dozen charges, most minor infractions of ASP regulations. The main complaints were against conducting an unauthorized mission that put the safety of Earth at risk . . . and treason."

Greyson groaned. All of Shyanne's arguments about corruption in government came back to haunt him. "I'm screwed. The director has no love for me. And that still doesn't explain why no one has questioned me."

"You were debriefed while you were unconscious."

"What? How?"

"A bit of new Consortium technology, a reward for bringing down Dempster's operation. It reads your thoughts and memories. The technology is still experimental, so it's taken the council a while to decipher the readings and make their ruling. So as to not skew any additional probes if they needed to delve further, you've been held incommunicado."

Greyson shuddered, glad he didn't remember the experience. The idea that his jailors had reached into his mind and now knew his secrets, his hopes, his fears, his dreams, felt like mental rape. Shyanne's fears of invasive government were well founded. He shook off his anger. "What did they decide?"

The grin spreading across Chalmer's face gave Greyson a prelude to his answer. "Not guilty on all counts!"

"I find it difficult to believe they cleared me of treason." Having served with ASP, Chalmer was well aware of the consequences of revealing one's UTD.

Chalmer smiled. "Well, it was strange. When I charged the Council with making public the cause of the treason charge, as mandated by Earth law, it was mysteriously dropped." The man's face reflected satisfaction with his legal maneuver. "The Council might not condone your actions, but they appreciated the results enough to give you a pass—this time. And to protect their secret, ASP went along.

"Because of your success in bringing an end to the pirate problem—there was a great deal of evidence in that fortress that linked Dempster to the attacks—the current ASP director has been promoted to third assistant to the Council, with a corresponding increase in pay and social standing as well as a decrease in his workload." Chalmer grinned. "What he doesn't realize yet is the position has no authority or power. He's now just a well-paid clerk."

"Shouldn't bother him much. He never really wanted to work hard, he just liked having the title and the money." Though Williams was basically an incompetent jerk, he wasn't an evil man and he'd helped pull Greyson's ass out of the fire. Greyson didn't begrudge the man his reward, such as it was, but he really couldn't care less what happened to his former boss; his thoughts had raced elsewhere. Finally, he could wait no longer. He had to know. "And Shyanne? What happens to her? Is she safe?"

Chalmer's smile faded. "I don't know."

"I told her about you. That if she needed help she should contact you."

"She hasn't."

Grayson could hear the hurt and helplessness in his foster father's voice. He'd found his daughter only to lose her again, all without ever getting to know her. "What was the Council's decision concerning her?"

"They were grateful for her help in the affair. Also, they were satisfied by the certainty in your mind that she wouldn't reveal . . . certain information." Despite his assurances that the room wasn't bugged, Greyson noticed, his foster father didn't mention the UTDs out loud. "They honored the pardons you promised her and her people on the condition that she never enter Earth or Consortium space again. Considering her crimes, it was the best deal she could get. But no one knows where she is. Shortly before we found you, her ship appeared and disappeared from the invasion force's sights. Fortunately, no one fired on it."

"The scan of my mind didn't reveal her location?"

"From what I learned through my source on the Council, that information was buried so deep in your mind that they feared they'd do irreparable damage if they tried to access it. The technology is still experimental, remember—on humans, at any rate. Since they were already disposed to forgiving you your trespasses, and because they had other things in mind for you, they didn't bother."

"Thank the stars!" Greyson rubbed at the sudden pain in his temple. For a second it felt as if he could still feel the probe digging into him. "What about . . . ?" He let his question trail off, because he didn't know how to reference Carter.

His foster father seemed to guess his meaning. "Some records seem to have been destroyed. ASP said something about a glitch in the system that wiped out certain recordings, certain recordings that would do no one any good should they come to light." His voice trailed off.

Greyson gave a sigh of relief. He would check in on his friend as soon as he could, just to make sure Carter was okay. But if the Council had spared Shyanne, it was very likely they'd ignore Carter's participation. "As soon as I'm out of here—I *am* getting out of here, yes?"

Chalmer nodded.

"I'll go to Shyanne with the news." She was his first priority. But would she even be on Uta? How would she react? Would she forgive him? Surely the Council making good on his promises would mitigate his lies and betrayal. Plus, she knew now what they'd been up against. She *had* to forgive him. She had to allow him to get to know their son. Without her, life stretched out before him without purpose or meaning.

"There's one other thing," Chalmer remarked.

"What else could there be?"

"Congratulations. The Council is offering you the position of ASP director."

"What?" Excitement coursed through him. For years he'd worked toward this goal, watched in helpless frustration as the current director's management rendered the agency less and less effective in stopping smugglers, pirates and slavers. He'd seen good men and women die or leave the agency in disgust at such incompetent leadership. Now he could do what needed to be done. With Dempster's organization smashed, and Williams out of the way, Greyson could strengthen control of Earth space and keep other criminal groups from gaining strength. More than anything, he could protect people from the threat of C.O.I.L. intervention. Everything he'd strived for, everything he wanted was within his grasp.

Everything but the one thing he needed above all else: Shyanne. And a new realization slammed into him. He couldn't have both.

Shy stood looking out over the ocean from the same plateau where she and Greyson had made love. A seabird wheeled high above. Its keening call sounded like the wail of a newborn baby.

Wrapping her arms around her thickening waist, she closed her eyes to the view and inhaled. The smell of brine and sea grass flooded her lungs. Like the waves crashing against the rocky beach below, memories surged, pushing her emotions to and fro. Logic had told her she had to leave him. He was dead and Rian needed her. But now grief, guilt and a tiny grain of doubt threatened to swamp her.

With a concentrated effort she pulled away from the undertow of memory before it dragged her so deep she'd never make it back to shore. The past was over and gone. She could allow herself no time for grief or tears. She needed to live and plan for Rian's future, for Uta's future—if any of them had a future.

Isolated on the fringe between explored space and the Beyond, well off any trade route, since she'd returned with *Independence* they'd heard nothing of what had happened in Earth space after Dempster's demise. She chafed against the silence. Knowledge conferred power. Power secured life. And life allowed for a future. There were still too many unknowns to feel secure.

Had she and Greyson stopped Dempster in time to prevent a C.O.I.L. invasion, or were Consortium troops even now working their way through the outer worlds, purging all life? Uta's council had discussed evacuating the planet, but even if they had a suitable destination and stuffed *Independence* to capacity, it would take months, perhaps years, to transport all the residents and the supplies they'd need to colonize a new world. After they'd discussed the situation, the votes were to stay and take their chances that Uta's location remained unknown.

Though she knew *Independence* would offer little protection against attack by the Consortium, it remained in constant orbit, alert, on guard, prepared to defend Uta. Able, Terle, Bear and Damon, along with Silky, stayed on board as crew, while Eldin and Brina were now both planet-side.

Without *Independence* out transporting goods, all smuggling operations had ceased. But life on Uta continued. For now they were simply forced to do without the goods smuggling had provided. She hoped they could make a go of it. So far, so good. The dead were buried. The injured were cared for. Buildings were being rebuilt, crops replanted. Life was returning to a semblance of normal.

Normal! Shyanne gave a humorless laugh. When had life ever been normal for her?

"Mom!" Rian's excited voice dragged her from her gloomy thoughts.

Watching him—healthy and strong, looking so like his father while dashing across the field toward her—lifted her spirits. Keeping him safe was worth any price.

Cheeks flushed, eyes bright, he skidded to a stop in front of her. "Look, Mom!" He gasped for breath as the words tumbled from his mouth. "A ship!" He pointed toward a growing speck in the sky.

She shielded her eyes against the glare of Uta's suns. The ship moved rapidly and silently through the atmosphere. It was headed straight toward where she and Rian stood, although they were hidden by trees. As it closed the distance, tension coiled inside her. It wasn't one of Uta's remaining ships.

ASP? ELF? Consortium troops? How had it got past *Independence*? Was this the beginning of an invasion and her friends were already fighting? Fear twisted her gut. In an unconscious gesture of protection, she rested one hand over her belly.

She tapped her head before she remembered her internal com link was still malfunctioning. With all the MAT units in constant use for medical and other necessary supplies, her com link had taken low priority. And Rian was too young to have one yet.

She grabbed his arm. "Run to town and sound the alert, then go to the caves." She wanted to take him straight to the caves, but someone had to warn the townsfolk and someone had to watch the invader.

"Ow, that hurts, Mom!" Her son grimaced.

"Don't stop for anything." She let go and forced herself to step back.

"Aw, Mom. I'm not a baby. I can help." He scuffed his feet against the trampled sea grass.

"You *are* helping. You're sounding the alarm."

"But, Mom, I—"

"Don't argue. Go. Now!" At his crestfallen look,

she softened her tone. "Tomas is at the caves. You can monitor things through the com. I'll send a message as soon as it's all clear." She lifted his chin with her fingertips and met his disappointed gaze. "Do you understand?"

"Yes, Mom." He turned to go.

"Rian," she called.

He stopped but didn't turn. "What?"

Though her heart still raced with fear, she grinned at his tone, the sulky inflection in his voice so similar to Greyson's. "I love you."

"Love you, too," he muttered.

Shy continued watching as her son broke into a run and disappeared into the trees. A moment later she heard the noise of the foreign ship landing behind her, and, finding a more suitable hiding spot, she waited to see what would happen next.

The light of Uta's suns sparkled off the spacecraft's sleek metallic form, and Shy considered it. Its landing struts hit the ground with a dull thud. Though it carried a full array of armaments, this wasn't a patrol or battle ship. Its design bespoke wealth and comfort, as well as speed and power. Curiosity and anticipation edged out fear. This was a space yacht.

As a smuggler she'd seen her share of cruise ships and private yachts, though none compared to this one. It was a beauty. Shy guessed it would comfortably hold ten to twelve passengers plus a crew of five. And though the smaller ship would easily fit in this ship's docking bay, its elegant lines reminded her of the *Lady Hawk*. Against reason, hope unfurled inside her.

She stepped forward. Though her com link wasn't working, she was sure the ship had a vid link and an exterior microphone. She stepped into the open. "Unknown ship, identify yourself!"

As the ship's hatch opened, her breath locked in her throat. Hand on her belly, she waited, knowing whoever emerged would change her life.

A man appeared in the opening. Hope turned to lead, weighing down her heart. It wasn't Greyson. The older man moved slowly down the ramp, and she stiffened against the urge to curl into a ball of misery. She didn't know him. Still, something about him—the mussed, gray blond hair, the way his lips tilted up on one side, the confident set of his broad shoulders—struck a chord in her memory.

Only feet separated them. His sea green gaze eagerly searched her face. Recognition dawned. She knew this man. Chalmer Dane. Her father.

Memories slammed into her: His strong arms cuddling her small frame. The comforting smell of his spicy cologne. His deep, compelling voice reading yet another bedtime story. With a gasp, she sucked air into her lungs and staggered. She looked around wildly for something real and solid to latch on to.

Another man followed Chalmer out of the ship. This one was as much of a shock, for he was the man she'd called father: Stewart Kedar. He smiled at her, a familiar, beloved smile. More memories battered her fragile emotions. Heart racing, she moaned. Tears blurring her vision, she stared in disbelief. To keep from crumbling she locked her knees.

The two men spoke as one.

"Shyanne."

"Anna."

She looked up as still another figure appeared at

the top of the ramp. His hand shading his eyes against the glare of the suns, he stood tall and strong . . . and alive. For the first time since she'd left him, his name slipped through her lips.

"Greyson."

Reality dissolved.

Chapter Twenty

Greyson caught Shyanne as she collapsed. Cradling her limp form in his arms, he carried her aboard the ship. Their faces creased in concern, Chalmer and Kedar followed, hovering behind in uncertainty.

Gently he lowered her into one of the lounge chairs in the main cabin. When he tried to straighten away from her, her hands clamped around his forearms. Her eyes flew open. "You! You bastard! You're alive!"

Rage flashed in her eyes. He reeled back in shock as she pummeled his chest. He knew she'd be angry, but he hadn't expected her to physically attack him. He caught her flailing fists and pulled her close.

For a second she struggled in his hold; then she sagged. Her body heaved as sobs racked her. He looked at Chalmer and Kedar in helpless dismay. Both shrugged.

Using his position as ASP director, he'd commuted the remainder of Kedar's sentence and commandeered the Dane Enterprises yacht. Not that Chalmer objected. During their trip to Uta, Greyson had come to know the two men he called Father. Chalmer would always be his true sire, but calling Kedar by that title felt comfortable as well. Both men had contributed to the man he'd become.

For all their differences in background and position, in many ways the two were alike. Neither could handle his daughter's pain—or would willingly face her justifiable wrath.

"Cowards," Greyson called as they backed hastily out of the room.

Holding Shyanne, he sank into the chair to wait out the storm. Her tears soaked his shirt. Her scent—sea air and sun-warmed woman—surrounded him. Her warmth seeped into his soul, easing the cold empty knot residing there. For the first time in months—*years*—Greyson allowed himself to relax, to let tension and fear drain away. If necessary he'd stay like this forever, waiting. Soon enough she'd demand answers. Soon enough she'd make the choice that would determine the course of the rest of his life.

Her soft body went rigid against him. When she jumped to her feet, he jolted in surprise.

"We have to contact *Independence.* You were in stealth mode, I'm sure. They'll believe Uta is under attack. I sent Rian . . ." Without waiting for his response, she headed unerringly toward the yacht's bridge.

Worry dogged him as he followed. Nothing had gone as he'd planned. Though what he'd expected from Shyanne he wasn't sure.

He caught her hand before she could hit the com. "*Independence* already knows we're here."

She whirled around. "When? What?"

"We contacted the *Independence* when we entered Uta's space. This is a diplomatic envoy, not an invasion. Because of our part in stopping the piracy and preventing a C.O.I.L. intervention, Earth government has declared Uta and all the outer-world planets adjacent to Earth space as proscribed planets."

It was the best of all possible outcomes, considering Earth's probationary status. This rendered Uta and other independent human colonies unclaimable by any Consortium world, protected them without stripping their freedom. Both Greyson and Chalmer had negotiated long and hard in the Earth Council to secure these concessions before he'd admitted to any coordinates.

"Earth asks that each world consider joining Earth, but doesn't insist they do so. The price of protection has already been paid."

He saw the rage drain out of her. She sagged into the captain's chair and stared up at him. Tear tracks streaked her pale cheeks. He stood in silent expectation as her gaze roved over him. He knew the exact moment it landed on the emblem emblazoned across his left breast. Pain flickered in her eyes, and then they went cold.

"Congratulations, Director. It seems you've gotten everything you wanted. Position. Power. Control."

"Not everything."

The hard line of her lips softened. "Why are you here?"

"To bring you the pardons I promised." Afraid of seeing rejection and anger in her eyes, cognizant of the wrongs he'd done her, he sank to his knees in front of Shyanne and bent his head. "And to beg forgiveness."

She stood and stepped away, presenting him with her back. "I forgave you long ago. But it means nothing. You're the director of ASP. I'm an ex-smuggler. An outcast and exile. Your life is on Earth. Your duty and career are there. I can never return, so we can never be together. I survived losing you twice. I can't do so again."

He noticed she was touching her belly with one trembling hand. He came to stand behind her. Her sweet scent rose on the heat of her body. "No, I'm not."

Confused, she turned. "Not what?"

"Not the director of ASP."

A flicker of hope rose in her eyes as they searched his. His own hope lurched to life in response.

"But that emblem—"

"I accepted the position long enough to make a few changes, to find a replacement and pardon my father."

"B-but why? You worked your whole life to become director. It meant everything to you. You'll be good at it."

"Perhaps, but my successor will do better." He smiled at the memory of being able to promote the other man. "Carter Kincaid cursed me to hell and back, but he accepted the position."

Shyanne's lips twitched. "The man will certainly shake up the agency."

Staring into his beloved's still-wary eyes, Greyson took her hands in his and held them to his chest. "Compared to what I'd have to give up for that job, it means nothing. Without you, I have nothing, I *am* nothing. I love you, Anna Shyanne Kedar Chalmer, my ex-smuggler, my star raider. Forgive me. Be my love, my life, my wife."

She jerked her hands free and threw her arms around his neck. "Yes. Yes. Yes and yes!"

He grinned down at the love shining out of her

eyes and teased, "There's a lot we need to talk about. Things we need to do. Plans we need to ma—"

She pulled his head down and covered his mouth with hers, and he couldn't find the desire to resist. "Later," she murmured against his lips. "Much later."

Epilogue

Uta, five years later

Greyson looked up from his desk as a small blonde whirlwind blew into his office.

"Daddy!" Four-year-old Arianna bounced across the room and into his lap. He leaned back in his chair and nuzzled his daughter's sweet-smelling neck.

She giggled, then squirmed away. "Uncle Eldin says you come now."

It was time! It was early! Greyson's heart raced with both excitement and fear. He wanted to dash out the door to Shyanne's side, but forced himself to remain calm so as to not frighten Arianna.

He didn't resist as she tugged him toward the door. Once outside the building, Greyson wasn't surprised when Arianna abandoned him in favor of her beloved older brother, Rian.

"Hey, Dad. Uncle Eldin says it's time."

Worry etched the boy's rapidly maturing face. Hovering on the verge of manhood, Rian made Greyson proud. In the last few years they'd forged a strong, loving bond, but Greyson couldn't forget the years he'd lost.

Oblivious of the tension in the air, Arianna lifted

her arms. "Piggy ride!" she insisted. Rian forced a grin, swung the girl up onto his shoulders and galloped off.

Greyson watched the two with a smile. His concern for Shyanne dampened for a moment by the sight; Rian would keep his sister occupied until everything was over.

As he rushed through town toward home, Greyson reminded himself Shyanne had been through this twice before. She'd be fine. Though Rian's birth had been difficult, Arianna slipped easily into the world, into his arms and into his heart. Though he didn't slow his pace, he turned his thoughts away from possible complications. Because there wouldn't be any. There couldn't. Because of Shyanne, Greyson's life was far different than he'd ever imagined it would be—far different and far better than he'd ever hoped.

He ignored friends' greetings and didn't stop to check out newcomers. His duties as Uta's planetary director included approving or denying emigrant status, but that was the smallest portion of his responsibility. The largest part of his time was taken up handling negotiations with the Consortium for admittance into C.O.I.L. Though Shyanne still had her reservations about the move, even she had finally admitted to the wisdom of joining the Consortium. Greyson was thankful for her support. Her position as head of Uta's governing council gave her a lot of sway with the people.

So much had happened since he'd returned to Uta, not the least of which was the birth of his adorable daughter who so resembled Shyanne at the same age.

With the reward money they received for stopping Dempster, Uta had become a thriving, self-sufficient colony. Their population had doubled each year until he no longer recognized every face.

Chalmer relocating a portion of his business to the planet helped solidify ELF's commitment to providing protection to Uta, too. Not that they needed it with three Kedar-designed, Dane-built battle cruisers now orbiting the planet under Able's command.

Greyson's route home took him past the new hospital, run by Eldin. He didn't stop. Shyanne had chosen to give birth at home. He rushed past the even newer school building where Brina now served as teacher and principal.

Greyson's gaze swung toward the busy spaceport. To Shyanne's dismay, Damon, Bear, Terle and Silky had chosen not to settle planet-side. Using their reward, they'd purchased a larger version of *Lady Hawk* and continued gallivanting across the galaxy. Fortunately they limited their activities to legal trading—mostly. If they sometimes straddled a fine line combating the still prevalent slave trade, they were careful not to get caught. It helped that ASP director Carter Kincaid turned a blind eye to their quasi-legal rescues. To Shyanne, Rian and Arianna's delight, the quartet visited often.

Breathing hard, not from exertion but from adrenaline, Greyson paused on the porch. He was about to become a father again.

A high-pitched wail pierced the air. Greyson dashed inside. He didn't pause to acknowledge Chalmer or Kedar as he headed to the bedroom. In the last few years the two men had settled their differences and become fast friends as well as business partners.

Shyanne lay propped on the bed. Sweat matted her hair to her head and her skin looked drawn and pale, but her smile was radiant. One blanket-wrapped bundle rested in her arms, while Matha helped Eldin clean another squirming, wailing infant. Though he'd known they were having twins, the sight of the two babies filled him with wonder.

Greyson knelt next to the bed. "In a hurry, were you?" he asked.

Shyanne's smile widened. "There's a lot to be said for *some* C.O.I.L. technology. It was quick and I barely felt a thing."

"Here's your son." Matha handed him the crying, blanket-clad bundle. She and Eldin then left the room. Greyson barely noticed.

"Son?" He and Shyanne had decided to be surprised by the babies' genders.

"*Sons*," Shyanne answered. "Meet Stewart and Chalmer."

"Which is which?" He studied the identical infants, one suckling contentedly on his fist. The other's face scrunched as he wailed his displeasure.

"This is Chalmer." Shyanne nodded toward the baby cuddled peacefully in her arms. "The squalling one in your arms is Stewart, of course."

At that moment Stewart's cries stopped. With wide, unfocused baby eyes he looked up at Greyson and began to coo.

Greyson eased himself onto the bed next to Shyanne. In a little while Matha would bring in Arianna and Rian. Later they'd introduce their sons to their grandfathers and the rest of the world. But this moment was just for Shyanne and him: a reward for the long, hard journey they'd traveled to get here . . . and a promise of what was yet to come.

ELISABETH NAUGHTON

THERON—Dark haired, duty bound and deceptively deadly. He's the leader of the Argonauts, an elite group of guardians that defends the immortal realm from threats of the Underworld.

From the moment he walked into the club, Casey knew this guy was different. Men like that just didn't exist in real life—silky shoulder-length hair, chest impossibly broad, and a predatory manner that just screamed dark and dangerous. He was looking for something. Her.

She was the one. She had the mark. Casey had to die so his kind could live, and it was Theron's duty to bring her in. But even as a 200-year-old descendent of Hercules, hc wasn't strong enough to resist the pull in her fathomless eyes, to tear himself away from the heat of her body.

As war with the Underworld nears, someone will have to make the ultimate sacrifice.

MARKED

ISBN 13: 978-0-505-52822-3